For Best and Worst

Marie Nicole Harper

My roots are in Alabama's sod,
I'm southern by the grace of God,
Coach Bryant taught me the meaning of pride,
Forever and ever, I'll be yelling Roll Tide!
(Author unknown)

Southland Bookworks, LLC

FOR BEST AND WORST

****

The author is grateful to singer/songwriter Mac McAnally for permission to include a part of the song, written and recorded by him, "Back Where I Come From," in the introductory pages of this book.

Library of Congress Cataloging-in-Publication Data is available.
ISBN-13: 978-0692373279
ISBN-10: 0692373276

Printed in the United States of America
January 2015

Some say it's a backward place,
Narrow minds on a narrow way,
But I make it a point to say,
That's where I come from.

Back where I come from,
Where I'll be when it's said and done,
And I'm proud as anyone,
That's where I come from.

Back where I come from,

I'm an old (Alabamian).

From the song, "Back Where I Come From"
Written and recorded by singer/songwriter Mac McAnally

Acknowledgements

I was inspired by many people, many places, and many things. All of the credit, of course, goes to my Lord and Savior Jesus Christ. With him all things are possible. The following lists a few of the many things that my Heavenly Father has done in my life.

First, he gave me the privilege of being made by Woodrow Graham and Gladys Ruehl Graham. Mama and Daddy loved me, nurtured me, disciplined me, and sacrificed greatly for me. I miss them so much.

God couldn't have done any better than to set me down where he did, Cullman, Alabama. Though I didn't always appreciate Cullman; as time passed, I came to realize that it's a place, a community of individuals, although they may not show it in day to day life, who genuinely care about others and continually strive to make not only Cullman a better place to live, but to make this world a better place for all of us.

God has given me so many great friends and blessed me with a great extended family. I love them all. And yes, God has put individuals in my life that I feel like I could have done without. While I will probably never look upon these individuals fondly, they made me strong.

SONGS FOR YOUR PLAYLIST TO LISTEN TO WHILE READING

- Jack and Diane recorded by John Cougar Mellencamp.
- Back Where I Come From written and recorded by Mac McAnally, also recorded by Kenny Chesney.
- Rock & Roll High School recorded by the Ramones.
- Yea Alabama recorded and performed by the University of Alabama Million Dollar Band.
- Song of the South recorded by the group, Alabama.
- Wagon Wheel recorded by Darius Rucker and others.
- My Home's in Alabama recorded by the group, Alabama.
- Copperhead Road recorded by Steve Earle.
- The Boys of Fall recorded by Kenny Chesney.
- Deacon Blues recorded by Steely Dan.
- The South's 'Gonna' do it Again recorded by The Charlie Daniel's Band.
- The Tide is High recorded by Blondie.
- Southern Voice recorded by Tim McGraw.
- Brick House recorded by the Commodores.
- Sweet Home Alabama recorded by Lynrd Skynrd.
- Bama Breeze recorded by Jimmy Buffett and the Coral Reefer Band.
- Suds in the Bucket recorded by Sara Evans.

CHAPTER 1

Kristie Tidwell gazed at her reflection in the ladies' room mirror on the second floor of the Renaissance, a private club in her hometown of Wentworth, Alabama. The pale blue empire waist dress hung perfectly on her slimmed down body, Its V-neck accentuated her near perfect bust line, and served to elongate her short neck. The double strand pearl choker and pearl drop earrings worked well with the dress.

Even though it was the middle of June, Kristie chose a dress with puffed sleeves that hit a few inches above her elbows because she had big arms and cameras made them look bigger.

Her dark brown hair hung just below her shoulders in thick curls, with no trace of the summertime humidity frizz that often plagued her this time of year.

The crown of multi-colored silk summer flowers that she would wear on her head sat on an antique dresser awaiting her oldest and best friend, Jennie Browning Stewart, to return and help her get it placed just right.

Three shades of eye shadow ranging from light tan to medium brown brought out her bright blue eyes. It's weird, thought Kristie, that shades of brown can accentuate blue. Her dark red lipstick was perfect, and so were her naturally white teeth.

The only imperfection that one might point out would be Kristie's legs. She had some freckles and blemishes on her legs, likely inherited from her mother and maternal grandmother. Years of sun bathing and lying in tanning beds didn't help either. A decade ago, pantyhose would have minimized those spots, but in the twenty-first century, pantyhose were off-limits. Thank goodness for the spray-on kind.

Kristie then looked down at her painted toe nails through her open-toed black patent leather dress shoes. While not exactly comfortable in high heels, Kristie was determined to wear them on her wedding day, and had practiced walking around in them at her house for a month. As soon as this "shindig" was over, the heels would be coming off, and probably not worn again.

Even though she was into her forties, Kristie was beautiful, but wasn't every bride on her wedding day?

The dress Kirstie chose was light blue, remarkably close to the color of robin eggs. This shade of blue was one of her best colors because it accentuated her dark hair, blue eyes, and ruby lips. It was empire cut to draw attention to Kristie's bust line. She considered herself lucky in that area. She was not too small and not too large, just a perfect 36-D. The neckline plunged just low enough to show a classy amount of cleavage, and the puffed sleeves gave it a youthful look. The material was a stretch type knit, allowing Kristie to move without difficulty. The flared skirt, hitting about two inches above her knees, flowed freely as she moved around. This was a good length for Kristie, since her legs were shapely.

In searching for something to wear on her head, she tried on many hats, including floppy garden hats, but nothing would work with her dress. Not being fond of hats anyway, Kristie, instead, chose a crown of silk summer flowers of various colors, fashioned similarly to the headpiece that Jennie wore when she married Forrest Gump in the movie.

Kristie could have easily passed for thirty-five, thanks to slow aging genes passed down to her from both sides of her family. On the Tidwell side, no one aged, and gray hair was rare for both men and women. When her dad died, his hair was salt and pepper. While her mom grayed early, she always looked young. Unfortunately, Kristie inherited the gray gene, but that could always be remedied in a cheap, painless manner.

Kristie started thinking about her mama and daddy. She missed them so much, and even though they would have had their doubts regarding the direction Kristie was taking her life, she wished they were here.

Most of the folks who had looked after her, along with her friends and cousins while they were growing up had passed. Her generation was now the adults. Scary, thought Kristie, as she stared out the window watching more guests enter the Renaissance.

Giving the hair one more scrunching and spray, Kristie noticed, that as guests were arriving, her hubby-to-be was standing outside the building in his dark suit greeting everyone. Yes, this was a bit unorthodox, but why be normal?

Kristie smiled because that was her Eric, the world's most down to earth and caring gentleman. It had taken her a long time to find Mr. Right, but now that she had found him, she was going to make him the happiest man in the world. Kristie had so much love to give, but until now, never had the chance. Now she would have that opportunity with a new husband and stepdaughter.

CHAPTER 2

Kristie was upstairs getting all prettied up, and Eric had no doubt that she would be the most beautiful bride ever.

Eric Channing was about to be married for the second time, and he hoped this would be his last time. Lasting six years, his first marriage was to a woman several years his junior. And while both had decided they did not want children, Gina managed to get pregnant with their only child after they officially separated, and were heading down the path to divorce. When a brief reconciliation failed to work, both decided that it was better to be apart and raise their child, rather than having the child grow up in a household where the parents didn't love each other.

There were no bridesmaids or groomsmen. Kristie's best friend, from when they were children, Jennie Stewart, would up standing up with Kristie. Eric's daughter, Tanya, would be standing up with him, along with his sister, Sandy. Brother Roger, living in South Carolina, was not able to attend. Because Kristie's dad was deceased, her cousin, Barry Tidwell, would be giving her away. Phil Stewart, Jennie's husband and a minister, would perform the ceremony.

Eric was having second and third thoughts about the wedding, but assured himself this was normal. Friends were telling him that he could always run away, but this was nothing but good-natured ribbing, wasn't it? At any rate, Eric was ready to get this over with, go on their wedding trip to Key West, and get on with their lives together as husband and wife.

Of course, he loved Kristie, but he had been a bachelor for most of his adult life, and was concerned about how he would adapt to a wife at this stage.

The night before, Kristie lay snuggled up to Eric on their last night to be single. Tomorrow she would be Kristie Tidwell-Channing. Because of her age and professional reputation, Kristie decided to hyphenate her name. It sounded professional and Eric liked it. He thought the hyphenated name sounded classy, just like the southern lady he was planning to marry.

Before falling asleep, Kristie and Eric talked about life together as a couple, there would be Alabama football games, concerts, political discussions, church, plus socials with friends and family. It seemed too good to be true. Spinster Kristie Tidwell, only child of Bobby and Mary Tidwell, would no longer be a spinster. Eric, who was married for six short years would be her husband. Eric, who was a womanizer in his younger days, but never picked up a sexually transmitted disease or fathered a child, except Tanya, would grow old with her. After kissing Eric tenderly, Kristie fell asleep in the crook of Eric's arm.

CHAPTER 3

As time for the ceremony to start was drawing closer, Kristie continued to sit by the big window at the Renaissance and stare at the guests who were rushing in at the last minute.

Oh no! There's Wiley Martin, and that woman with him must be his wife, Anabelle. Kristie would recognize him anywhere. Even though chemotherapy had done a job on Wiley's once thick hair, and he was using a cane for support, some things about him were unmistakable after all these years. The woman with him looked exactly like she imagined Anabelle Martin to look. She was short and petite, with straight blonde hair falling into a bob just below her earlobes. The above the knee peach suit she wore was stunning, and she walked with confidence in her taupe stiletto heels.

So that was Anabelle Martin, the perfect wife of which Eric spoke so highly. She and Kristie were physical opposites. Kristie's dark hair was long, falling to just below her shoulders, plus she was five foot six, the average height for a woman. Since early childhood, Kristie had struggled to keep her weight in check, sometimes winning the battle, sometimes not.

Once the handsome bad boy of their class, Wiley's days on this earth were now numbered. Even though Kristie and Wiley grew up in the same church, Wiley had never said a friendly word to Kristie in his life, and she wondered if he would be nice to her today. He made fun of her weight, and even tripped her when they were in the seventh grade, causing her to fall on some gravel, skinning both of her knees. After the fall, Wiley and his buddies laughed and walked away, leaving a humiliated Kristie to pull herself up, gather her books, and rush to her next class with both knees bleeding.

Kristie speculated that the last time she had spoken to Wiley was during their freshman year at the University of Alabama when she came face to face with him at Bidgood Hall. She greeted him with a "Hi Wiley," and he greeted her with a "Hi Kristie."

Would Wiley, in some way, trip her today, just to embarrass her? How would she treat Wiley today? He came as a friend of Eric's, not as a friend of hers. Kristie decided she would be cool and aloof. "Hello Wiley, so lovely to see you. Thank you for coming." And she would say this without cracking a smile.

Jennie arrived in the ladies' room, announcing that the Renaissance was filling up with guests, mostly folks with whom they had attended high school. The guest list was confined to only those who were in the bride and groom's high school graduating class, and their guests. When planning the wedding, Kristie started out small, knowing there would, inevitably, be "wedding creep."

Eric, Tanya, and Sandy were having their pictures made in one of the downstairs rooms, and the photographer would be up there soon to make their pictures. Also, cousin Barry was standing outside the ladies' room waiting to give Kristie away.

"Now, we just have to get this headdress on you, and we'll be ready to get married," said Jennie.

Once the headdress was in place, Jennie and Kristie left the ladies' room and walked into the small room next door where Barry was waiting.

The photographer bounded up the stairs and took the photos of Jennie and Kristie, Barry and Kristie. When Sandy and Tanya arrived, upstairs, the photographer finished the pre-wedding picture taking.

The music had begun. Jennie was standing at the top of the stairs. Kristie, on Barry's arm, stood behind her. Barry whispered to Kristie. "There's still time to escape. We can sneak out using the back stairs, then drive to I-65, and head north or south before Eric finds out what happened."

"I guess I'll go through with it," laughed Kristie. "But I'll be glad when this is over, and we can unwind."

The newlyweds planned to go back to Kristie's house for their wedding meal and wedding night. Both were older, and this was the real world.

CHAPTER 4

Suddenly, screams were coming from downstairs, and Barry said, "You two ladies stay here, and I'll see what's happening."

Kristie heard someone ask, "Who knows CPR?"

What happened? Was something wrong with Eric? He is on heart medication and wears a CPAP mask to bed. In about a half minute, Barry came running up the stairs and told Kristie and Jennie that Wiley Martin had slumped from his chair onto the floor, and the paramedics had been called. He was still breathing and had a pulse.

"Well, isn't this just lovely?" Kristie said out loud as she headed straight for the ladies' room, and to the window overlooking the street in front of the Renaissance.

Jennie rushed in after Kristie and suggested that they pray for Wiley as they awaited the arrival of the paramedics.

"That sorry son of a bitch has just ruined my wedding, no way am I praying for him."

Shocked at Kristie's outburst, Jennie turned away from her and said she was going downstairs to get Phil.

"Whatever!"

In what seemed like a matter of minutes, the paramedics drove up to the front entrance, got out of the ambulance, grabbed a gurney, and rushed into the building.

Should Kristie do the classy thing and go downstairs to check on Wiley, one of Eric's best friends? If he made it through today, he would not likely be around for very much longer. No, this was supposed to be her day, and guess who had ruined it? Wiley Martin!

The next thing Kristie saw was the paramedics carrying Wiley out on a gurney, and following close behind was Eric with Wiley's wife, Anabelle. Eric assisted Anabelle into the ambulance, then crawled in there with her. Kristie found herself hating Eric, hating his friendship with Wiley Martin, and hating that he had encouraged Wiley Martin to attend their wedding.

Just as Kristie was checking her cell phone to see if Eric had tried to call or text her, Jennie and Phil entered the ladies' room. Phil took one look at Kristie and insisted they pray. Phil, always in control prayed for God to give them strength as his will is carried out today. The back door of the Renaissance was appealing to Kristie.

Phil reminded Kristie that food and guests were downstairs. She needed to decide what to do. Re-checking her phone, Kristie saw that Eric had still not tried to call her, so she called him, getting the voicemail. Before she could leave a message, cousin Barry came up the stairs with Eric's phone which he found in one of the small downstairs rooms.

"Oh great," an exasperated Kristie screamed, and then couldn't hold it in any longer, and burst into tears.

Jennie suggested that Barry and Phil go back downstairs and tell the guests to go on ahead and have something to eat, but leave the cakes alone. If Eric returned soon, the ceremony would take place, and then the cakes would be cut and served.

Jennie reminded Kristie that her guests were anxious about her, and it would be gracious if she went downstairs to mingle with them until Eric returned.

"I guess that would be the right thing to do, just let me fix my makeup and hair, and I'll be right down."

After requesting that Jennie, Phil, and Barry leave her alone, Kristie, in robotic style, began applying more makeup. After a few squirts of hairspray and some scrunching to the hair, she was ready to go downstairs and greet her guests.

As she reached the foot of the stairs, everyone in the room turned and clapped, with some of the ladies giving her condolence hugs. Cindy Smith, one of the girls with whom Kristie had grown up in church, suggested that she might want to go Wentworth Medical Center, and at least find Eric, to see what was happening.

Cindy was right. Wiley and Anabelle's Mercedes was parked at the Renaissance. Someone would need to drive it to WMC for Anabelle, and Eric would need to return to the Renaissance, whether the wedding took place or not. Then it occurred to Kristie that she had no vehicle of her own here. She had ridden up here with Phil and Jennie, and was planning on leaving with her new husband in his truck.

Shortly after Kristie appeared downstairs, the local photographer, hired to take pictures, approached Kristie, looking somewhat embarrassed, and announced that he had another job in twenty minutes. Kristie had no choice but to let him go, assuring him that he would get paid. She would contact him later to settle.

While Barry and Phil offered to go to WMC and get Eric, Kristie felt it would be better if she went, remembering she had a set of keys to Eric's truck. She was not crazy about driving that "big ole thing," but would manage.

Dressed in her pale blue wedding dress and the black patent leather heels, Kristie climbed into Eric's truck and headed to WMC. Entering the hospital, she walked toward the main waiting room to see if Eric was there. Not only was he there, his big arms were also encircling the sobbing Anabelle.

Eric spoke about Anabelle as though she were a saint, always commenting about how attractive she was. Eric thought she and Wiley made a perfect couple. It was too bad they never had children, because any children they made would have been beautiful.

Kristie walked over to the sofa where Eric and Anabelle were locked in what could have been mistaken for an intimate embrace. For a moment neither looked up. Eventually, Eric raised his head and jerked out of the embrace. Lifting her head, Anabelle turned to Eric and asked if this was his bride to be.

At that very moment, Kristie started seeing spots before her eyes, her vision doubled, and she became dizzy. Making her way to an empty chair in the waiting room, she sat down and kicked off her shoes, not having said anything to either Anabelle or Eric.

Before Eric could check on Kristie, a young man, who appeared to be a doctor, walked out of the elevator and into the waiting room, asking for the family of Wiley Martin. When both Eric and Anabelle looked at him, he motioned for them to follow. Eric released Anabelle, but she softly asked Eric to go with her. Eric then arose from the sofa, helped Anabelle up, and the two of them followed the young doctor.

When her dizziness passed, Kristie stood and went to the restroom. As she settled back into the faux leather waiting room chair, her phone went off. It was Jennie telling her that most of the guests had departed and, except for the cakes, most of the food and punch was gone. Also, the room reservation was elapsing in about twenty minutes. At this point, Kristie told Jennie that Eric and Anabelle went to talk to the doctor and hadn't returned.

Jennie, feeling Kristie's pain, offered to pack up the cakes and take them to Birmingham. She and Phil would also gather up Kristie's things from the upstairs ladies' room and bring them to her at WMC.

When Jennie and Phil arrived at the hospital, Eric and Anabelle had not re-appeared. So, Kristie thanked Jennie and Phil for their friendship and loyalty, and everything else, and told them to go back to Birmingham.

A few minutes after Jennie and Phil had departed, Kristie went to the receptionist's desk to inquire about Mr. Wiley Martin and his whereabouts. After some time, the older woman returned and said that Mr. Martin had passed away a little while ago, and that Mrs. Martin had surely left the hospital by now.

"WHAT!" Kristie shrieked. Today was supposed to have been the best day of her life, and it was turning into the worst day of her life.

The receptionist, who thought Kristie was rather harsh, said, "I'm sorry."

"Where is Eric, my husband to be?" Kristie muttered as she walked out of the hospital, not knowing quite what to do. When she looked to where she had parked Eric's truck, it wasn't there. IT WASN'T THERE! Could it have been stolen? Or, did Eric and Anabelle take it without waiting for her? Here was Kristie at Wentworth Medical Center in Wentworth, Alabama without transportation. It looked as though the man she was supposed to marry today had abandoned her at the altar.

Kristie was calm, and she was surprised that she was calm. I'll just call over to their house, yes, that's where they are, at Wiley's house. However, when Kristie tried to get the number, she was told it was a private number. What in the world does Wiley Martin need with a unlisted number? This is Wentworth, Alabama, and he is indeed no celebrity.

Kristie then remembered that Eric's cell phone was in her purse, and decided to check his contacts. To her surprise, he had Wiley's and Anabelle's phone numbers, mobiles and landlines. The address of their house was also stored. After calling the numbers and getting only voicemails, Kristie called for a cab to pick her up at the hospital and take her to the Martin home in the upscale Wentworth neighborhood known as Summer Lakes.

Upon arrival, Kristie spotted Eric's silver pickup truck parked outside the Martin home. After paying the cab fare, she walked to Eric's truck and peered inside. A cell phone was lying on the front seat, must be Anabelle's. The house appeared to be quiet, which Kristie thought was a little strange. As word of Wiley's death spread, surely some folks would go to the house to pay their respects.

When knocking and ringing the doorbell failed to bring anyone to the door, Kristie decided to turn the knob, thinking the door would be locked, but it wasn't. Guess things had not changed that much in Wentworth, Alabama. Kristie walked into the foyer, thinking an alarm would go off, but no, it did not appear that an alarm was even set. Once again, this was Wentworth, Alabama.

Before Kristie could call out, she heard muffled sounds coming from upstairs. Still in her light blue wedding dress, sans the black patent leather heels, Kristie hurriedly climbed the ornate staircase, following the sounds into Wiley and Anabelle's bedroom.

What she saw caused her to gasp and crumple down on the polished hardwood floor. There on the king-sized bed, intertwined, were Anabelle Martin and Eric Channing.

While Kristie's knees buckled, and she fell to the floor, no sound came from her throat, and she could only lie in a heap while Anabelle and Eric appeared oblivious to her presence. Kristie was forced to listen to their screaming and panting.

"I think I'll go downstairs and make sure the doors are locked."

There was more heavy breathing before Kristie heard Eric's feet hit the floor.

"What the hell, Kristie, what the hell are you doing here, and how did you get here?" yelled Eric, as he grabbed Kristie roughly by her elbow, jerking her up into a standing position.

"I'm looking for you, my husband to be, the man that I was to marry today."

"Look, sweetie, Anabelle needs me. Wiley wanted Anabelle and me to be together after he was gone, but when you and I got engaged, Wiley was disappointed, and requested that I continue to, well, be here for her."

Staring at Eric in his birthday suit, Kristie screamed at the top of her lungs. "THIS IS WENTWORTH, ALABAMA, Y'ALL ARE SICK, YOU'RE JUST SICK!"

"Honey, you'd be surprised at what goes on in this town. As Bobby and Mary Tidwell's chaste daughter, you couldn't be any dumber. While you went to work, attended meetings, and did your little career things, I didn't just sit around and wait for you to leave the office. I visited Anabelle almost every day."

"And Wiley said, of all the girls on the planet, why did I have to choose you. Yeah, I was going to marry you. With your career and all, it would be easy to keep Anabelle company and be your doting husband. When a respectable amount of time had elapsed after Wiley's death, I was going to fall in love with Anabelle and her petite little body, and divorce you. Do you still want to get married? I'm sure Phil can perform the ceremony after church tomorrow."

After Eric's tirade directed toward her in Anabelle's bedroom, in front of Anabelle, Kristie stood there attempting to get her words out, but couldn't say anything. She, instead, was making noises like those of stroke victims who could no longer talk. She strained and strained, but the words wouldn't emerge.

CHAPTER 5

"KRISTIE, KRISTIE, sweetie! What's wrong" Are you okay? You had a bad night, an awful night. I tried to wake you up a couple of times, but I couldn't get you to respond, and frankly, I was getting scared and almost called the paramedics."

Kristie managed to open her eyes and look at the man who was with her and said, "Eric?"

"Yeah, were you expecting someone else?"

"What a dream, no, what a nightmare! I dreamed you left me at the altar, and later I found you with another woman."

"Hmmm," smiled Eric, and said as he rubbed his chin, "Just who was I with?"

"Oh shut up," said Kristie, angry at him for no reason other than the dream.

"I want to know."

"Later. We have to be at a wedding in a few hours."

Eric then proceeded down the hall to the second bathroom where he was going to take a shower, while Kristie headed toward the master bathroom for her shower. She was glad Eric didn't want to shower with her on this, their wedding day. He hogged the water leaving her feeling like she was getting used water. Showering together was overrated.

Kristie sat down on the bathroom stool and looked at her reflection in the mirror. She was still reeling from the dream and was mad at Eric, who had done nothing. She was also nauseous and had a dull headache, but nothing a little Pepto-Bismol and an extra strength Excedrin wouldn't cure.

Finally, Kristie managed to turn on the water and step into the shower. When she emerged from the shower and stepped back into the bedroom, she found Eric, sitting on the bed with a towel wrapped around his middle.

"Come on, please tell me who I left you at the altar for?"

"Hillary Clinton," replied Kristie.

After making exaggerated choking noises, Eric replied, "Oh come now, who was it? Someone I know, someone in the class?"

Just then, the familiar strains of *Yea Alabama* came from Kristie's phone. The call was from Jennie's home phone. When Kristie answered, Jennie asked her how she was feeling. Then Jennie told her she loved her and indicated this day was going to be a happy one for her because was not the bride. Jennie went through this many years ago, and once was enough. Jennie also said Phil wanted us to pray as the day was getting started. Jennie then called Eric on his cell phone so that the four of them were together on a teleconference.

Phil prayed, asking for God to bless Kristie and Eric, and guide them as they found their way in Holy Matrimony. A few last-minute details for the wedding were discussed before Kristie and Jennie hung up.

Kristie's plans for the morning were to dress in shorts and a top for the ride up to Wentworth with Jennie and Phil. Then she would dress for the wedding in one of the rooms in the Renaissance. Everything she needed was already packed in her car that she was going to drive to Jennie's and leave until after the wedding.

"Should I put on my makeup now, or wait until we get to Wentworth?"

"Well, I intend to put on my makeup now," replied Eric. "Someone just might see me without it on the way up there, and heaven forbid anyone should see me without makeup." Was that woman fussy about her appearance or what?

"I think I'll put it on now and do touch ups when I get to the Renaissance," said Kristie in a serious tone.

Eric was sitting in Kristie's living room watching Fox News on her big flat screen when she came into the room and announced that she was heading to Jennie and Phil's. Eric stood and took Kristie in his arms. Kissing her passionately, Eric told her that he loved her more than anything on earth.

While Kristie was riding up to Wentworth with Jennie and Phil, Eric was driving his truck. After the wedding, they would leave in the truck and stop at Jennie and Phil's to retrieve Kristie's SUV. Then they would return to Kristie's house in the Birmingham suburb of Helena where they would spend their wedding night. On Sunday, they would spend the day lounging around and getting used to being Mr. and Mrs. Eric Channing.

On Monday, they would transition to Kristie's convertible and head south to Key West for a wedding trip, before returning to the real world where Kristie planned to immediately resign from her position at work. Eric would continue his sporadic work as a freelance writer for several hunting and fishing magazines. Football games, concerts, cookouts with friends, and evenings watching O'Reilly and Hannity would all be a part of their life together.

It seemed like déjà vu. Kristie sat on the window seat in the ladies' restroom of the Renaissance in Wentworth, staring out the window as guests arrived. Because the guest list was confined to the folks in their graduating class and their immediate families, Kristie knew everyone who was entering the Renaissance.

Suddenly, she saw someone she didn't recognize, a heavy-set woman with salt and pepper hair was walking toward the entrance of the Renaissance. Perhaps she was someone who didn't go to class gatherings, but just wanted to come to the wedding.

As in her dream, Jennie helped Kristie get dressed and adjusted her flowered headpiece. The photographer took pictures, and Phil came up to pray with Kristie, Jennie, Sandy, Tanya, and Barry.

Kristie looked beautiful in her pale blue dress and pearl accessories. Eric looked handsome and manly in his dark suit, white shirt, and crimson and white tie.

As soon as Phil pronounced Eric and Kristie husband and wife, instead of *Mendelsohn's Recessional*, the music played was *Yea Alabama*.

About half of the thirty attendees stood up and clapped their hands while the other half remained seated, some shouting *War Damn Eagle*.

Kristie, Eric, Tanya, Sandy, and Barry made up a small receiving line to greet the guests. As the mystery woman drew closer, Kristie still didn't recognize her. Both Tanya and Sandy hugged her. When she got to Kristie and Eric, Eric gave her a big hug and said, "Anabelle, I'd like for you to meet my wife, Kristie. Kristie, this is Wiley's wife, Anabelle."

To the bride and groom, Anabelle said, "I had to admit Wiley to the hospital yesterday, he's not doing well, but I wanted to come to the wedding and meet Kristie."

"Thank you for coming, Anabelle," mumbled Kristie, as she was relieved that the dream version of Anabelle Martin didn't fit the real-life Anabelle Martin.

At the reception, the guests were treated to miniature quiches, melon balls, both chicken salad and pimento cheese sandwiches, and nuts. The groom's cake was decorated with an Alabama Crimson Tide theme, and the bride's cake was decorated with a tropical theme. The punch was your standard lime sherbet and club soda, a favorite of Kristie's.

When it was time for the bride and groom to return to their dressing rooms, Jennie accompanied Kristie upstairs, telling her she looked beautiful, but exhausted and somewhat drawn. Could something be wrong on her wedding day?

Kristie laughed and told Jennie she was way too observant, informing her that she had a nightmare last night where Eric left her at the altar, and she found him later with someone else. Jennie laughed and said, "I wonder if anyone actually enjoys their wedding day."

Eric and Kristie ran out of the Renaissance, amid showers of birdseed, and got into Eric's truck, which was decorated tastefully. Instead of heading south to Birmingham, Eric turned the truck in the direction of Wentworth Medical Center.

"Do you mind if I visit Wiley before we leave town and then leave the state for a couple of weeks?"

"I guess not."

The newlyweds drove in silence to WMC. Getting out of the truck, Eric asked Kristie, "Are you coming in with me?"

"If you don't mind, I'll stay here in the truck. You said yourself that Wiley was less than enthused when you told him we were engaged. While I only wish the best for him, and that his suffering is minimal in his last days, we weren't friends, and it's a little too late to start up a friendship."

"Suit yourself, but it's going to get hot out here."

"I'll manage."

Entering Wiley's hospital room, Eric found a sedated Wiley and a somber Anabelle.

"Oh Eric, it was so kind of you to come. Where's Kristie?"

"Sitting in the truck."

"Oh, I see. Wiley's been heavily sedated to ease his pain, but go on ahead and talk to him."

So, Eric told a dying Wiley he loved him as a friend and would catch up with him on the other side.

When he returned to the truck about fifteen minutes later, Eric told Kristie that Wiley, more than likely, would not come out of the hospital alive.

"I'm sorry to hear that. I never cared for Wiley, and still have problems with him, but I will pray for God to take care of him."

Eric and Kristie drove to Birmingham in silence.

CHAPTER 6

"What's the matter now?" hollered her dad, Bobby Tidwell, from outside the bathroom door where her mom was holding her head while five-year-old Kristie threw up in the toilet.

"The fish she ate for supper just didn't agree with her."

"Something's wrong with that child, and we're going to have to do something about it," growled her dad. "Most of the time she won't eat, and when she does, she gets sick."

When it looked like all the fried fish, French fries, and hush puppies had come up, Mary Tidwell splashed some water on Kristie's face. Then she gave her a few sips of Coca-Cola to drink, walked her to her bedroom, and tucked her in under the covers.

Doors were never closed in the Tidwell household, and Kristie could easily hear most of the conservation her mama and daddy were having in their bedroom.

"All of the children in her kindergarten and Sunday School classes are much bigger and stouter than she is. They can run faster, play better, and do just about everything better than she can," commented Bobby. "Why, she can't even color between the lines. Jennie gets gold stars every day at school, and I think Kristie's only received one in the five or six months since we put her in that private school."

Mary, fearing her already upset child would overhear their conversation, quietly told Bobby that they would discuss it tomorrow.

Kristie tried to keep silent as the tears flowed from her eyes. Something was wrong with her. Her daddy hated her, and while her mom loved her, she felt as though her she got exasperated at times.

While Kristie was trying to hide her sniffles and tears, Mary, overhearing her daughter's sobbing, appeared at the door of her bedroom telling her there was no reason for her to cry. She was a big girl now. When Mary returned to their bedroom, she whispered to Bobby that Kristie may have heard him. Again, Bobby grumbled, "Well, I hope so, she needs to start eating, quit getting sick, put some flesh on those bones, and start doing things as well as the other kids her age."

Kristie hated the private kindergarten where she was enrolled. Being one of the smallest children in the class, she was always getting pushed and knocked around. This made her feel that the other kids didn't like her. During the school year, the two teachers complained to Mary and Bobby, telling them that Kristie wasn't keeping up with the other kids and should repeat kindergarten.

Kristie's birthday was on November 8, and Bobby and Mary put her in kindergarten in September when she was four and would turn five in November. In Wentworth, the public schools would only admit a child to first grade if he or she turned six by October 1. So, Kristie would have had to wait anyway to attend public school.

However, this private school would take some children into the first grade even if their birthdays fell after October 1. But it looked like little Kristie would fail kindergarten anyway, and would have to wait another year to get into the first grade.

When it was time to register Kristie for next year, Mary registered her for kindergarten. Knowing this was the best thing for Kristie, Mary still hated that Kristie would be separated from her best friend, Jennie Browning. Jennie was doing great in kindergarten, and her birthday was in September. Therefore, she could have gone into the first grade without having attended the private kindergarten.

Located on the outskirts of Wentworth, the Tidwell house was not in a subdivision. Therefore, Kristie, an only child, had no one to play with unless her mom or dad drove her to someone's house or vice-versa. Also, Kristie's only real friend was Jennie Browning, who lived about ten minutes from the Tidwell house. If Kristie and Jennie were separated, Kristie might be a lonely little girl with few, if any, friends. While she had cousins her age, they were boys and didn't have much of anything to do with their only girl cousin.

Shortly before the school year ended, Mary received a call from one of the teachers saying they had changed their minds. Kristie was doing much better in kindergarten, and they felt she was ready for the first grade. She was registered, and everything was set for her to start school. Kristie did struggle for a while, but when things clicked, they clicked. Bobby and Mary were pleased that Kristie didn't have to go through another year of kindergarten, and she would be in the same class as Jennie.

Over the summer, Kristie did some growing up, resulting in Mary and Bobby feeling satisfied with their daughter. However, Kristie still wouldn't eat much, and would get sick if she over-ate. This was a source of displeasure for Bobby and Mary. Kristie's maternal grandmother, who took care of Kristie when Mary was working, fussed at her saying she needed a tonic to make her eat.

As a result, Kristie still felt like there was something terribly wrong with her, and at times felt unloved and unwanted. Of course, that wasn't the case, but children sometimes get weird notions. People still talked about how thin and small she was, with Mary griping about Kristie's appetite to anyone who would listen.

One day, during lunch, after Kristie began the first grade, she had the misfortune of sitting by her teacher. As usual, Kristie picked at her food, with the teacher telling her she had better get busy and clean her plate. When Miss Blaylock went to another table to talk to another teacher, Kristie took her barely touched plate to the window where the children put their plates when they were finished eating. The teacher saw this and rushed back to get Kristie, marched her back to the room, said some harsh words to her, then giving her a lick on her behind with her hand.

This was the first and last spanking Kristie ever received at school. Miss Blaylock then marched Kristie back into the lunchroom and told her to sit down. Some of the children were laughing at her.

Kristie was terrified her mama and daddy would find out about the spanking. What in the world would they do to her if they found out? Probably give her a whipping for getting a whipping. At the end of every six weeks, the teachers would have a conference with the parents. As the day for the meeting drew near, Kristie fretted that the teacher would tell her mama and/or daddy she had given her a spanking.

After attending the conference, Mary came home and told Bobby what Miss Blaylock had said about Kristie. Kristie was doing fine except for her eating. While Kristie was relieved that Miss Blaylock didn't tell her mama about the spanking, Mary and Bobby talked to her, saying that she was just going to have to try to clean her plate at lunch.

Something once again kicked in between the first and second grade, and Kristie started to eat. Mary was more than glad to let Kristie have what she asked for, a second piece of fried chicken, a second helping of mashed potatoes, or even a second piece of chocolate cake. Kristie would eat, often forcing her food down because she knew it pleased the grownups. Also, Kristie's stomach problems disappeared, and she was rarely sick.

As the weight came on, everyone seemed pleased until Kristie gained too much weight and became a chubby little girl. Of course, that didn't please anyone either. Her daddy called her fat, and at times told her he was ashamed of her. This was especially tough on Kristie, because all little girls want their daddy's approval.

Being overweight didn't help Kristie with making and keeping friends either. Sometimes the girls would play with her, sometimes they wouldn't. Even Jennie Browning seemed to pull away from Kristie, telling her she didn't want to be friends with her at school because others would not play with her if she hung out with Kristie.

In addition to being overweight. Kristie had freckles. While the grownups told her the freckles were cute, she didn't believe it. And to top it off, Kristie had hair neither she nor anyone else could manage. There was just nothing physically attractive about poor Kristie. Her mother told her she would never be a beauty, and her dad remained ashamed of her because of her looks.

CHAPTER 7

Bobby Tidwell was an outgoing person and had many friends; one of which was a guy who lived about a half mile south of the Tidwell's. This guy drank heavily and would often stop by the Tidwell house unannounced, and as Mary would say, "three sheets in the wind." He always commented about Kristie's weight calling her a little fat youngin.

By this time in her life, Kristie was used to having things like this said to her. She was never going to please anyone, and no one would ever like her. First, she was too thin and wouldn't eat. Now she was too fat and ate more than she should. Nothing she would ever do in life would be right or good enough.

If Kristie were a parent, she wouldn't have allowed anyone to talk to her child like that old drunk did. Also, if Kristie had children, she would not force them to eat because of what happened to her when she was a child. That was then, and this was now.

One Saturday afternoon when Kristie, now a beautiful young career woman, was visiting Bobby and Mary, the old drunk stopped by the house, and Bobby invited him in.

"Kristie, you remember Johnny Cole, don't you?"

Pursing her lips and staring daggers through the rough old gent, Kristie said, "Yes, Mr. Cole, I remember you."

After a short visit, Bobby walked Johnny Cole to his car.

"Bobby, you have a beautiful daughter and a fine wife. Neither of them likes me, and I guess over the years I've given them good reasons."

At supper that evening, Bobby told Mary and Kristie what Johnny had said.

"Johnny can be nice when he wants to, and when he's not drinking," commented Mary.

"I didn't like him when I was growing up, and I don't like him now, and I don't plan on liking him anytime soon," replied Kristie.

Even though Kristie was a beautiful, successful young career woman, there was resentment, and even hate, festering insider of her. This distressed Bobby considerably.

The old drunk passed away several years before Bobby died. Kristie remembered her mama telling her about his death during one of their bi-weekly phone calls.

"Well, I'm glad."

"Now Kristie, that's no way to be."

CHAPTER 8

Thinking about Wiley, Kristie and Eric rode in silence, waving to the folks honking their horns at the newly married couple. When they were about half way to Birmingham, Eric started talking about his and Wiley's escapades in their younger days. At one point, Kristie gave Eric a rather displeased look.

He said to her, "I'm sorry, I know you don't care for Wiley and would rather not hear about him, especially two hours after we were pronounced husband and wife."

"Oh, before I forget, open the glove compartment, there's a few things in there you might like."

"Salad dressing?"

"Smell again. Passion Fruit Tequila, your favorite. From what I understand, you downed a few shots before going to the reunion.

"How'd you know?"

"Oh, I know."

"Want one?"

"No, I'm driving."

"Well, I'm not, and I'm going to have one, or all three."

"That's my girl. And have I told you that I love you. I really do.

"Actually, I don't think you have since this morning."

"I love you, I love you, I love you. Is that enough?"

"For now, you can stop. I love you too. You can stop saying it for maybe another five minutes."

Kristie's left hand grabbed Eric's right hand. Things were good, and they could only get better.

Their wedding meal was lasagna, salad, garlic bread, a hearty Chianti, and lime sherbet for dessert. The table was set, and all that needed to be done was heat the lasagna and the garlic bread, and open the Chianti.

Arriving at the house after picking up her SUV at Jennie and Phil's, Kristie took the garlic bread out of the fridge and put it in the oven to warm. In about fifteen minutes, she would reheat the lasagna in the microwave. The salad would come out of the fridge, and dinner would be served.

While eating, Kristie and Eric both acknowledged they were exhausted. Maybe when you were twenty-five, you could have a wedding, a reception, a nice dinner, and still have enough energy to make love the entire night. But not when you were Eric and Kristie's ages. After doing some token cleaning up, Eric and Kristie consummated the marriage, but just barely. Eric rolled off Kristie and was snoring within what seemed like less than a minute. Sorry girls, but he's taken, laughed Kristie to herself.

CHAPTER 9

When Kristie began high school, she discovered something that would be with her always, makeup. It covered those freckles and made Kristie look half-way decent when she wore it, which was every day. After discovering makeup, Kristie then had her hair cut in a short style. For the first time in her life, she could do something with it. Overnight, Kristie became attractive, except for her weight. She also started taking an interest in clothes, and found herself attracted to some of the boys at school.

By this time, Kristie was used to not being liked, used to being called fat, used to being by herself and not part of any social groups at school. They say what doesn't kill you, makes you strong, and the strength Kristie developed during her younger years definitely helped her deal with difficulties life threw at her in later years. She learned to take criticism and bounce back. She also mastered the art of being alone.

Kristie was smart, and Bobby and Mary expected nothing less than top notch grades from her. She didn't mind studying because she knew good grades would get her into a good college and out of Wentworth.

At a Wentworth football game during her sophomore year, she was sitting with a group of girls and observed the couples who were attending, including Jennie and her new boyfriend. Kristie also watched the dance team and cheerleaders. They were having a great time because they weren't fat. It was at this moment that Kristie decided she needed to lose weight. She was indeed attractive enough to have dates and be accepted, but the weight was holding her back, the only real thing holding her back.

Deciding to go on a diet, she ate lean meats with lots of salads and veggies. Soon, the weight came off, and her clothes got too big. Mary, pleased with her daughter's efforts, was happy to buy Kristie new clothes. Bobby was also pleased with Kristie's efforts and encouraged her to continue. In addition to Mary and Bobby, most of the girls at school were proud of her and supported her. Even Jennie came around and didn't mind talking to or being seen with her at school.

But much to her disappointment, many of the boys didn't notice her weight loss. A number of them, including Wiley Martin, continued to make fun of her and treat her like they did when she was fat. Kristie never expected Wiley, Johnny Morton, and Jake Stanley, the bad boy trio, to treat her with any sort of respect. However, she hoped that a couple of the other guys would be nice to her, and maybe even ask her out.

But little did Kristie know, there was one guy in her class who did want to ask her out, Eric Channing. Eric was secretly proud of Kristie, but was scared of what some of the other guys, especially his friend, Wiley, would think, should he ask her for a date. Also, Kristie belonged to the smart, talented crowd, and he didn't. Eric's grades were average, and even though he knew he could do better, he didn't care about academics. Kristie might consider him beneath her.

Even though she had lost weight, making her one of the most attractive girls at WHS, a few of the girls and most of the guys failed to see the new Kristie. And if they did, they wouldn't acknowledge her weight loss.

Being smart, Kristie was taking college prep courses. It was understood she would go to college, the University of Alabama. But it looked as though Kristie would have to wait until she left Wentworth to be accepted by her peers.

During the summer between her sophomore and junior years, Kristie did have a few dates, but none of the guys were from Wentworth. A cousin in Birmingham fixed her up with a guy who was a friend of her boyfriend's. Also, some friends in Tuscaloosa fixed her up a couple of times with guys they knew. Because these guys were cute and didn't know about Kristie's overweight past, she began to enjoy her teenage years that summer.

At the beginning of every school year, new students would arrive. They would accept Kristie, but had to wonder why she was not accepted by so many of the other students. Frustrated, Kristie tried her best to be friendly to everyone. When that didn't help, Kristie came to the unfortunate conclusion that high school was not going to be memorable for her. So, she lived for the days when she could "blow" this place and head to college.

On the first Saturday in February, Wentworth High School held its annual Miss Wentworth Pageant. The competition was open to any female student attending Wentworth High. All of the popular girls entered the pageant, and so did Kristie, now a senior. During the weeks leading up to the pageant, some of the students would make snarky remarks about Kristie entering the contest. Even though she did her best to ignore the comments, she was hurt.

To determine the next Miss Wentworth, fifteen finalists were selected, then five, then the runners-up to Miss Wentworth. Kristie made the top fifteen, and the top five. In the countdown, Kristie was named first runner-up.

When the pageant was over, the girls rushed back to the classrooms designated as dressing rooms, hugged one another, and went on to meet boyfriends, family, or other friends. Many of the girls hugged Kristie telling her how proud they were of her. A couple of the guys did also. Because Kristie was meeting her parents and riding home with them after the pageant, she saw no need to change out of her gown. Grabbing her casual outfit and makeup bag, she went to find her mom and dad.

It was the morning before her high school graduation, and the class had just finished rehearsing for the big event that evening. School was still in session for the underclassmen, but seniors could take their exams early, and Kristie was finished with high school studies. As she drove out of the school parking lot in the family car, she said to herself, this time tomorrow, it will be over, and I will never have to come to this place again.

Kristie wasn't feeling well that morning, but wasn't feeling so bad that she wouldn't be able to attend the ceremony. She had a headache, and her stomach was slightly upset. She thought it might be nerves, but there was nothing to be nervous about. Getting into the family car to head home, Kristie saw some of her classmates getting into cars together to possibly cruise their favorite hangouts one last time. She, though, was going home to lie down and take it easy. In just a few hours, it would be over. She would be leaving WHS, never to return.

It wasn't as though Kristie was going to the other side of the world. She was only traveling one hundred miles southwest to begin summer school at the University of Alabama, a place where she could start a new life.

The graduation ceremony ended, and Kristie was marching up the aisle of the Wentworth High School auditorium to the strains of *Pomp and Circumstance*. Give it about twenty minutes, and she would never have to see this place again for the rest of her life. In two days, she would begin her college career at the University of Alabama. She would make new friends and hopefully have lots of dates, both of which were minimal during her high school years.

After the class emptied out of the auditorium, the class members, congregating outside and facing the auditorium, sang the Wentworth High alma mater and did the class cheer. Then everyone proceeded on to the gym to turn in caps and gowns, say their goodbyes, and go their separate directions.

Kristie flung off her cap and gown, turned them in, and hurriedly walked toward the gym doors to catch up with her mom and dad, a couple of their friends, and a childhood friend of Kristie's who had attended one of the county schools.

In Kristie's haste to get out of the gym, she almost ran into bad boy, Wiley Martin, and his girlfriend, who was a junior and next year's head cheerleader. A few of the other bad boys and their girlfriends were also hanging out next to the gym doors. Included in that group were Eric Channing and his pretty girlfriend, Rita McDonald.

While Kristie was confirmed as a school beauty by her first runner-up place in the high school beauty pageant this past winter, some students still thought of her as a plump teenager with braces and unruly hair.

After Kristie inadvertently brushed up against Wiley, he turned around and gave her an aggravated smirk. Wiley had plans to attend the University also, but the campus was large, and she wasn't planning to hang out with him while they were in school there. He could just go to hell as far as Kristie was concerned.

As she rushed past this group, she heard a couple of voices saying, "Goodbye Kristie." Feeling that it wasn't a sincere farewell, Kristie threw her arm up for a brief wave, not turning around. Following that somewhat rude gesture, she thought she heard some laughter coming from the group, which made her want to show them another gesture, but she resisted.

What Kristie failed to see was the way Eric Channing, even with his girlfriend draped all over him, stared at her as she went out into the night to join family and friends.

CHAPTER 10

Eric Channing was the oldest of three children born to Jack and Dorothy Channing of Wentworth, Alabama. His siblings included his younger sister of three years, Sandy, and the youngest, Roger, who was six years younger than Eric.

In school, Eric generally ignored Sandy and Roger because that's what older brothers did. Besides, there was something a little different about Roger.

Blessed with athletic ability, Eric participated in every sport played at Wentworth High. While he was told he had some artistic talent, he had no interest in developing it. As far as his studies went, he was an average student, making mostly Bs and Cs. His parents felt he could have done better and been a part of the accelerated group, but again, Eric didn't care. He didn't want to do anything except play sports, drink alcohol, hunt and fish with his friends, and be with his girlfriend, Rita. On Sunday afternoons, it was common for Eric and his friends to race up and down the hills and hollows of Wentworth at top speeds just to prove they could do it. Beer, whiskey, and cigarettes were usually involved.

Eric was lucky that his parents didn't give him a hard time about his extracurricular activities. While he was sure there were times his parents knew he was tipsy when he came home, they seemed to close their eyes to such things.

When he was a junior at Wentworth, Eric started dating Rita McDonald, a sophomore. From their first date in early fall, until Eric's graduation, the couple was always together, holding hands or with their arms around one another. It was assumed by Eric and Rita, and everyone else in school, that they would eventually get married.

When they were alone in Eric's older model car, Eric would drive with one hand, and have the other hand on Rita's thigh, just above her knee. When it was time for romance, they would get in the back seat of Eric's car. But if they were lucky, Eric would take Rita to a small farmhouse in a community just south of Wentworth. The farmhouse had a couple of bedrooms with single beds, but not much else. The father of a friend of Eric's owned this small farm, and the friend would often allow his friends to use the house for whatever teenage boys wanted to do.

Eric was looking forward to the Miss Wentworth pageant and seeing Rita in the pageant. She should do well because she was one of the prettiest girls at WHS. When Rita didn't place, she and Eric were somewhat taken aback. To make matters worse, when leaving the school, they found themselves walking behind first runner-up, Kristie Tidwell. Of course, Eric thought Rita should have won the pageant. Or did he? As he walked behind Kristie, he couldn't help but notice how Kristie's lemon-yellow gown cascaded over her slim, but rounded hips. Also, her long dark hair hung in sexy waves over her shoulders. Up ahead was a handsome older couple, smiling as they saw their daughter. As Kristie approached them, her dad took her makeup bag, and both parents hugged her.

As Eric and Rita walked past the Tidwells, Rita smiled at Kristie's mother, but didn't say anything to Kristie, neither did Eric. He had other things on his mind for the remainder of the evening.

Eric's high school graduation ceremony took place in the auditorium, but the gymnasium was where the seniors met to put on their caps and gowns. Then they returned afterward to turn in their caps and gowns, say their goodbyes, and leave WHS as alums.

At one of the gym doors, Eric and Rita gathered with Wiley Martin and his girlfriend. Standing with them was Jake Stanley, who was with a girl from one of the county schools, and Jim Winston, another class bad boy, and his girlfriend, Hannah. Jim and Hannah, along with Eric, Wiley, and Jake, had just graduated. Suddenly, Kristie Tidwell, in an apparent hurry to leave, brushed up against Wiley Martin's back.

"Oh, I'm so sorry," said Kristie, not pausing to say goodbye to anyone.

"Low down too," muttered Wiley under his breath.

Then some of the others in the little group yelled, "Goodbye, Kristie."

Not turning around, Kristie held up her right hand in a farewell gesture.

While Eric Channing had no romantic thoughts what-so-ever regarding Kristie Tidwell, he did think she was gorgeous. But he would never ask her out because he had a girlfriend he loved and hoped to marry one day.

But as Kristie was walking away with her back to the group, something kind of snapped inside Eric. He wanted to run after her, hug her, and tell her that he enjoyed being in school with her. But he didn't. How would Rita act? Would Wiley and the rest of the guys make fun of him for being nice to Kristie Tidwell?

"It would be great if I never had to see her again, but she will be at the University, and so will I," said Wiley.

"Actually, I hope she has a good time in college, because everyone was so hard on her here, and for no good reason," said Rita McDonald. "Wiley, why do some of y'all hate her so much?"

"She's a fat slob."

"No, she's not."

"Well, she used to be."

"So, you hate her because she used to be overweight?"

Later that night, in Eric's car, where he and Rita were in the backseat, Eric again thought of Kristie. What was she doing now? He knew she dated some; guys from other schools in the county, and there was that rumor about a guy from Tuscaloosa who she occasionally saw. Thoughts of Kristie vanished as soon as Rita's clothes were off.

When Wiley and his girlfriend were in the backseat of his late model car, his girlfriend, Carol Ann, mentioned Kristie, and admonished him for being difficult on her.

"Is this be nice to Kristie Tidwell day?"

"No, it's just that she's smart, talented, pretty, and has a good personality. You and some of the other guys were horrible to her."

"I don't think she's that pretty. Look, in less than three months, I'm going off to college. Let's not fight."

"Okay, but when you get to the University, don't give Kristie a hard time, please."

"Oh, all right."

CHAPTER 11

Two days after high school graduation, a Wednesday, Kristie's mother drove her to Tuscaloosa for summer school freshman orientation. Orientation would last until Friday and included registration for summer classes. At Alabama, summer school was divided into two terms or semesters. The average load was two courses or six hours per term.

Kristie had never been as happy in her whole life, as she was on this day. She was out of Wentworth, and the world was her oyster.

On Thursday night, there was a dance for the incoming freshman in the recreation room of Tutwiler Dormitory. Shortly after she arrived, a cute guy asked her to dance, and they danced almost every dance together until the end. The guy wrote down Kristie's name and the phone number of her room. Unfortunately, she never heard from him.

Like most freshmen, Kristie learned that her study habits in high school weren't going to cut it in college. She found herself studying hard to get Bs in math and Cs in psychology and sociology. A senior who lived a few doors down room from Kristie told her if she made As and Bs in high school, she would likely make Bs and Cs in college.

It was the second semester of the summer term, and the football players had arrived on campus to prepare for the upcoming season. Because the cafeteria in Bryant Hall was not yet open, the players had to eat at Tutwiler. Some were flirty and winked at every girl they came in contact with, while others were full of themselves and kept their noses stuck up in the air. They were Alabama football players and the desire of every female on campus.

Some of Kristie's dates were good looking, and some were not. Many of the girls on campus were bleach blondes with breasts which stuck out so far you would think they could fall forward at any moment. While her hair, face, and figure were above average, she didn't appear to have what it took to get the eye of a football player or some other popular campus hunk. While her best friend at the dorm had started dating one of the seniors on the team, she wasn't inclined to fix any of her friends up.

A few days later, a girl living down the hall knocked on Kristie's door and said, "Chip Reynolds, a freshman football player from Colorado needs a date for Saturday night. Would you like to go out with him?"

"Sure," said Kristie.

Kristie and Chip had a great time on their first date and started seeing one another.

Late in the summer semester, on one of those rainy, humid days, Kristie was rushing back from class trying her best to keep the rain off. Her hair was a mess, and she was meeting Chip for lunch. Would she have a few minutes to repair the damage the rain had done before he arrived? As Kristie hurried through the door, closing her umbrella, she ran smack into a guy who had also entered the dorm and stopped abruptly as soon as he walked through the entrance.

Kristie immediately said, "Oh, I'm so sorry." The guy turned around, and it was none other than Wiley Martin, who was probably on campus at freshman orientation and having lunch at Tutwiler. Kristie said no more and headed straight for the elevators to go to her room.

Upon arrival, she put her notebooks down and freshened her hair and makeup. While Kristie was doing her thing, Chip called from downstairs and said he needed to be back at Bryant Hall in an hour for a meeting, and wouldn't have time to hang out after lunch.

After meeting up with Chip in the Tutwiler lobby, they went up the stairs to the cafeteria. After going through the lines and selecting their food, they found an unoccupied table and sat down. Chip was getting the eye from most of the girls in the dining hall. Kristie was in "hog heaven" having lunch with one of the cutest boys on campus and a football player to boot. The encounter with Wiley Martin was forgotten.

When Chip went to get ice cream, Kristie looked around to see if any of her friends were there. Instead, she looked into the eyes of Wiley who was sitting with some guys two tables away. Neither acknowledged the other. Had Wiley seen her with Chip, and did he know that he was a football player? It shouldn't matter, but, for some reason, it did.

Walking out of the cafeteria, Chip seemed distracted. When leaving her in the lobby to go to his meeting, he barely touched Kristie's shoulder, telling her that he would see her later. The way Chip left her was disappointing. Kristie headed for the elevators to go up to her room and study for a while.

Was Kristie as happy as she thought she would be when she was finally out of Wentworth? She had friends who truly wanted to be friends with her, and the guys were nice to her. However, she was new to the dating experience since she had dated so little in high school. Could that have been obvious to Chip, or maybe some of the other guys she went out with who never called her for a second date? Also, classes were hard; much harder than in high school, and she had to buckle down and study to get those Bs and Cs.

While no one would argue that Kristie was an attractive young lady, and wore fashionable clothes, some of the other coeds seemed to have something she didn't. Many came from wealthy families and were sharp dressers, never wearing anything twice. She was told by an upperclassman that her clothes still had a high school look to them, and she should be making the transition to more college suitable apparel.

Was Kristie trading one set of challenges for another set of challenges? Was this what life was about? Instead of studying, Kristie curled up on her single bed and went to sleep.

CHAPTER 12

While Kristie's freshman year was a difficult one, her sophomore year began with promise. She decided that sorority life wasn't for her because she was much happier hanging out with her girlfriends at Tutwiler who were not Greek. She also had a couple of friends who were locals, and she hung out with them at their houses. Kristie was seeing someone when her freshman year ended, but with the semester ending, so did the relationship.

She no longer worried about dating or guys, and instead, wanted to concentrate on her studies. Besides, she was always getting asked out, but no one yet seemed to be the one.

One Sunday afternoon in the fall, Kristie was hanging out in a friend's room. A cute petite brunette entered and asked if they knew anyone who would like to go out this evening with a friend of her boyfriend's. They were going over to some apartments to grill steaks. David's date couldn't make it, and they already had steaks marinating and daiquiris in the blender. The Brunette's name was Teri, and she looked right at Kristie and said, "Can you go?"

"Well sure," replied Kristie. Teri told her to go get into some jeans and off they would go.

Kristie had never met Teri, and it was on their way over to the apartments that she found out that Teri was practically engaged to one of the football players. Kristie's date, even though only a sophomore, was a starter for the team. But Teri told Kristie not to get her hopes up about David, because he was seeing a girl, and would likely continue seeing her. Oh, well, thought Kristie. Why can't I ever be in the right place at the right time, doing the right thing?

David Strayner was easily the best looking guy that Kristie had ever been out with, and he proved to be a gentleman also. Kristie discovered that athletes are generally the same, no matter where they attended school, and the University was no different. Most of the football players drank heavily, and would get into anything they could get into. David seemed different, though. When the cookout was over, he drove Kristie back to the dorm, parked the car, took her hand, and they talked for a little while. Then they kissed for about five minutes. After walking her to the dormitory doors, he gave her a peck on the cheek and said he would call her either tomorrow or Tuesday.

Sure enough, on Tuesday night, David called Kristie, and they talked for a little while. The ballgame was out of town that weekend, and David would be leaving with the team on Friday, and returning with the team Saturday evening. He asked Kristie if she would come out to the airport to meet the team when they arrived back in Tuscaloosa after the game.

Because Kristie didn't have a car, David suggested she ride with Teri. In fact, he called Teri, and she said it would be okay. Since the team was required to ride the buses from the airport to Bryant Hall, he also suggested that she and Teri drive to Bryant Hall from the airport. Then he and Kristie could meet up and go out for a little while.

After the game on Saturday, which Alabama won, Teri and Kristie drove out to the airport to meet the team. Because this was not a particularly big game, few folks were there. Teri spotted her boyfriend, Garrett, and right beside Garrett, was David. David gave Kristie a big hug and kiss on the cheek, putting his arm around her as the team members walked to the buses that would take them to Bryant Hall.

After the buses departed, Teri and Kristie made their way to Bryant Hall where David was awaiting Kristie in the lobby. After taking her to a local steakhouse for dinner, he suggested they go to a friend's apartment. This friend and his roommates were out of town, but David had a key, and was welcome to use the apartment anytime he needed a place to chill, to take a date, or whatever.

When he and Kristie arrived at the apartment, David turned on the stereo and turned out the lights. Kristie and David made out for a couple of hours before David had to be back at Bryant Hall. Coach Bryant wasn't pleased with how the team performed, even though Alabama had won. So, they were having an early morning practice. The time that Kristie was alone with David, he was a perfect gentleman, making no improper advances. Whatever happened to the girlfriend Teri said he was seeing? When he dropped her off at the dorm, David asked Kristie if she would like to have Sunday dinner with him at Bryant Hall tomorrow, and she said yes. Sunday dinner at

Bryant Hall was a big deal. The athletes could bring friends and family for Sunday lunch with excellent food. Because Teri was traveling to Birmingham for a family dinner, she would not be there with Garrett.

After arriving with David at Bryant Hall, Kristie noticed that most of the athletes had dates with perfect figured and perfect featured blondes. While Kristie wasn't the homeliest thing on the planet, the other girls made her feel frumpy. Furthermore, most of the girls were in sororities, and Kristie had de-activated from her sorority after her freshman year.

After going through the cafeteria line, David and Kristie sat at a table with Beck Johnson and his girlfriend, Suzanne O'Hara. Kristie and Suzanne were sorority pledges together last year. The stunning Suzanne asked Kristie how she was doing.

"Fine, and you?"

"Just wonderful!" Suzanne continued to chat about things the sorority was doing, especially for the upcoming homecoming weekend.

Soon, senior linebacker Josh Tatum and his wife, the former Corolla beauty, Denise, joined them. Denise had been in a different sorority than Suzanne and Kristie before she and Josh married. She now served her sorority in an advisory capacity. Thus, the talk was all about sorority activities by the girls and football by the guys. While Kristie could talk football with almost anyone, she wasn't about to try to talk about it with three Alabama football players. So, while they were having lunch, Kristie didn't talk much. In fact, neither Josh and Denise, or Beck and Suzanne showed much interest in her.

After lunch, David took Kristie back to the dorm, telling her he had to study this afternoon and would call her tomorrow night. After Sunday dinner, Kristie felt somewhat dismayed. She was not a part of the sorority set, and as such, felt like she didn't fit in with many of these folks. Teri would be returning soon, and maybe they could do something together later that evening.

Kristie had made a new friend in Teri Sharpe. Always acting crazy and goofy, Teri was not the type of girl you would expect a football player to be with. Kristie and Teri would meet for meals in the dorm, walk to class together, go shopping together, and just hang out and talk. Teri was glad that Kristie and David were getting along because Teri was also uncomfortable with many of the girlfriends of the players.

Besides Teri being away, Kristie's roommate went to her parents' house for the weekend and was not due back until that night. Kristie felt lonely and a little disappointed that David had not suggested they study together. So, she decided to take a textbook downstairs to the rec room in the dorm and do some studying. It would get her out of her room for a while.

But Kristie could not get her mind on her studies. Instead, her thoughts kept wandering back to David. Was she falling in love with him.? Then her thoughts turned to the folks in Wentworth, notably, Wiley Martin. Kristie had not seen Wiley lately. Was he still dating

Carol Ann Tucker, little Miss Wentworth High School? Carol Ann should be a freshman somewhere now. Then her thoughts went to Jake Stanley and Johnny Morton. Together with Wiley, they had formed the bad boy trio of Wentworth. She thought Johnny Morton was still at Auburn, but didn't think Jake was attending college.

Kristie would love for the three of them to know she was dating David Strayner of the Alabama football team, also a starter as a sophomore. In fact, she would love for everyone she went to high school with to know she was dating David. But just how could she let everyone know? Not being able to keep her mind on studying, Kristie returned to her room, bored.

Shortly after getting back to the room, the phone rang. It was Garrett, Teri's boyfriend, who wanted to know if Teri was in Kristie's room.

"No, I don't think she's back from Birmingham," replied Kristie.

He and David were downstairs and wanted to know if the girls would like to go to a late afternoon movie. Kristie said she would love to go, but Teri wasn't back yet.

David grabbed the phone and said, "Let's go without her, and maybe she will be back by the time the movie's over."

That sounded like a plan to Kristie, so she went downstairs, met up with David and Garrett, and they drove to the movie theater in David's car. Garrett was a fun person to be with, plus he and Teri were great together as a couple.

After the movie, Garrett called Teri to see if she was back from Birmingham, and she was. The three of them drove to the dorm to get Teri, and then went out for pizza. This was just a simple date, but Kristie was having such a great time being with David and hanging out with Teri and Garrett.

After eating, Garrett suggested that they go to the Moon Shadow, which was a hotel in Alberta City, where the manager gave discounted rates to athletes and fraternity guys. While Kristie certainly didn't mind being alone with David in an apartment, this was a hotel/motel. Teri acted like she and Garrett did this often.

At the men's dorms, guys could have visitors anytime. But Bryant Hall, the athletic dorm, was an exception. No women were ever allowed upstairs. Therefore, the athletes needed places to take their dates. So, the Moon Shadow, as sleazy as it sounded made sense. Still, Kristie was apprehensive.

When she and David arrived at the room, they talked for a few minutes and then started making out on one of the two double beds. Once again, David was a perfect gentleman and didn't try anything.

The next weekend was homecoming at the capstone, and David asked if she would spend homecoming with him, and she replied, yes. Being a football player, he would not be able to go out on Friday night. Then there was the game on Saturday afternoon. Come Saturday night, they would go out.

CHAPTER 13

Homecoming weekends were stressful, and not having a date was disastrous. Making it worse, lots of guys had hometown girlfriends they would invite to homecoming, leaving many girls scrounging around for dates. Last year Kristie went out with three different guys for homecoming weekend. A date with one guy on Friday night, another for the ball game, and then another one for Saturday evening. It was not a fun weekend.

For this homecoming, she would spend Friday evening with Teri, then go to the game with her and some other girlfriends of team members. She and David would go out Saturday night together. Also, Jennie Browning was coming in for homecoming to be with her boyfriend, Daniel, an engineering major. They had been seeing one another since Jennie was a senior in high school. Jennie was planning on staying in the dorm with Kristie, and Kristie was anxious to talk to Jennie about David.

Late Friday afternoon, Jennie arrived at the dorm to get ready for her date with Daniel. And, of course, Kristie bent Jennie's ear telling her about David. Jennie was excited for her friend and felt she deserved this.

Kristie and Teri were planning to spend a quiet evening at the dorm after going out to eat at one of Tuscaloosa's better restaurants. Also, Teri had bought beer for them to drink as they passed the time.

While Jennie was getting ready to go out with Daniel, the phone rang, and it was Daniel wanting to talk to Kristie. Daniel's brother, a senior at Wentworth, was also in town for homecoming. Kristie knew Jeff and considered him a friend. Would Kristie like to keep Jeff company tonight?

"Not really, I have plans to go out to dinner with Teri, and then we're coming back here to drink beer."

"Okay, replied Daniel. "But could you at least go to the game with Jeff?"

"I suppose," replied Kristie, although going to the ball game and being seen with high school senior, Jeff Robertson, was not what she had envisioned for homecoming.

While Teri was disappointed that Kristie wouldn't be joining her and the other girls for the game, she was on board with Kristie going to the game with Jeff Robertson. However, Teri did remind Kristie that she needed to be waiting for David outside the dressing room after the game to greet him. She would need to ditch Jeff, and head off to the dressing room about five minutes before the clock ticked down.

On Saturday morning, Daniel and Jeff picked up Jennie and Kristie for the game. They were going to walk to Daniel's apartment which was across the street from the stadium and have lunch.

Well, who should show up at Daniel's apartment but Wiley Martin and Ross Turner. Ross and Daniel were in the class ahead of Wiley, Kristie, and Jennie. Ross hung out with the wild crowd as did

Wiley, and Kristie was surprised to see them at Daniel's because Daniel didn't hang out with that group. Of course, there was Kristie with high school senior, Jeff Robertson. Wiley, no longer seeing Carol Ann, was with another Wentworth girl. Ross was also with a girl from Wentworth. Couldn't these Wentworth guys find women to go out with them who weren't from Wentworth? Kristie didn't even acknowledge Wiley and Ross.

As time to go to the game approached, the group crossed the street and made their way to the student gates. Because no seats were reserved in the student section, the students would arrive at the stadium when the gates opened to rush in and grab the best seats. Fortunately, two guys who lived next door to Daniel had already gone to the stadium to save seats. For the next home game, it would be Daniel's turn to get to the stadium early to get seats for the group.

With five minutes remaining in the game and Alabama way ahead, Kristie left the group and headed to the home team dressing room to meet David. Girlfriends, moms, dads, family, and friends of the players were standing outside the dressing room. While David's parents attended every home game this year, they were not able to make it to this one because of prior commitments. Kristie had never met them and wondered if she ever would.

Seconds after Kristie arrived at the locker room entrance, Teri and the other girlfriends showed up. Since Kristie had been seeing David for only two weeks, she was not a part of the little girlfriend clique that Teri was a part of. Garrett came out and gave Teri a hug, and said hello to the others. Then out came Beck Johnson to retrieve his blonde girlfriend, Suzanne, who was also a member of the homecoming court.

Finally, David emerged and spotted Kristie. He immediately ran up to her giving her a hug and a chaste kiss. He then took her by the arm and said he needed to be at Bryant Hall for a short time before going out. Would she care if he walked her to Tutwiler, and then picked her up in a couple of hours? Kristie did care, but there was nothing she could do about it.

After the games at Bryant Denny Stadium, there were football boosters, many with small children, who would want autographs, hanging out at Bryant Hall. Kristie knew that girlfriends would sometimes accompany players to Bryant Hall after Tuscaloosa games, but for some reason, David didn't want her with him. Oh, well, she'd be with him later this evening, and that's what counted. Also, he didn't say anything about her going to Bryant Hall to have Sunday lunch with him the next day.

Kristie used her free time at the dorm to re-do her hair, change clothes, and get a little something to eat from the snack bar. David didn't give her a time that he would come back for her, but said he would call her when he was leaving the dorm. The game ended between 5:00 and 5:30. When David said he would pick her up in a couple of hours, she thought it would be between 7:30 and 8:30. But come 8:30, she had not heard from him. When it was getting close to 9:00, the phone rang, she expected it to be David, but it was Teri indicating that Garrett and David were still tied up at Bryant Hall. Terry suggested they go out and do something away from the campus. What else was there to do?

In Teri's car, they drove over the river to Northport to eat at one of the quaint old restaurants in old town Northport. With this being homecoming weekend, it was crowded, even though it was after 9:00, and there was a twenty minute wait to get a table. Because there were no seats at the bar, Teri and Kristie strolled along the street until their table was ready.

Teri seemed a bit on edge, but reluctant to talk. Also, Kristie wondered why David didn't call her and tell her that he couldn't get away from the athletic dorm to take her out on homecoming Saturday night. When they were seated at the restaurant, Teri indicated that Garrett gave her some cash for them to go out and have dinner if he and David were held up.

When dinner was over, and the girls left Northport, heading back over the river toward Tuscaloosa, Teri blurted out, "Let's drive by the Moon Shadow."

Something was bothering Teri. Driving through the wooded maze of units, they spotted Garrett's car. Kristie couldn't help but gasp, and Teri said, "I knew it."

Well who is he with?" asked Kristie.

"Could be one of many, or maybe more than one, who knows."

Teri and Garrett seemed like a perfect couple, and Kristie admired them.

"I wonder if David's here also."

"No, he isn't. But what I'm about to tell you is not going to make you happy."

"Well, what?" Kristie screamed.

"You know the date David had for the cookout that was your first date with him?"

"Yes."

"She and David have been dating since last summer. They're both from Nashville, but they didn't meet until they arrived here last year. Mazie broke the date with David that night because her grandfather in Nashville had a heart attack. They didn't think he would live, so Mazie went home to Nashville to be with her family."

"Her grandfather passed away, and now that he is buried, Mazie's back. She showed up with her well-to-do parents at Bryant Hall after the game. When David dropped you off at the dorm after the game, he thought he would be back in a couple of hours to get you. But things got sticky. So, David is not here, he's with Mazie and her family, having dinner at the Yacht Club with some Tuscaloosa friends."

Teri asked Kristie, "Are you ready to go back to the dorm?"

"Aren't you going to stay here and see who Garrett comes out with?"

"No, I don't want to know."

As Kristie and Teri walked through the Tutwiler lobby, they found it deserted. Most everyone was out for the evening because this was homecoming, the biggest date night of the year.

Kristie was going to her room to change clothes, then she would go to Teri's room where they would probably spend the rest of the evening talking. As Kristie was getting into her raggedy jeans and sweater, the phone rang. Should she pick it up? If she did, the other party would know she was at the dorm on homecoming Saturday night. So, she let it ring until it stopped.

When she arrived at Teri's room, Teri told her that David had called her room because he couldn't get anyone to answer in Kristie's room. He was through with Mazie and wanted to know if they could get together.

"Through with Mazie?" Kristie screamed.

Mazie went off to spend the evening with her parents at the Stafford Hotel, and David wants to see you."

"Wait a minute, I'm second fiddle to Mazie?"

"No, but he needs to talk to you. He's in his room now, and I'm supposed to call him as soon as I can find you. Just talk to him, and see what he has to say."

"Okay, get him on the phone."

Teri called David and handed the receiver to Kristie.

"Will you meet me downstairs in about ten minutes:

"Sure."

Kristie ran back to her room, put on what she had worn to dinner, and went downstairs to await David's arrival. When he arrived in the lobby, Kristie ran up to him and they hugged and kissed the empty Tutwiler lobby.

Because David had a curfew at Bryant Hall, he and Kristie only had a couple of hours to spend together. They got in David's car and drove to the back of the dorm and parked for a while. David apologized to Kristie for the botched evening. When Kristie asked him about Mazie, David indicated there wasn't much between them now, and he wanted to be with her. True or false, Kristie fell for it.

David and Kristie ended up in the backseat of David's car. Even though there was lots of heavy breathing, David was still quite the gentleman, something for which Kristie was thankful. If things worked out between them, there would be plenty of time for the other stuff. Now, they were two young people who were attracted to one another and having a damn good time.

Because she was happy, Kristie didn't think of Teri, and that they had seen her boyfriend's car parked at the Moon Shadow Motel. Upon returning to her room and feeling guilty, she called Teri to check on her. When Teri answered the phone, Kristie apologized profusely for thinking only of herself.

Much to Kristie's surprise, Teri didn't seem upset by the way Kristie had acted. In fact, she didn't appear that upset about Garrett lying to her and being at the Moon Shadow with someone else. One thing did bother Kristie. David did not ask her to have Sunday lunch with him at Bryant Hall; whereas, Garrett and Teri were having lunch there tomorrow. Could things just work out for everyone for a change? There was always a catch, a snag, something to keep a near perfect situation from being perfect.

After Kristie hung up the phone, Jennie arrived, and they talked for a while. When Jennie asked Kristie how her evening was, Kristie replied that she had a great time with David and liked him. When Kristie asked the same of Jennie, Jennie replied that things were okay. Was anyone happy this homecoming weekend? Apparently not.

Daniel was seeing someone else, a girl Kristie had some classes with. Of course, Kristie said nothing, wanting no part of any private little wars.

Kristie and Jennie slept until a ringing phone woke them up. It was Daniel wanting to know when Jennie would be ready to leave so they could have lunch before Jeff, on his way back to Wentworth, could drop Jennie off at Samford University in Birmingham. Jennie quickly showered and dressed, hugged Kristie, and off she was after another homecoming weekend.

Jennie was gone, Teri was having Sunday lunch at Bryant Hall, and Kristie's roommate was at church, and going to Morrison's Cafeteria to eat afterward. Kristie was by herself. While the Tutwiler cafeteria was open, she didn't want to be seen down there. Anyone who was anyone was out for Sunday lunch. So, Kristie didn't eat, and truthfully, she wasn't hungry.

Apparently, Teri didn't indicate to Garrett that she saw his car at the Moon Shadow the night before, because Garrett dropped her back at the dorm late Sunday afternoon. But Teri did get the low-down on why David didn't ask Kristie to have Sunday lunch with him. David, instead, drove to Birmingham to have lunch at The Club with some Alabama boosters. This would be illegal today, but it was okay at the time. Why didn't David just say that he was going to Birmingham for lunch? Guess Kristie would never know.

CHAPTER 14

David and Kristie continued to see each other through football season and the end of the semester. So did Teri and Garret, who became officially engaged. Alabama was ranked number two in the polls and would be going to a major bowl. Once the bowl destination, the Sugar Bowl in New Orleans, was announced, Garrett and David arranged for Kristie and Teri to attend the bowl game. Garrett and David would have to travel to New Orleans with the team, but would drive back with the girls in Teri's car afterward.

Mary and Bobby were not happy about Kristie attending the bowl game. However, after doing some heavy duty lying to the effect that Teri's parents would be there to chaperone, they relented and allowed her to go.

Before the bowl game, Coach Bryant kept a tight rein on the players. They were not allowed to be seen on Bourbon Street, much less in a bar, and heaven forbid, be caught with something alcoholic. That left Teri and Kristie to experience what New Orleans had to offer. And what a time they had. Choosing to avoid the other girlfriends as much as possible, Teri and Kristie acted silly and giggled, doing their best to act as unsophisticated as possible. The other girlfriends would have been appalled at their behavior.

There were a couple of nights that Kristie and Teri were able to have dinner with David and Garrett. But the guys had to watch everything they did because someone on the coaching staff just might be hiding out in the next booth or behind a wall. Of course, girls were forbidden on any of the floors of the hotel where the players were staying. At times, Kristie found herself thinking that dating a football player wasn't all that it was cracked up to be. To be truthful, she was uncertain about the relationship with David. Would she rather be with someone who could spend more time with her and be there when she needed him?

When Kristie approached this with Teri, Teri said that she often felt the same way, and also felt that the other girlfriends, the perfect featured/figured blondes would say the same if given doses of truth serum.

Game day arrived, and Kristie and Teri were seated in the New Orleans Super Dome awaiting kick-off. Because they were using player comp tickets, their seats were with the other girlfriends, the perfect featured/figured blondes. The blondes had frozen smiles on their perfect little faces just in case the TV cameras panned their section. Teri knew them and made sure that Kristie was included in any of their conversations.

While they were concerned about their men, Kristie was concerned about the ball game. She didn't care if David had a good game, she just wanted Alabama to win. Alabama football was something special to Kristie, and nothing whatsoever could change that. Kristie and Teri were as nervous as cats, but the blondes weren't fazed as long as their men played well.

After a back and forth game, Alabama pulled it out. In the fourth quarter, David was unable to break up a crucial third down pass, but did get the receiver down on Bama's seven yard line. After three tries, Bama's opponent moved the ball to within inches of the goal line. Fourth and inches, this was critical, the play of the game. If the opposition scored a TD, they could tie it. If Bama held, they could run the clock out and win. Fourth down and inches. Well, it was more like an inch.

On a play that would be remembered for decades, the Tide held on fourth down. After taking over and running out the clock, Alabama had won one for the ages.

Kristie and Teri were in tears, hugging each other. The blondes were also cheering, but were quick to make sure their hair was perfect should the camera focus on them. Kristie watched as Coach Bryant was given a piggyback ride on the shoulders of the players to the center of the field to shake hands with the opposition's legendary coach. It was a moment that would live forever in the minds of the Alabama faithful. Kristie loved the Tide, and there was no greater feeling than the one she was experiencing now.

When the game was over, the girls stayed a few minutes to listen to the bands and witness the awarding of the trophy to Coach Bryant. After the presentation, Kristie saw David sprinting to the locker room. The girls needed to head there also.

Kristie and Teri met up with David and Garret outside the locker room with David twirling Kristie around and around to celebrate the

Bama victory. They decided to return to the girls' hotel room, and decide on a restaurant for dinner. Then they would go to the famous New Orleans establishment, Pat O'Brien's, for drinks and a real celebration. On the walk back to the hotel, there was noticeable tension between David and Kristie. David said little, and Kristie said nothing.

When they entered the lobby of the hotel, David told Garrett and Teri to go on up to the room. He wanted a minute alone with Kristie. Because the lobby was crowded with many folks returning from the game, David took Kristie by the arm and escorted her to an alcove off the lobby.

"Look, my mom and dad arrived last night after driving from Nashville."

"Why didn't they come to the dressing room?"

"I asked them not to, and told them I would get with them later."

"Excuse me; I would like to have met them."

"I would like for you to have met them also, but there's some stuff going on that you wouldn't understand."

"I wouldn't understand, what do you mean?"

"They like Mazie and want us to get married. You know, two prominent Nashville families joining together."

"Who am I, Kristie Tidwell from Wentworth, Alabama, and not good enough for them? The Tidwells aren't exactly white trash."

"It's not that."

"Then what is it?"

For the first time since they started seeing one another, Kristie thought she and David were going to fight.

Scowling at her, he said, "I think I had better go over to Mom and Dad's hotel and spend the evening with them."

"Why don't' you come up to the room, call their hotel room, and then decide what you want to do?"

"Okay."

David was wearing his traveling uniform, a crimson blazer, navy blue pants, white button-down shirt, and a crimson and white striped tie. This screamed that he was a member of the football team, resulting in several people approaching him to shake his hand and ask for autographs as he and Kristie were walking to the elevator. Kristie learned that whenever this happened to back away, smile, and say very little while David flashed his toothy grin and made small talk with the fans.

Arriving at the room, they found Teri and Garrett watching another bowl game on TV. David immediately sat down on one of the beds and retrieved the phone book from one of the nightstand drawers to look up the number of his parents' hotel. When Kristie fell back on the other bed where Teri was sprawled out, Teri mouthed to her, "Is something wrong?"

"Sort of."

By this time, David had located the phone number and was calling the hotel. When he was connected to his parents' room and talking to one of them, Garrett came over, sat on the bed and whispered, "What's wrong?"

David's upset because his mom and dad are here. He feels like he needs to have dinner with them, instead of celebrating with us or me. Apparently, this small town girl from Alabama is not good enough for the crème de la crème of Nashville.

"Oh," whispered Garrett and immediately said, "I'm not going to let him do this to you. He asked you down here as his date, and while the time he's been able to spend with you before the game was limited, he's pond scum if he doesn't take you out tonight."

Garrett Jenkins certainly had his faults and could be a real jerk at times, but deep down he was a principled and caring person. In fact, from the time they first met, Garrett and Kristie had gotten along. Until his untimely death, Kristie considered Garrett Jenkins her soul mate.

When David hung up the phone, three sets of eyes were on him.

"They're going to Metairie to have dinner because they don't want to deal with the quarter this evening. In fact, they asked if the four of us wanted to meet them up there. There's lots of stuff going on in Metairie, and we'd escape the crowds of the quarter."

"Yes, but if we stay in this area, we won't have to drive anywhere," replied Garrett. "Besides, I heard Namath might show up at Pat O'Brien's later this evening."

"Namath at Pat O'Brien's, hmm," said David. "That place will be a zoo."

Kristie was uninvolved in the conversation. She didn't care where they went if she was with David.

"Is that okay with you, Kristie?" asked Teri.

"What?"

The quarter's going to be crazy, so we're going to try to get a table at Kolb's Steakhouse on this side of Canal for dinner. Then we'll go to Pat O'Brien's and hopefully get seats in the piano bar."

"Sounds fine to me."

In fact, it sounded great. Kristie could most certainly get into a steak after the seafood and Cajun cuisine she had been dining on for the past few days.

Garrett, who had connections, or at least thought he did, tried to get in touch with one of the travel personnel for the team to see if they could get reservations at Kolb's. When he was not able to reach the guy at his hotel room, the four of them went at it alone, anticipating a rather long wait. But when Garrett called to make a reservation for four, he was told they could seat his party in thirty minutes. So, off went four young people, two of them were celebrities for the moment. Alabama should move up to number one, David and Garrett were the men of the hour, and Teri and Kristie were their beautiful ladies.

After a quick trip back to the team hotel where David and Garrett shed their travel uniforms for something less conspicuous, the four of them arrived at the restaurant. The maître d immediately escorted them to one of the better tables at the establishment. Lots of Bama fans were dining there, and some of them came up to the table to shake hands with the guys and get autographs. While Garrett hated this sort of thing, David lapped it up.

Dinner was excellent with the foursome splitting two appetizers, oysters Rockefeller and stuffed mushrooms. Kristie, being in the mood for a steak, ordered the medium sized filet mignon, cooked medium rare, with a baked potato and salad. The guys each ordered large T-bones, with Teri ordering a shrimp pasta dish. When it came time for dessert, they ordered bread pudding with whiskey sauce and praline ice cream.

At that time, the drinking age in Louisiana was eighteen, so all were legal. The guys were drinking Jack Daniels and water, and the girls were drinking rum and coke. Kristie knew she would probably drink hurricanes when they got to Pat O'Brien's and didn't want to mix liquors. It seemed like every time she looked up, another round of drinks would appear at the table. When it was time to pay the check and leave, they were surprised that it was already paid. When the guys tried to find out who had paid for their pricey meal, the waiter said that the person wished to remain anonymous, but wanted to thank them for making Alabama proud.

The foursome left the restaurant, headed a couple of blocks east, crossed Canal Boulevard, and entered the French Quarter. Because Teri and Kristie had roamed all over the quarter leading up to the game, no one was interested in walking up and down the famous

French Quarter streets. Instead, they continued to Bourbon to St. Peter Street and on to Pat O'Brien's.

David and Garrett escorted the girls to the entrance of the establishment where they spoke a few words to the elderly gentleman dressed in white and green. The host smiled and told them to follow him, as he led them to a table in the piano bar close to the famous dueling pianos. As soon as they were seated, another gentleman dressed in white and green took their drink orders. The girls ordered hurricanes while the guys stuck with JD and water.

There were two ladies at the piano bar; one was wearing a large floppy Alabama hat. Looking around, Kristie recognized two former Alabama players who were now in the NFL. Both had beautiful girls draped all over them, and were on their way to becoming inebriated. Also sitting at the same table were two girls who looked out of place. They were unattractive, and no one was paying any attention to them. While girls like that hung around the football players in Tuscaloosa, and Kristie knew who these girls were, the ones here didn't look familiar. They were groupies and felt the need to be around athletes, or anyone famous, for that matter. Why would anybody want to debase themselves in that way?

Scattered around the room were players from both teams, and fans of both teams. It seemed like every other song played was *Yea Alabama*. That suited most everyone in the bar. At one point the pianists played a popular romantic song, and David, who had his arm loosely around Kristie, brought her in closer and began to kiss her. The song didn't last long, but then, there was *Yea Alabama*.

It was between 1:30 and 2:00 when the four of them left Pat O'Brien's. Garrett's roommate for the trip was one of the married players, and while he was not allowed to stay with his wife before the game, he was spending the night with her at her hotel tonight. Thus, Teri and Garrett could go to Garrett's room where girls were now allowed, and David and Kristie could go to her hotel. They were going to spend tomorrow morning in New Orleans, then head back to Tuscaloosa, classes, and the real world.

CHAPTER 15

David and Kristie were high when they returned to the room. As soon as the door closed, David grabbed Kristie and started kissing her passionately as they both stumbled over to one of the beds, falling backward onto it. They both kicked off their shoes, and Kristie removed her wool blazer. David was a little more than high. Yes, he was drunk. While Kristie and David had done some fooling around in the three months they had been seeing one another, they never went all the way, and Kristie always kept her clothes on. While David wanted to go further, he did respect Kristie and was not going to force her into something she didn't want to do.

What was going to happen tonight? They were two kids, yes kids, alone in a hotel room with no curfews and no other restrictions. After several minutes of just kissing on the bed, David began unbuttoning his shirt with one hand. When his shirt was off, he put both hands inside Kristie's sweater. Kristie had let him do this before, but now he started pulling her thin turtleneck sweater over her head. Never had she let him get this far. But plied with alcohol, and happy because of the victory, Kristie let him pull her sweater over her head. He then reached back to unhook her bra.

"Don't," whispered Kristie.

"Yes, baby."

Tonight was different, though, and Kristie let him remove her bra. But she was still fully dressed from the waist down, pantyhose and all. Then David put one of his hands on the inside of her thigh and moved it up all the way to her panties.

This time Kristie said, "David, you know better than that."

"Please baby, I've held out for so long, don't continue to torture me. At least take those pantyhose off. I hate pantyhose."

Kristie was beginning to get nervous. She had never been this far before and was scared. She wasn't using birth control because she didn't need it, plus she still had hopes of saving herself for marriage. One thing Kristie was sure of, was that she had to go to the bathroom and told David she would be right back. While in the bathroom, Kristie saw her velour bathrobe hanging on a hook on the door. The robe was full length, and Kristie thought it looked appealing. She took off her skirt and pantyhose and put the robe on.

When she left the bathroom, Kristie found David asleep on his stomach, snoring. He couldn't have done much anyway, she thought, as she crawled into the bed beside him and was soon asleep herself.

Kristie and David awoke to the ringing of the telephone. It was Teri calling from a house phone downstairs wanting to know what kind of "state" they were in, and when could she come up to the room. David, now fully awake, was running his hand up and down Kristie's back.

"Give us ten minutes," Kristie told Teri.

David informed Kristie that the last thing he remembered was leaving Pat O'Brien's. Then he spotted Kristie's turtleneck and bra on the floor, and realized that he was shirtless, and his pants were unzipped.

"Did we?"

"No."

Kristie quickly grabbed the turtleneck and bra off the floor. Then retrieved her skirt and pantyhose from the bathroom and put them in her suitcase. David zipped his pants and put his shirt on. When Teri arrived, nothing looked awry. Kristie was sitting up on the bed in her long robe, and David was lying back on the bed, but fully dressed.

"Where's Garrett?"

"He's downstairs talking to some goober-head. It's amazing how Garrett will pick out the biggest goof in the room and start up a conversation."

Garrett was a character all right, thought Kristie. Sometimes she wished she was with Garrett instead of David. Garrett made her laugh and wasn't that hung up on being an Alabama football player. David, however, did enjoy that distinction and didn't have Garrett's sense of humor.

"Well, what do we want to do before we head back?" asked Teri.

"I have to get back to the hotel to take a shower and gather up my stuff," said David.

"And I need to get presentable," said Kristie.

"Ok, said Teri. "David, you go back to the hotel, shower, and get your stuff, and meet us back here. Kristie, start doing your thing now, and when you finish, I'll get in the shower. Then how about we go for beignets and coffee, then head home?"

"I need to check on my mom and dad," said David.

"Then do it," said Teri.

Kristie was already in the shower trying to hurry as fast as she could so they would have more time in the quarter. That left David and Teri in the room with David talking to his parents at their hotel. When he got off the phone, he told Teri that since his parents had not seen him except on the football field during the game, they wanted him to ride back with them. While not the shortest route from New Orleans to Nashville, they would go through Tuscaloosa and drop David off.

"But that was the plan, we would ride back together," said Teri in an agitated voice.

"I know, but it's not that big of a deal, only a four to five hour drive."

"Kristie's going to be disappointed."

"Yes, but so are my parents if I don't ride back with them."

With that, David gave Teri a friendly hug and said he would see her back in T-town, not bothering to wait for Kristie to get out of the bathroom.

When he got to the lobby, David saw that Garrett was still talking to some Bama fans who were hanging out. When Garret saw David, he approached him and asked about plans for the rest of the day. After telling him he was riding back with his parents, Garrett frowned but said okay. Then he asked David to give him some cash to finish taking care of the girls' hotel room. David and Garrett had agreed to split the cost of the room, and had already paid the lion's share, but there would be some incidentals remaining on the bill they would need to take care of, such as parking. David took two twenties out of his wallet and handed the cash to Garrett, saying if he owed him more, he would settle when they were back in Tuscaloosa. With that, David headed out the door and back to the team hotel two blocks away.

By the time Garrett arrived at the girls' room, Teri was in the shower, and Kristie was sitting on one of the beds, dressed in jeans and a sweater, putting on her eye makeup.

"Did you know David was riding back with his folks?"

"Yes."

"I'm sorry."

"Not your fault."

"David's been kind of a shit on this trip and I feel bad for you. But I tell you what, it's getting almost time for lunch, and I'll take the two of you out for a nice lunch before we start driving back."

"Fine by me," replied a dejected Kristie.

When Kristie finished her eye makeup and stood up to fix her hair, she found herself face to face with Garrett. He looked at her, smiled, and casually caressed her shoulder. Then, looking toward the bathroom, yelled, "Teri, how much longer are you going to be in there?"

"Hold your horses, I'll be out in just a minute."

When Teri came out, she was set to go. All she had to do was gather up her stuff. Kristie was ready, and was sitting in one of the chairs with her bags at her feet. In less than fifteen minutes, the three of them left the room, checked out of the hotel, and left their luggage with the bell captain to be picked up later.

"Well, ladies," Garrett said, offering one arm to Teri and the other one to Kristie, "Where will it be?"

"How about Acme Oyster House, we haven't been there yet?" said Teri, quite the seafood person.

Both Kristie and Garrett agreed, and off they went to Iberville Street.

Within five minutes of their arrival, the hostess seated them at a table next to fair-haired boy, Beck Johnson, and his perfect-featured, blonde girlfriend, Suzanne O'Hara. While the five of them were chatting, Suzanne asked Kristie about David.

"Oh, he's riding back to Tuscaloosa with his mom and dad. They didn't have much time together while we were down here."

There were some team members in the restaurant, most with girlfriends, and Kristie started feeling like a fifth wheel.

Then much to her embarrassment, she saw an older man and his wife, a couple from Wentworth who attended church with her mom and dad. Kristie didn't want them to see her, especially since she had ordered a beer. So, Kristie made every effort not to look their way. But after a few minutes, she heard a "Hi there, Kristie." The Wentworth couple was on their way out of the restaurant. Kristie, being her usual gracious self, introduced them to Garrett, Teri, Beck, and Suzanne. After everyone shook hands and exchanged pleasantries, the couple left. Thank goodness, they didn't ask for autographs, thought Kristie.

When they were finished eating, Garrett took care of the check and asked the girls if there was anything else they wanted to do before leaving. Both were ready to get out of there. New Orleans is a great place, but after several days, Teri and Kristie were anxious to get back to the real world.

Back at the hotel, they had the car brought up, and their bags loaded in it. Even though the car was small, the bell captain could fit their bags into the trunk and backseat, leaving a space for Kristie to sit in the back. If David and his stuff had been included, they would have been in a little bit of hot water. So, things did work out.

Despite being deserted by David, Kristie had a great time riding back with Garrett and Teri. They were so funny together and went out of their way to make sure she didn't feel like a third wheel. But, they were always like that. Back at school, they would ask her to go places with them even if David couldn't come along. While Garrett was not as good-looking as David, he was okay by Kristie.

CHAPTER 16

Kristie and Teri walked wearily into the dormitory, both going to their respective rooms. As Kristie tried to go to sleep, her thoughts turned to David. Where was he at this very minute? Was he back at the athletic dorm or was he still with his parents? But what a trip, and what an experience; plus, Alabama was once again number one.

It was the day before registration, so Kristie decided to straighten the room for her roommate's eventual arrival, wash some clothes, and maybe go out to visit her friends who lived in Tuscaloosa.

Visiting the friends, she did, and returned about 11:00 that evening. She had just put on her nightgown, and was getting ready for bed when Teri, looking solemn, came into her room and asked her if she had a moment to talk.

"Sure."

"David's not coming back to school. He's transferring to Vanderbilt to study pre-med, and maybe try out for the football team.

"What, are you serious? Is he crazy?"

"Mazie's pregnant and it's his. He's going to marry her right away and continue with his schooling at Vanderbilt. "

Kristie, caught off guard, turned over on her bed and didn't say anything for a few minutes.

"It's the talk of the athletic dorm. Garrett said his parents came to the dorm and packed up David's things, carting them away. David didn't even come by to bid his teammates farewell. David's father did leave $500.00 with one of the dorm counselors to give to Garrett to cover anything he might have owed Garrett for the bowl trip. Between Dr. Strayner and Coach Bryant, all the details had been worked out.

When did David know that Mazie was pregnant? Was it before the bowl game or afterward? How long had this marriage been planned? Did David know Mazie was pregnant when he was trying to go all the way with her on their last night in New Orleans? Kristie didn't want to ask these questions because she didn't want to know the answers. Maybe she would find out later.

What a way to start a new semester? Kristie couldn't believe her luck. Well, yes, she could. Nothing had ever gone right in her life, and things certainly weren't going well for her now. She thought if she ever got away from those horrible Wentworth people, her life would surely be better, but now she just wanted to die.

That night she got little sleep and had some horrible dreams. Getting out of bed and going to registration was one of the hardest things she ever did in her life. But Kristie did it, and got the classes she wanted.

Coming in from registration, Kristie ran into Marty Jacobs, a girl who had lived down the hall from her during their freshman year. Marty had transferred to Troy University, but was now back at UA. She was beautiful and loved to party. Whenever you went somewhere

with her, you were in for an adventure. Marty asked her if she wanted
to go for a walk that afternoon, and Kristie said sure.

They ended up at a party at some guy's house, staying out until
almost dawn. Then the two of them had to get up for their first day
of classes.

This wasn't the way Kristie wanted to begin the second semester
of her sophomore year, but it was what it was, and she muddled
through. In her accounting class, one of the senior football players,
also in the class, sat beside Kristie and told her that everyone on the
team was shaken about David, and all that had happened. David, a
scholar and an athlete, was the last person in the world they thought
would get a girl pregnant, drop out of school and football, and get
married.

Even though Kristie was dating lots of guys, nothing worked out
that semester. With the end of the term getting close, Kristie decided
to get a two-bedroom apartment for summer school, and hopefully
the rest of her college days, with Teri and two other girls. The four of
them got along great, and Kristie's mom and dad were pleased that
Kristie had such down to earth friends. Mary and Bobby weren't into
the sorority thing, and didn't like Kristie dating a football player.
According to Bobby, "Anytime you get involved with somebody
popular, you're bound to have trouble. I wouldn't want to be married
to Marilyn Monroe."

Kristie laughed and said David Strayner was not exactly in the
Marilyn Monroe category. "Well, he's pretty popular." That was one

of her dad's famous sermonettes that Kristie would remember forever.

Kristie, Teri, and Chloe, who lived on Kristie's floor in the dorm, moved into a unit at Rock Creek apartments for the first summer semester. Cindy, the other girl who lived on Kristie's floor, would be joining them for the second summer term. Again, Kristie had lots of dates, and lots of fun with Chloe, Cindy, and Teri, but no real boyfriend.

After fall classes began, Kristie was sitting at a table in one of the Bidgood Hall break rooms, talking to a guy in her finance class. Another guy, who couldn't have been more than five feet nine inches tall, sat down with them. Her classmate introduced her to Jerome Peterson, his best friend from high school and best man at his wedding. As it turned out, Jerome had some relatives who lived in Wentworth, and they began a conversation. Jerome had sandy colored thick curly hair, glasses, and a deep voice. He was no David Strayner, but very few guys were. Kristie found herself attracted to him. Plus, he lived with a roommate in an apartment complex that was just around the corner from Rock Creek.

The guys went to their respective classes, and Kristie left to go back to her apartment in the new car that her parents had purchased for her earlier in the summer. Later that night, Jerome called Kristie and asked her out for the football game the following weekend in Tuscaloosa. She accepted. When Kristie told Chloe about her new friend, Chloe said she kind of knew him. They went to high school together, but Jerome was a year ahead of her. She also told Kristie that Jerome was a major nerd in high school, but maybe he had changed. This didn't please Kristie, but she had already agreed to go to the ball game with him, as well as out with him on the Friday night before the ball game.

The weekend came and went with Kristie having a great time with Jerome. Saturday night after the game, they joined Chloe and her boyfriend at his apartment for a party. Afterward, they went to Kristie's apartment to be alone for a while. Jerome not only was a great kisser, but he looked incredibly handsome without his glasses; something that Kristie made a point of telling Chloe. Besides, Chloe's boyfriend, a law student, was no prize himself.

Kristie and Jerome continued seeing each other into the spring semester with Kristie falling in love. Forget jocks, this scholarly guy was for her. She wanted to marry him, have his babies, and live happily ever after.

This relationship wasn't meant to flourish either. Jerome was afraid of commitment. He was accepted into Stanford's graduate accounting program, one of the best in the nation, and wasn't about to enter graduate school in California with a wife tagging along.

Would Kristie ever find someone? She had gone from jocks to nerds, and couldn't seem to zero in on that right person who would fall in love with her and marry her.

At the start of her senior year, Kristie, Cindy, and Chloe were still sharing the Rock Creek apartment. Teri, who was still engaged to football player, Garrett Jenkins, had dropped out of school and rented a small apartment for herself. Garrett was talking about getting married at the end of the semester and wanted Teri to set up housekeeping at this apartment for them when they did marry. The girls, especially Kristie, missed Teri.

If Kristie took a heavier load this semester, she would complete her requirements for her degree, and decided to do so. Her breakup with Jerome threw her for a loop, and she was ready to move on. With this goal in mind, she concentrated on her studies and didn't go out except to go to football games.

Leaving the apartment and Chloe and Cindy was emotional because the girls were close. Teri was getting married in January, and Chloe was getting married to the lawyer in June. Cindy, having three more semesters before she could graduate, was moving into another apartment complex with a friend she had met in some of her classes.

Kristie left the University of Alabama with a degree in Business Administration and her whole life in front of her. Wentworth, however, was the last place she wanted to be. The thought of living there spurred her to seek job opportunities in Dallas, Atlanta, and Birmingham. After two months, she was offered a job in Atlanta and accepted it.

CHAPTER 17

Eric was awarded a football scholarship to play for Georgia Southern University, a Division 2 school. Georgia Southern was in Statesboro, Georgia, a long way from Wentworth and Rita. Being young and in love, they could endure anything, even the pain of being separated. Eric would go off to play football at GSU, and when Rita graduated a year later, the two would get married and live happily ever after.

During the idyllic days after Eric's graduation, he and Rita went out almost every night and sunbathed at the Wentworth Community Swimming Pool every day. Sometimes they would go to nearby Jones Lake with friends to water ski. While those who observed them thought they were the luckiest couple on earth, there was a wedge of some kind between them.

Eric reported to GSU in the middle of July, with the other incoming freshman football scholarship players, to begin fall training.

On the second day in pads, Eric, attempting to tackle a somewhat slippery running back, got tangled up, with the back falling on Eric's right knee. He had never been in so much pain in his life.

Even though he was rushed to the medical center in Statesboro, the hospital staff couldn't give him anything for the pain until they had the verbal permission of his parents. Unfortunately, it took a couple of hours to get them on the phone. After giving their authorization to sedate Eric, his mom and dad traveled the six hours to Statesboro to sign the paperwork. Poor Eric lost his freshman year of football. From summer until at least October, Eric's life would be one of constant pain and rehabilitation., resulting in his loss of enthusiasm for playing football. All he wanted was to be with his girl.

As Thanksgiving approached, Dorothy and Jack decided to travel with the rest of the family to Statesboro to be with Eric. They would stay at a hotel and have dinner at the one buffet restaurant that was open, serving turkey, dressing, and the trimmings.

Since Eric's departure from Wentworth, he and Rita wrote each other, but rarely talked on the phone. Wouldn't it be great if Rita would accompany the Channings to Statesboro for Thanksgiving? So, Eric called Rita's house one week before Thanksgiving and asked to speak to her when her mother answered. Mrs. McDonald hesitated and said that Rita wasn't home, and she didn't expect her for a couple of hours.

Of course, how could he have been so stupid? Thursday night was band practice and cheerleader practice. Rita would not have been at home. When he called the following Friday afternoon, Mrs. McDonald answered the phone, and once again seemed hesitant when she told him Rita was not home.

Failing to catch the busy and popular Rita again, Eric decided to talk to Mrs. McDonald about her traveling to Statesboro with his parents for Thanksgiving next week. After hearing Eric's invitation, Mrs. McDonald stuttered and said the family already had plans to spend Thanksgiving with relatives in Dothan. But she indicated that she would have Rita call him when she returned home for supper in a couple of hours.

When Rita returned home to eat before going out with her new boyfriend, a senior at Crystal Springs, Mrs. McDonald insisted that she call Eric and break up with him.

"That boy has a right to know so he can get on with his life." Mrs. McDonald preferred Eric to the guy Rita was now seeing. And while she wished Rita and Eric would get back together, she knew that Rita needed to be upfront with him.

Reluctantly, Rita dialed the number of Eric's dormitory and asked for him when some other guy answered the phone.

"Just a minute."

"Hello.

"Eric?"

"O baby, I've missed you so much it hurts. Just thinking about seeing you and being with you has kept me going through this nightmare of a semester."

"Ugh, Eric, I don't believe we should see each other anymore."

"WHAT?" screamed a desperate Eric.

"We're just different people, that's all."

"When did you decide this?"

"After you left for Statesboro."

"Do you have anything against Statesboro and Georgia Southern?"

"No"

"But what is it?"

"We're just growing apart."

"Is there someone else?"

"Well."

"Well, what?"

"I've been seeing this guy who goes to Crystal Springs."

"Crystal Springs," Eric screamed. "That redneck backwater place!"

"It's not a redneck, backwater place! Look, I really have to go."

"If that's what you want," replied a shocked Eric.

At that point, Eric thought he was going to faint. His therapy session had been rough that day, to the point that he was almost sick to his stomach, and to hear this news; it couldn't get any worse. Not knowing what else to say, Eric quickly got off the phone, limped back to his room, lay face down on the bed and cried. What had he ever done to deserve this? He was, for the most part, a good kid while growing up. Sure, he smoked, drank, and fooled around, but he never used drugs, nor had he shoplifted, or been involved in other pranks like many of his fellow students and friends.

Here he was, unable to play football, and may never play football again. Also, he was stuck in Statesboro, Georgia, a place he never heard of until GSU offered him a football scholarship. He also had failing grades. Could life get any worse? Yes, it could, because next week was Thanksgiving and he would have to face his family, having failed at everything.

Eric stayed in his room the whole weekend, refusing to eat and do his therapy exercises. His roommate, Brad, another freshman football player from Savannah and a womanizer, told Eric not to worry. He would introduce him to some of the girls he knew, and Eric could have his pick. But the prospect of other girls didn't make Eric feel any better. Rita was his girl, his first love, and was supposed to be his last love. They were going to get married after she graduated from high school. She would move to Statesboro where they would have a good life until he graduated. Then he would get a job, and they would start a family.

By Sunday night, Brad finally convinced Eric to go out with him for burgers. Also, there was a party off campus that evening, and he convinced Eric that they needed to attend. Girls would be at the party, plus beer, and maybe some of the hard stuff.

Eric did need to shower, shave, and get some fresh air. So, he agreed to go with Brad, who drove a nice car that he parked one block from campus. At the burger joint, Eric discovered that he was hungry, and polished off two double cheeseburgers, fries, and a large Coke, before the two headed to the party.

Being faithful to Rita, and being immobile for a while after the injury, Eric had not been on one date, nor had he been to one party, and the semester was almost over. He was glad to pay the $3.00 the host was charging everyone who wanted to drink from his keg. After a few beers, Eric was feeling better than he had felt in a while.

Besides, there were a lot of cute girls attending the party, and Eric wasn't the worst looking thing on the planet.

As the party continued, Eric found himself talking mostly to an attractive brunette who was from Palmetto, Georgia, a suburb south of Atlanta. The girl, whose name was Kim, talked incessantly about her family. Her parents were quite well to do and wanted her to study abroad, but being the southern girl that she was, she wanted to stay in the south, particularly in Georgia. She planned to attend GSU for two years, then transfer to the University of Georgia to complete her undergraduate studies. After that, who knows? Maybe graduate school at Emory, a prestigious school in the Atlanta suburb of Decatur.

Kim and Eric made out for a while on the floor in a corner of the small one-bedroom apartment, until Brad nudged Eric with his foot and said it was time to leave. Through her dad's connections, Kim, a freshman also, wasn't living in the dormitory. Instead, she had a luxury apartment about three miles from campus. She also drove a nice car. When they parted ways for the evening, Kim gave Eric her phone number, and he promised to call her the following day.

At approximately 3:30 on the Wednesday before Thanksgiving, the Channing family was heading toward Statesboro, Georgia, approximately six and a half hours from Wentworth. Driving straight through with minimal stops, they hoped to arrive at their hotel between 10:00 and 10:30.

CHAPTER 18

Jack Channing wasn't the worst person to ever walk the face of this earth, but he did some living in his younger days. He was fond of the ladies, and they were fond of him. He did have some run-ins with the law, but always managed to land on his feet.

Jack met and married Dorothy Channing when he was twenty-three, and she was nineteen. Both came from poor families. All thoughts of other women vanished the day Jack first laid eyes on Dorothy while having breakfast to relieve a hangover at a roadside cafe near the small north Alabama town of Falkville. Dorothy had been working as a waitress since graduating from high school a year and a half earlier. After six months of proper courting, Jack and Dorothy were married at the Morgan County courthouse, and spent their wedding night in a small trailer in the backyard of Dorothy's parents' house.

Because both were ambitious, and didn't want to remain poor, Dorothy continued to work, and both worked hard. Seven years later, Dorothy gave birth to the couple's first child, a healthy baby boy they named Eric. Three years later, along came Sandy, a daughter. Then, as if on cue, three years after Sandy arrived, Dorothy gave birth to the couple's last child, a boy they named Roger.

While Jack remained technically faithful to Dorothy until after Roger was born, he just couldn't tame that wandering eye. Being a foreman at one of the plants in Wentworth gave him opportunities to pluck from the incoming stream of young women destined to a life of factory work until they either married up, or retired with thinning gray hair, wrinkles, and varicose veins.

It was no secret that Jack was partial to his first born, Eric, who had looks, athletic ability, artistic ability, and could do well in school if he studied. Jack would have been thrilled if his son had received a football scholarship to Alabama or Auburn. However, it appeared that the coaches in Wentworth were unable to develop the players into what it took to play at a Southeastern Conference school. So, Jack was content with Eric receiving a scholarship, even if it was to a smaller school in Georgia. At least expenses for his college education would be paid.

CHAPTER 19

The Channing family pulled into the Ramada Inn parking lot in Statesboro at 10:30 pm on the Wednesday before Thanksgiving. When they were settled into their rooms, Dorothy called Eric's dorm and was surprised that Eric answered the phone. He was one of five or six guys, and a graduate dorm manager, who remained on campus for the Thanksgiving weekend. Dorothy told her son that the family would come and get him around 10:00 the next day, and take him to the hotel for a family visit. Then they would go out for Thanksgiving dinner at the Plantation Inn, a Statesboro establishment that would be serving a Thanksgiving buffet.

Eric was in a good mood Thanksgiving morning because he had seen Kim on Tuesday. She picked him up at the dorm, and they went to her apartment where they cooked steaks and drank daiquiris. Then it was on to Kim's bedroom where she let Eric take a few liberties. Kim was leaving on Wednesday afternoon for Palmetto where she would be spending Thanksgiving with her family. Then on Saturday, the family would drive to Atlanta to Grant Field for the Georgia-Georgia Tech game.

At 10:00 sharp, Dorothy Channing appeared in front of Eric's dorm in the family car. Not having seen her son since the days following his injury, she was shocked at his appearance. He had put on quite a bit of weight, making his clothes ill-fitting. And who was cutting his hair? Athletes at Georgia Southern could not have long hair or facial hair, but someone with rusty scissors, maybe even Eric himself, had done a number on that once nice head of hair. On the ride to the hotel, Dorothy detected an aura of sadness that seemed to engulf him.

When they arrived at the hotel and the adjoining rooms the Channings had reserved, Eric shook hands with his dad and hugged his younger siblings. Once Wentworth's and Alabama's football seasons were discussed, the conversation lagged to the point of embarrassment. Eric's grades weren't good, but he didn't want to discuss school and classes. No one asked about Rita because the family knew from Sandy that she was seeing someone else.

After deciding that the family would go to the Plantation around 2:00 pm for dinner, Eric, Sandy, and Roger stayed in one of the rooms so they could talk, while Jack and Dorothy watched TV in the other room.

As soon as Eric was alone with his sister and brother, he wasted no time in asking Sandy about Rita. According to Sandy, Rita had started seeing this guy, a senior at Crystal Springs. He was cute, but short. The guy didn't play football or do much of anything. When Rita heard about Eric's injury, she decided that he would never be a college football star, and lost interest.

When it came time to leave for dinner, the family piled into the one car, drove ten minutes to The Plantation, and had a good holiday meal of turkey, dressing, and the trimmings. After dinner, Dorothy and Jack dropped Sandy and Roger at the hotel and took Eric to his dormitory where they wanted some private time with him. Jack and Dorothy wanted to know about Eric's progress in rehabbing his torn-up knee, and they also wanted to know how his grades were.

Unless something radically changed, Eric would be placed on probation the next semester for his Ds and Fs. He wouldn't be allowed to participate in spring practice, knee permitting, unless some strings were pulled. After a protracted conversation, Jack and Dorothy ascertained that Eric's knee, while healing nicely, might end his college football career. He was also close to flunking out of school.

On an impulse, Jack told Eric he wanted him to come back to Wentworth, re-think, and go from there. He could get him a job at the plant, and then Eric could decide what he wanted to do with the rest of his life.

Even though he was devastated over Rita, Wentworth was not in short supply of good looking women. He also missed his high school friends. Wiley was at Alabama, Johnny was at Auburn, but Jake was still in Wentworth working for one of the four large manufacturing plants located there. Since beginning school in Statesboro, Eric hadn't been in contact with anyone from Wentworth. It would be great to hang out with his buddies, taking up from where they left off after graduation.

So, it was decided that Eric would talk to the freshman football coach first thing Monday morning about getting out of his agreement to play football for Georgia Southern. He was also going to ask if he could drop his classes with incompletes and quit school. If his parents needed to talk to the coaches, counselors, or anyone else, Jack and Dorothy were prepared to make another trip to Statesboro to do so.

For once, things went Eric's way. He saw his freshman football coach early Monday morning. The coach, a tough ex-military guy, was happy to let the injured, less than perfect bodied Eric, out of his scholarship and pull some strings allowing Eric to drop out of school with incompletes. In fact, Eric could leave school as early as that evening. When he called home to tell the family the good news, his mother said that she and his dad would be in Statesboro tomorrow afternoon to bring him home. Before noon on Wednesday, the Channing family car was loaded with Eric's clothes and other incidentals, and the three of them headed toward Wentworth, Alabama. On Thursday morning, Jack had scheduled an appointment for Eric at the HR office at the plant. He had arranged for another foreman to hire Eric to wash equipment. While not the most glamorous job in the world, Eric would be paid some money while he decided what he wanted to do. Eric started his new job the following Monday, three and a half weeks before Christmas.

As soon as Eric settled in at his parents' house, he got in touch with Jake Stanley, one of the class bad boys. Jake was working at a plant on the opposite side of town and had moved into his parents' basement where he had his own kitchen with appliances, a bathroom, a television, and a telephone. Jake had a girlfriend he planned to marry, but he was having too much fun, even in Wentworth to get tied down.

Jake had always been heavy into alcohol and tobacco, but now he had discovered the delights of marijuana and found a reliable dealer who lived in a small north Jefferson County town. Soon, Eric was spending almost every evening at Jake's basement apartment, drinking and smoking pot.

Because there was a substantial amount of physical exertion required with his job, Eric quickly lost the extra weight he added at GSU. With his income, he bought some new clothes and got his hair cut by a professional. Jake even fixed him up with some local girls who were friends with his girlfriend. Most of these girls never blinked an eye when Eric tried to remove their clothes and go all the way with them. In fact, Eric was having sex, real sex, on a regular basis and loved it. Jake was spending most nights with his twenty-one year old girlfriend, who lived in a trailer in the western part of Wentworth County. Therefore, Eric was free to bring his women to Jake's apartment for trysts.

Both Jake and Eric considered themselves lucky that their parents didn't mind their comings and goings, even at odd hours. Eric would get home from the plant around 4:30, take a shower, and change clothes. Most of the time, he would have supper with the family around 6:00, then he would be off to Jake's apartment for who knows what, beer drinking, pot smoking, and womanizing.

As Christmas drew near, Eric knew many folks would be heading home from various colleges and universities. Wiley would be home from the University of Alabama and Johnny would be home from Auburn. Being anxious to see his old friends, Eric called their moms, asking when Wiley and Johnny would be home. It's going to be great, Eric thought, to have the guys back together again.

On the day that Wiley was to arrive from the University, Eric called his house and found out that Wiley had gone out with his girlfriend, Carol Ann. But Wiley's mom said she would be sure to tell Wiley to call him. Eric stayed at his parents' house the following night, not going over to Jake's, because he didn't want to miss Wiley's call. Much to Eric's disappointment, Wiley never returned the call.

The next day, during their thirty-minute lunch break, Eric called Wiley's house again. This time Wiley answered the phone and seemed happy to hear from Eric, but didn't sound like the old Wiley Martin. When Eric asked him about getting together, perhaps this evening, Wiley indicated that he and Carol Ann were going over to Johnny Morton's parents' house for dinner. When Eric asked about the next evening, Wiley said he was taking his girlfriend to a dance that one of the high school sororities had every year during the Christmas holidays. Wiley's girlfriend was the president of the sorority, and they would be first to go in the lead out. Eric then suggested to Wiley that maybe they could get together between Christmas and New Year's before Wiley had to go back to the University.

Eric had been to the big sorority dance a couple of times with Rita and wondered if Rita would be attending, even though she wasn't a member of that sorority. Had his life deteriorated or what? Last year he was a stud, dating a pretty girl, and planning to play college football somewhere. Now, his football career and college career were over, and he was dating, well, not actually dating, but having sex with women who worked in factories.

While you could only attend the so-called cotillion by invitation, just about anyone who was anyone at Wentworth High School received an invitation to it. His sister, Sandy, had some cute friends, and Eric wondered if any of them had an invitation and needed a date. When he approached Sandy about this, she said she would call a few of her friends, but thought that anyone with an invitation already had a date. And sure enough, after a few phone calls, Sandy couldn't find anyone who might want to go with Eric.

The day of the dance, a Saturday, Eric was at one of the area's strip malls, finishing some Christmas shopping for family members. As he pulled into one of the parking spaces near the anchor store, he couldn't help but notice a dark-haired beauty coming out of the store toting some packages. As she made her way to a large Chevrolet sedan, Eric realized it was Kristie Tidwell. Her hair was perfect, and so was everything else. She was stylishly dressed in a long skirt with high-heeled boots. Over her shoulder was a trendy looking bag. Plus, the sunglasses she wore gave her a movie star look.

Kristie got in the Chevy, which was apparently the Tidwell family car, and drove off. Wow, she sure looked fantastic, thought Eric. Wonder if she's going to the dance tonight? Then he realized, probably not. She was a University of Alabama co-ed and wouldn't have time for such foolishness. Besides, Kristie wasn't in a high school sorority, and wouldn't have received an invitation to this dance now that she had graduated. Forget the dance, he wondered if Kristie had a date tonight. It would sure be nice to go out on a real date with someone he would be proud to be seen with in public. No, Wiley Martin wouldn't let him live it down if he went out with Kristie Tidwell.

But wait, hadn't Wiley Martin blown him off? Who cares what Wiley thinks or says, he was going back to the house, do what he could to find Kristie, and ask her out for the evening. He would take her out to eat, then maybe to a movie, and who knows what else.

Eric raced home and immediately paged through the Wentworth phone directory until he got to the Tidwells. Oh man, there were so many. What was Kristie's dad's name? He couldn't remember. So, he started at the top and planned to all every Tidwell in the book, but after about ten tries with no luck, he gave up. Little did he know that Kristie's dad was William Robert Tidwell, listed as W.R. Tidwell, the last Tidwell entry in the Wentworth phone book. Also, there were two groups of Tidwells in Wentworth County. The group to which Kristie belonged lived on the west side of the county, while the other group lived on the east side of the county.

Shortly after giving up on locating Kristie, the phone rang, and Eric picked it up. It was Jake telling Eric that he and his girlfriend/fiancée and a couple of her cousins would be at the basement apartment that night. He wouldn't be able to come over for his usual beer drinking and pot smoking. It was the Saturday evening before Christmas and Eric was spending it at home with mommy and daddy. What fun!

CHAPTER 20

After the Channing family decided they would have barbecue for supper that Saturday evening, Eric drove to a local barbecue restaurant to pick up the food. As Eric was waiting in line, he heard a female voice behind him say, "Is that you, Eric Channing?"

Eric turned around and was face to face with Mrs. James, the guidance counselor at the high school. Mrs. James asked him how he was, even though she already knew about the injury he had incurred at GSU. Mrs. James, the nicest person on the Wentworth High School faculty, was genuinely interested in helping the students, and was never judgmental.

When Eric told her he had dropped out of school and was working at the plant, Mrs. James informed him it was still her job to counsel students, even if they were no longer in high school. She invited him to visit her so they could talk about some options that might be open. When Eric indicated he was on the clock and couldn't make it to the school during school hours, Mrs. James said she would stay late to see him. Knowing he had nothing to lose, Eric made an appointment with Mrs. James on the first Monday after school was back in session after Christmas.

On the day of his appointment, Eric hurriedly left the plant and drove to Wentworth High school where Mrs. James was waiting for him in her office. Thinking he had nothing to lose, Eric spilled the beans about his unfortunate time at Georgia Southern. He even told her he had failing grades and would have surely flunked out had the coach not intervened and made sure that he dropped his classes with incompletes. Mrs. James pointed out several colleges in Alabama that might be a good match for him. She was upfront, though, indicating that his grades combined with his SAT score last year were insufficient to get him into an Alabama, Auburn, UAB, Birmingham Southern, or Samford.

Thanking Mrs. James for her assistance, Eric promised to read the literature and get back to her in the next ten days. He would like to stay in North Alabama, but the two leading colleges in the area, Jacksonville State and the University of North Alabama didn't appeal to him. Many Wentworth graduates attended those schools, and Eric, for some reason, wanted to go someplace where there were few, if any, Wentworth folks. In the Birmingham area, there wasn't much to choose from either. His grades weren't good enough to get him into Samford, Birmingham Southern, or UAB. But one of the things that Mrs. James asked him to consider was attending a junior college for two years, get his grades up, and then try for an Alabama, Auburn, etc.

Attending a junior college appealed to Eric with Calhoun in Decatur and Snead in Boaz located close to Wentworth. He was also interested in Troy and Montevallo. With Calhoun located thirty minutes from Wentworth, Eric could commute. He had a car, and he was sure that his parents would agree to spring for tuition. Also, he could continue working at the plant until summer when he would enroll.

He called Mrs. James and told her he wanted to pursue enrolling in Calhoun in the summer. She thought it was a great idea, especially if he had a goal of getting into a college where the academic standards were above average. Thus, they decided that Eric could apply to Calhoun to start in the summer and would work at the plant up until that time. Hopefully, he could save enough money for commuting expenses and other incidentals.

Feeling better about himself, Eric invited a new girl who had just begun working at the plant over to Jake's for the evening. Much to his surprise, the girl showed up with two six-packs of beer and a friend. Oh great, thought Eric, I'm not getting any tonight, these girls just want to get drunk. Getting drunk was only part of it. Within thirty minutes, both girls had taken their clothes off and were begging him to do the same.

Hours later, Eric woke up in Jake's bed with nothing on and no sign of the girls he was with earlier. Eric admitted that he loved being with two women, but there was just something wrong about it. Rita would have been mortified had Eric suggested they participate in something like that.

Even though it was fun while it lasted, Eric couldn't shake the feeling that he had been a part of something "dirty" last night. And the girls, from the neck up, were pitiful. Both had decaying teeth and bottle blonde hair. So, he had gone from the super cute and classy

Rita McDonald to a couple of women who were likely over thirty, with rotten teeth.

CHAPTER 21

For once in his life, Eric felt he did the right thing by applying to Calhoun. He was accepted for the summer session where he could complete four courses. Fortunately, he had a boss who understood Eric's attempt get an education, and told Eric if he needed a break from school to earn extra money, he would gladly re-hire him. While spending most of his free time at Jake Stanley's garage apartment smoking pot and drinking beer made Eric feel utterly worthless, he was pulling himself up by his boot strings. Maybe in a year or two, he would be attending Alabama or Auburn.

In anticipation of his new life, Eric limited his visits to Jake Stanley's to the weekends, but still drank beer and smoked pot when he was there. He occasionally enjoyed the company of a woman, but hadn't had a real date with a girl he wasn't ashamed to be seen with since his last date with Kim at GSU. And he wanted to have a real date with a girl who wore an above the knee skirt, a sweater, pantyhose, and stylish shoes. But where was he going to find that type of girl?

Duh! Lots of good-looking girls attended Wentworth High School. Surely Sandy could fix him up with somebody classy and pretty. Late one night, Eric knocked on Sandy's bedroom door, asking her to let him in. When she did, he asked her about some of the girls at Wentworth that she knew. Sandy assured him that he could get a date with most any girl, because this time last year, he was a popular jock dating Rita McDonald. Rita and Wiley's girlfriend, Carol Ann, were "Little Miss Everything's" at Wentworth High School.

"Is Rita still dating that guy?" asked Eric.

"Uh huh."

Retrieving last year's yearbook, she and Eric reviewed the academics' section looking for girls for Eric to ask out. This was Eric's senior yearbook, and he saw many pictures of himself, including some of him and Rita walking hand in hand across campus. Wanting someone who was a looker, Eric flipped to the Miss Wentworth section where he viewed last year's Miss Wentworth. He wouldn't kick her out of bed, but she was a senior last year and was now attending Auburn. First runner-up was Kristie Tidwell, who was now at Alabama. Having tried to call Kristie before Christmas, Eric asked Sandy if she knew how he might be able to contact her. Sandy told Eric that there were rumors that Kristie was dating a football player at Alabama. Maybe he would ask Wiley if he ever saw Kristie at the University.

After looking at the photographs of the girls who were in the top fifteen and were still in high school, Eric settled on three that Sandy didn't think had boyfriends. Sandy lent him her student directory, so he could call the girls. Also, this year's Miss Wentworth pageant was coming up in a week or so, and he should make his plans to attend.

The first girl that Eric called accepted his invitation to go to a movie on Saturday night. Wow, a real date with a real girl, it had been way too long. According to Sandy, Julie Yarborough, now a senior at WHS, had plans to attend Jacksonville State University after she graduated. Having been on the drill team and an accomplished dancer, she was planning to try out for the Jacksonville State drill team, and wanted to major in special education. Perfect, thought Eric. Even though women were now entering traditional men's fields such as law, medicine, and business, Eric, somewhat old-fashioned, thought that men should be men and women should be women.

For their date, Julie wore a short skirt and a tight sweater with chains around her neck. Her bobbed blonde hair reached the bottoms of her earlobes. After the movie, they went for hamburgers at one of the high school hangout places where Eric saw a lot of folks he knew, mostly dating couples. While he and Julie were eating, Kristie Tidwell walked in with Sara Johnson, a senior at WHS this year. Apparently, Kristie was home from the University and spending an evening with her friend, Sara.

"Isn't that Kristie Tidwell?" asked Julie. "She sure looks great. Her hair seems to have gotten thicker also. While some folks used to treat her shabbily, I thought she was pretty. Guess that's what going to the University of Alabama and dating a football player does for you."

"She doesn't look as good as you," said Eric, when, in fact, Kristie was miles ahead of Julie in the looks department. Having expectations for later, Eric did everything he could to flatter Julie.

When Kristie and Sara had their orders, they sat at a booth next to Julie's and Eric's booth. Sara waved at Julie and asked her about one of their classes, while Kristie said nothing, not even cracking a smile. In fact, Kristie looked as though she was too good to be seen at a fast food hamburger place in Wentworth on a Saturday night.

While Kristie and Sara were still eating, Eric and Julie left. Where should he take Julie tonight for a spirited make-out session? Jake Stanley and his girlfriend were spending the night at her trailer, so Jake's apartment was a possibility. But would that make Julie nervous? Eric had no intention of having sex with Julie, but he hoped to get the sweater off her. Maybe they should go to one of the places where high school students went to park. Would Julie drink beer? He doubted it. She was serving as president of her church's senior youth group this year.

Eric decided to take Julie to the local reservoir to park. If things went well, he might suggest going over to Jake's. After a few minutes of kissing, Eric reached under Julie's sweater, and she didn't flinch. Instead, she started sticking her tongue further down Eric's throat. At this juncture, Eric said that Jake Stanley's apartment was vacant for the evening, and suggested they go there.

"Sounds like a great idea," Julie whispered in his ear, inserting her tongue into his ear as well.

To his surprise, Julie accepted a beer and allowed Eric to steer her into the bedroom where he got her to lie down. Julie let Eric take her sweater off, but not her bra, so Eric managed to get what he could. After all, Julie was supposedly a nice girl.

Eric didn't hear the basement door open. Jake entered the bedroom reeking of bourbon and cigarettes. Eric immediately tried to hide Julie while she could get her sweater back over her head. He stood up to help Julie get off the bed, so he could have her back to her parents' house by curfew.

Jake, who had a fight with his girl and got nothing that evening, pushed Eric aside, grabbed Julie, and forced her down on the bed. With one quick movement, Jake pulled up her skirt, pulled down her pantyhose and panties to around her ankles and was unzipping his pants. Roughly shoving his hand between Julie's legs, Jake venomously exclaimed, "Tight and dry. We'll fix that. Then Jake pulled his pants off and began to force himself onto Julie.

"Jake, what in the hell do you think you're doing?" screamed a frightened Eric. "Stop that."

At that point, Eric grabbed at Jake and tried to pull him off of Julie. But Jake was stronger than Eric and shoved him to the floor. This can't be happening, thought Eric. He knew that Jake had practically no morals or scruples, but he never thought his buddy would be capable of rape.

Grabbing a ceramic lamp, Eric hit Jake over the head with it. Jake then got off the bed and took a swipe at Eric, who was able to dodge it, grab the nightstand beside the bed and throw it at Jake. The blow knocked Jake over and pinned him to the floor with the nightstand on top of him. Eric then grabbed a couple of chairs from the kitchen and put them on top of Jake's legs to further render Jake helpless. He then started cursing and yelling for Eric to get that stuff off him.

Eric called the operator who connected him to the Wentworth City Police Department. When Eric couldn't remember Jake's address, the dispatcher traced the call, and sent a car with two of Wentworth's finest to Jake's address. The policemen arrived in a few moments to find a crying Julie and a cursing Jake, still trapped on the floor by the nightstand and chairs.

One of the policemen removed the furniture, jerked Jake to his feet, and read him his rights while handcuffing him. The other called headquarters to ask for a female officer to be sent out to question Julie. Then the officer began questioning Eric, asking him what had happened, reminding him he had to tell all, and he did.

Julie said there was little penetration. No blood or other fluids were found on the bedspread. Never-the-less, the policewoman said it would be best for an ambulance to transport Julie to the hospital to examine her for other possible injuries. A red mark had appeared on her face where Jake had slapped her.

Even though Eric was not a suspect for any wrongdoing, he had to go down to the police station to answer some additional questions and fill out some paperwork. Then, being only eighteen, the police would notify his parents and subsequently release Eric to them.

Wentworth had two newspapers, a daily and a community/weekly. The town also had three radio stations. But none of this would be in the media due to Julie being a minor.

Eric's parents arrived at the police station, none too happy about having to get out of bed to retrieve their son. But until this day, Eric had never been involved in a crime or with the police. As soon as they saw Erick, their hearts went out to him. It was evident that he had been crying, actually crying real tears.

Jack and Dorothy, with Eric, drove the family car from the police station to Jake's apartment where Eric picked up his car.

"What happened, son?" his father asked. Eric reiterated the story one more time as the two of them were about to enter the Channing driveway. Dorothy was right behind them in the family car.

As the three were heading into the house, Dorothy asked, "Think we need to go to the hospital and check on Julie? Next to Jake Stanley, I'm sure we're the last people that the Yarboroughs want to see, but I think we need to do it anyway."

The three of them turned around and got in the family car and headed toward the hospital.

As Dorothy predicted, the Yarboroughs were in shock, and Mr. Yarborough immediately ordered the three of them to leave.

After being examined, Julie was released. Even though this incident was not reported by any of the media outlets, by church time the next day, everyone in Wentworth knew about it.

A troubled Julie returned to school the following Wednesday. She needed to complete this semester to graduate, but instead of attending Jacksonville State University, she would probably go out of state to college. Jake Stanley was sentenced to six months in the county jail. And Eric continued to work at the plant washing equipment parts. As planned, he entered Calhoun Junior College for summer school.

Chapter 22

Much to Eric's surprise, he made two A's and two B's in his classes for the summer term. While he did spend time studying, he didn't have to burn the midnight oil. In the fall, he was able to schedule his classes on Monday, Wednesday, and Friday. Being free on Tuesday and Thursday, he took a job sacking grocery at one of the town's supermarkets. Being young and energetic, Eric could handle a schedule like this, and keep up with his studies, even though his chemistry class was giving him fits.

Because he no longer had anything to do with Jake Stanley, he stopped smoking pot and drank alcohol sparingly. Wiley Martin, who had snubbed Eric after he had dropped out of Georgia Southern, had called him a few times to go out and do something when he was home from the University. After breaking up with Carol Ann, Wiley had started dating another girl from Wentworth who was attending Auburn.

"Gee Wiley, with all those cute girls at the University, why do you stick to Wentworth girls who you can only see once in a while?"

"I don't know."

Always interested in what his former classmates were doing, Eric asked about the Wentworth people who were attending the University. Of course, he inquired about how Kristie was doing, and if Wiley ever saw her.

"I think she's dating a different football player this year. But I do know one thing; she has her nose stuck up in the air so high that if it were to rain, she'd surely drown."

Wiley still despised Kristie.

"Are you working the Saturday after Thanksgiving?" Wiley asked.

"Probably, why?"

"I have four tickets to the Auburn game, and they're not student tickets. Jamie is going with me, and I'm sure she can fix you up with one of her friends at Auburn. They'll be yelling for Auburn, but I'm okay with that."

"Thanks. I'd like to. I'll check and see if I can get off."

This was Eric's lucky day. His boss at the grocery store said he could have the Saturday of the Alabama-Auburn game off if he would agree to work the Friday before the game, the Friday after Thanksgiving. Eric told his boss he had a deal, and called Wiley to let him know he would be joining them for the game.

Eric was excited about going to the game. While he had been to a few Alabama games, he had never been to an Alabama-Auburn game. Also, Wiley's girlfriend had a foxy date for Eric, or so Wiley said. Now, if Alabama would just win the game. It had been an excellent season for the Tide, undefeated and ranked high in the AP and UPI polls.

Gameday was a cold one in Birmingham, and everyone dressed accordingly; hats, gloves, heavy coats and boots. Because Eric's date lived in Birmingham, he, Wiley, and Jamie drove from Wentworth to

Birmingham that morning, picked up Eric's date, and drove to Legion Field. Rhonda Jarvis was certainly attractive enough, but she seemed a little snobby, not that he cared about a girl's personality. He hadn't had a girl in his arms since Julie Yarborough, and he felt he was ready to get physical again.

About twenty minutes before kickoff, the foursome found their seats in the stadium and sat down to await the start of the game. Looking around after they had settled in, Eric spotted none other than Kristie Tidwell walking up the steps in the next section, her mom, dad, and another girl were with her.

When Eric told Wiley and Jamie that he had just seen Kristie with her parents, neither seemed to care.

"Who's the football player she's supposedly dating?" asked Eric to Wiley.

"David Strayner, starting cornerback," said Wiley.

"Big deal," Jamie piped in. "I couldn't care less about Kristie Tidwell. I hear she won't have anything to do with anyone in Wentworth except her parents."

"And can you blame her?" asked Eric.

"Maybe you should ask her out if you like her so much," said Wiley. "Frankly, I hope she gets a terminal disease and dies."

Guess there was no way to reconcile Kristie and Wiley.

After the game which Alabama won, the four of them went out to eat at a trendy Birmingham restaurant. Then they went back to Rhonda's house where Eric walked her to the door, got her contact information, and kissed her good night. He finally had a fun date with someone who wasn't white trash, and it was about time.

As the three of them were driving home, Eric's thoughts went to Julie Yarborough. He thought he heard that Julie's parents sent her to Emory University in Atlanta in hopes that she could start a new life after that tragic night. Jake Stanley had been released from the county jail, but Eric would have nothing to do with him, even though Jake had made several attempts to renew his friendship with Eric.

Eric finished the semester at Calhoun, making three B's and two A's, and was eager to begin the next semester. He planned to attend Calhoun for the upcoming spring semester, then work at the plant in the summer. When summer was over, he hoped to attend a four-year college, which he had yet to choose.

When it was time to choose a four-year college to complete his bachelor's degree, Eric applied to Alabama, Auburn, North Alabama, Jacksonville State, and West Alabama. All five institutions accepted him. After talking it over extensively with his parents, he decided on North Alabama, even though he once hesitated about going there.

Located in the northwest Alabama town of Florence, he could continue his fishing and hunting activities on and near Lake Wilson. Also, Eric's date for the Auburn game last year, Rhonda, had dropped out of Auburn and was attending North Alabama. She and Eric had continued seeing one another, and Eric thought she just might be the one.

On schedule, Eric graduated from the University of North Alabama with a degree in Marketing, and took a job as a pharmaceutical sales representative in Nashville. Rhonda, who graduated with a degree in Education landed a teaching job at one of the Huntsville schools. While their preference would have been to end up in the same town, they were less than two hours apart and could see each other on the weekends.

CHAPTER 23

Kristie's six-month evaluation for her job as customer service representative for the large Atlanta bank, where she was hired right out of college, was glowing, and so was her one-year evaluation. However, there was no mention of moving her into other areas to be trained in multiple bank operations. Much to her dismay, what they told her when they hired her was not true. They had no plans to train her in other areas. She had a business degree from Alabama, an excellent business school, and they wanted her. Telling her they wanted to start her as a customer service rep, but train her in other areas was only to get her to come to work for them.

It was about time for her to look for another job, something that would be a step-up from what she had. Also, Kristie was no longer enamored with Atlanta. She was finding it hard to make friends and meet guys, always looking forward to those weekends when she traveled either to Birmingham to see Chloe and her husband, or to Tuscaloosa to visit Cindy, who was still in school.

She wanted to move to Birmingham. Tuscaloosa was a little small for her, and Wentworth was out of the question. Having to go back to Wentworth was Kristie's greatest fear in life, and this fear spurred everything she did. Also, she learned through Chloe that Jerome Peterson had graduated with honors from the Stanford MBA program in accounting and had taken a job with a Big Eight firm in

Atlanta. Chloe had encouraged her to call Jerome, but she didn't have the nerve. Besides, she was no longer in love with him.

After a year of sporadically looking for a new job, Kristie landed a position with a large insurance company. She would go through a training program in Atlanta, and subsequently be transferred to a branch office somewhere in the southeast. While Kristie had never felt that she was a lucky person, this time she was. The company had an opening in their Birmingham office, and Kristie got to move to Birmingham, all expenses paid.

She stayed with this company for two and a half years before moving on to a smaller company whose corporate offices were in Birmingham. With this company, she found a home, and within a year, she had received a promotion and a substantial salary increase to go with it.

Kristie Tidwell was twenty-eight years old, smart, and beautiful. She had moved to Birmingham from Atlanta four years ago and had no regrets. Being an hour's drive away from her parents was important to her, along with living in a city that was manageable. Birmingham suited her.

A few months after her promotion, Kristie met a good-looking guy who said all the right things and treated her like a queen. However, the guy sold life insurance on straight commission for a local company and worked most of the time, including evenings and weekends. Kristie was okay with this because she too was into her career. Steve Conley was divorced with a ten year old daughter, and lived with his parents in a Birmingham suburb located on the other side of town from where Kristie lived.

After Kristie and Steve had been seeing each other for several weeks, Kristie called his office one afternoon to tell him that she was going out of town unexpectedly on business, and wouldn't be able to have dinner with him the next night. She knew he probably wouldn't be there, but intended to leave a message. When Kristie asked the receptionist if Steve was in the office, the receptionist replied no, and asked if this was Mrs. Conley. Kristie said no and hung up without leaving the message. Asking if she was Mrs. Conley wasn't something Kristie wanted to hear. Was Steve married, separated, divorced, whatever?

The next morning after Kristie arrived at the Birmingham Airport, she called Steve's office and was prepared to leave a message. To her surprise, he was in the office, but about to leave for an appointment. When she told him she was leaving for San Francisco and wouldn't be back until Friday, Steve seemed shocked.

Why in the world are you going to San Francisco?" asked Steve.

"I have to try to settle this big case for a reasonable amount. The judge has ordered representatives of all insurance companies involved to be present in his courtroom tomorrow morning."

"I didn't know your job required you to travel to places like San Francisco. When you said that you traveled, I thought you meant to places like Anniston or Montgomery."

"Nope."

"I guess there's a lot I don't know about you, but I'm looking forward to finding out more."

Yeah, and there are things I need to find out about you also, thought Kristie. Because she felt that this was neither the time nor the place to bring up the Mrs. Conley thing, Kristie told Steve she would see him when she returned.

Kristie returned from San Francisco late Friday afternoon to find several messages on her answering machine. One was from Steve indicating that he wouldn't be able to see her this weekend because there was a death in his family. He would call her on Sunday afternoon, and maybe they could spend some time together. Steve was a genuinely nice guy, and Kristie knew he and his ex-wife did have to spend some time together because of the child. As a result, she wasn't worried that he was married or still married. She had to ask, and would do it on Sunday.

Late Sunday afternoon, Steve called and wanted to come over and order pizza for supper. After eating, when they were lying in bed talking, Kristie blurted out, "Are you married?"

Steve hesitated and said, "On paper, yes. We'll probably be getting a divorce, but not now."

Steve told Kristie about his family life, but emphasized that the marriage, was, for all intents and purposes, over. He was living with his parents and planned to do so for a while. Steve also told Kristie that he wasn't intentionally keeping this from her, and he intended to tell her, but was waiting until he was sure that she cared for him as much as he cared for her.

Sadly, Kristie was falling in love, and accepted, like a fool, everything Steve Conley said to her. Maybe he would divorce his wife, Carol. Kristie didn't care for the name, Carol, because she knew several Carols and didn't like any of them.

New Year's Eve, universal date night, was approaching, and Steve had not mentioned anything to Kristie about plans. She was uncomfortable asking him, fearing that he would be ringing in the New Year with Carol, maybe kissing her at the stroke of midnight.

The thought made Kristie nauseous. But, much to her surprise, Steve informed her that his brother, the leader of a local band, was playing at some club on the other side of town. Steve was going to be there to assist his brother with whatever needed to be done. The brother was in the process of divorcing his third wife and chased anything in a skirt. Therefore, he shouldn't be upset if Steve was with someone other than the wife, nor would he tell on Steve.

Kristie wanted to be with Steve on New Year's Eve, and agreed to drive to the other side of town to be with him as he assisted his brother. Kristie took great pains to ensure that her look was perfect. Her low cut little black dress, cinched at the waist, coupled with black satin pumps, white lace pantyhose, and a classy gold choker necklace made her look like a princess. She was going to be with Steve tonight, kissing him at midnight. Then they would return to her apartment.

Kristie followed Steve's directions and arrived at the club shortly after 8:00 pm, parking close to the back, per suggestion from Steve. That way she could enter through the band entrance and not have to pay a cover. Spotting Steve's vehicle, she parked, got out of her car, and walked to the back door. When she tried to open it, she found it was locked. Pounding on it with her fists proved useless. Having no other option but to enter from the front, she made her way to the main entrance.

While Kristie knew this crowd was not exactly a crowd you might find at one of the Birmingham area country clubs, she was shocked to see women wearing jeans so tight that every crease in front and back was visible. These women were wrapped all over their men who had enormous beer guts. One man appeared to have his hand down the back of a woman's pants. And the music hadn't even started.

As Kristie approached the front door, one woman said to her, "Honey, you're not dressed appropriately, are you sure you're in the right place?"

The man with this woman let out a hearty belly laugh, and so did the woman. Not only were these people trashy, but they were old enough to be her parents. Kristie could never imagine Mary and Bobby going to a place like this. Nor could she imagine any of her friends' parents going to a place like this either.

Upon entering the club, Kristie surveyed the premises to find a way to get backstage. She approached the stage and was looking for a doorway or something that might lead there. From out of nowhere, a deep voice startled her and asked, "You looking for something, Miss?"

Kristie turned around to find an older man in a security guard uniform. "My boyfriend is the brother of one of the band members, and he's backstage. I'm supposed to meet him there. How can I get backstage?"

The guard/bouncer led her through the kitchen and opened a door leading to the back for her.

There was quite a bit of activity taking place with members of the band preparing for the show. A quick scan of the area produced no Steve. Then she saw him emerging from behind a curtain of some kind with a bleach blonde hanging onto him for dear life. When Steve spotted Kristie, he took the blonde's arms that were wrapped around him, unwrapped them, and escorted her to a chair. He then made his way over to Kristie, telling her to follow him. Kristie followed Steve to another enclave of the stage behind another curtain where he told her to wait while he fetched a chair for her.

When Steve returned, Kristie asked him, "Who was that blonde?"

"Chuck's wife. She's drunk as shit and horny as hell, plus she told me she has her sights set on me tonight."

"And?" replied Kristie.

"Well, you know me, I'm not about to take advantage of any woman in that kind of shape. You know how to go through the kitchen to get to the main area. If you want something to drink, go to the bar. If you're hungry, you can order something at the bar. There are signs to the restrooms. And when you're back here, please stay behind this curtain. It wouldn't be good if we're seen together as a couple."

"I thought your brother was okay with us."

"Well, he probably would be, but the drummer is Carol's second cousin, and even though he has a wife and several chicks on the side, blood is thicker than water."

Steve then sauntered off, telling Kristie he would check back to see how she was doing in a little while.

What was happening was surreal. Kristie was in a world where she didn't belong. She was a graduate of the University of Alabama and a young executive, who lived in a nice apartment in an upscale suburb of Birmingham. How in the world did she end up here, a sleazy joint in a run-down part of town? She should be dancing to the beat of a rock band at one of Birmingham's upscale clubs where the clientele were mostly under thirty-five and professional.

On top of that, Steve didn't want to be seen with her and hadn't even told her how gorgeous she looked, something he had never missed telling her when they were together. At least he had given her two twenties to pay for her supper and drinks.

Did she want something to eat? Not really. Something to drink? A beer, maybe. So off she went to the bar, sat down on a stool, and was ready to order something. Behind the bar was a middle-aged man with a gut and a cigarette hanging out of his mouth. His hair was slicked back in a pompadour, and he had a receding hairline. There was also a woman behind the bar, who, with her bright red hair, bright blue eyeshadow, and bad teeth, looked like she had been ridden hard and hung up to dry. This woman was too busy thrusting her cleavage at a customer to come over and take Kristie's drink order. However, after a few awkward minutes, the man turned around and saw Kristie, looked at her and said, "Yes?"

A Lite Beer, please.

Without saying anything, the man retrieved a beer bottle and placed it in front of Kristie, telling her that it would be $3.00. Kristie paid, left a tip, and went backstage.

Steve's brother's band was terrible, but the patrons didn't mind. Whenever a fast song was played, there were pelvic thrusts, boob thrusts, booty thrusts, and every salacious movement possible. When the band played a slow number, couples were straining against one another doing the slow pelvic grind. If Steve wasn't being such an asshole, this whole thing, nightmare that it was, might be the makings of a comedy series.

Since giving her the twenties for food and drink, and telling her to stay behind the curtain, Kristie had not seen Steve, neither had she seen the blonde floozy who was hanging all over him. She didn't like the music and was uncomfortable with the patrons; so much so, that every five minutes that elapsed seemed like an hour. She was not going to make it to midnight. And since Steve was not paying her any attention, why was she here? Yeah, why was she here? She wasn't comfortable and wanted to go home.

Kristie stood up and walked out the front door discreetly. However, as she walked to her car, couples were outside laughing and being romantic. She passed one couple where she swore it looked like the man had his hand down the woman's blouse. Classy! It took Kristie about forty minutes to get home. When she looked at her reflection in the mirror, her lipstick was gone, and her mascara was streaked. Would Steve try to call her in the next couple of hours? She doubted it. Would she ever see him again? She didn't know.

CHAPTER 24

Years later, Kristie and friend, Kay Murphy were heading down to the Alabama Gulf Coast for a few days at the beach. Three other friends would be joining them later. When everyone arrived at the condo, the girls decided they would go to one of the many local seafood restaurants for dinner.

At the restaurant, the five women were seated at a table next to five men. The men were having drinks and laughing. The guys appeared to be around Kristie's age, and a couple of them were good-looking. As Kristie eye-balled the guys, looking for wedding rings, one of them looked familiar. Could that guy be Wiley Martin? While some of the other guys looked familiar also, Wiley was the only one she felt safe about identifying, and she wasn't about to say anything to him. If Wiley or anyone else at the table recognized Kristie, none of them showed it.

Kristie had not seen Wiley since they were students at the University, but noted he still had his thick dark hair and crooked smile. The women ordered their drinks and dinner. Donna, one of the women, was sitting closest to the table of guys and overheard something said about Wentworth. Donna then said to Kristie that she thought one or more of the guys might be from Wentworth. Kristie shrugged it off and said she didn't recognize any of them.

One guy that kept eyeing the table of women, particularly Kristie, was Eric Channing. Eric had just gone through a divorce and to put it bluntly, he was looking for women. Eric wanted to talk to the beautiful dark-haired woman at the next table, but couldn't figure out how to do so without being obvious. Little did he know she was Kristie Tidwell, a former classmate of his and Wiley's.

Even though the guys arrived at the restaurant before the ladies, both groups finished dinner and were getting up from their tables simultaneously. As the girls were walking out, some of the guys were holding the doors open for them. The guy holding the door open for Kristie did not look familiar to her. She said nothing and neither did the guy, Eric Channing.

Kristie, a party girl, asked if anyone in the group was up for the Flora-Bama. There were no takers except for Donna, who had never been, and had always wanted to go. Because the group was in Harriet Bentley's huge Buick sedan, they went back to the condo where Kristie and Donna got in Kristie's Chevy Camaro and headed east toward the Flora-Bama.

Donna had only heard of the Flora-Bama and knew that it was on the Alabama/Florida state line. She wasn't expecting a falling down roadhouse whose patrons ranged from sailors and bikers to businessmen and women driving expensive cars. She was also taken aback at the clothesline full of bras strung over the main bar.

"This is not at all what I expected, and I don't like it," exclaimed Donna.

Kristie had ordered a beer, but said, "I guess I can run you back to the condo and come back. My hand's stamped so I shouldn't have to pay another cover charge, but I would like to finish my beer."

"You'd come back here by yourself?"

"Sure. In fact, this is a great place if you're by yourself. You can just blend into the crowd. There's an urban legend that Mick Jagger was here in the eighties and signed his name on the wall in the ladies' restroom."

When Kristie finished her beer, she drove Donna back to the condo, which was about five minutes from the bar. Much to the chagrin of Donna, who was old school, and felt that "proper young ladies" should not go to bars by themselves, Kristie dropped her at the entrance to the condo, telling her she would see her later.

During to the drive back to the Flora-Bama, Kristie shook her head. All Donna could talk about was going to the Flora-Bama. Then when we go, she decides in five minutes she doesn't like it and demands to be taken back to the condo. No respect for me and what I might want to do.

Kristie got back into the establishment without having to pay another cover charge. She ordered another beer, and sat at one of the long tables next to the tent, closest to the parking lot. She could hear the band that was playing under the tent, and kicked back to people watch.

Just as soon as Kristie got settled, who should come in and take seats not far from her, but the guys who were seated next to them at the restaurant earlier this evening. They were getting wasted, and a couple of them appeared to be looking for women.

There was Kristie, a sitting duck. The one who she felt sure was Wiley Martin was getting obnoxious, but he didn't seem interested in chasing women. Perhaps it was because of the wide gold band on the third finger of his left hand. So, Wiley had married. To whom, she wondered.

There was one guy in the group that kept looking at Kristie. In a few moments, he stood and started toward her. The guy didn't look like anyone she remembered. After sitting down across the table from her, he said, "Weren't you at the Perdido Pass Restaurant earlier this evening with some other ladies?"

"Yes, girls' beach trip."

"Where are y'all from?"

"Birmingham. What about y'all?"

"Wentworth."

"Oh, okay." Kristie wasn't about to tell the guy she grew up in Wentworth because that would mean having to talk to Wiley Martin, something she wasn't prepared to do.

"What happened to your friends?"

Kristie told him that three in their group weren't much for going to bars and the other, Donna, didn't like the Flora-Bama.

"I take it you like to party."

"Yeah, but I'm not a wild child."

"Neither am I."

How am I going to get out of this, thought Kristie? I'm not attracted to this guy in the least, and I don't want to tell him that I have roots in Wentworth. Kristie and the mystery guy chatted for a few minutes and found they had some things in common such as Alabama football. They discussed last year's national championship and the coaches succeeding Coach Bryant. Eric knew about football, and Kristie guessed that he must have played football in high school and maybe in college. She tried to remember some of the football players who were in high school with her, but this guy didn't seem like any of them. So, Kristie asked him if he was originally from Wentworth or did he grow up somewhere else. He was Wentworth born and bred.

"Oh, by the way, I'm Eric."

"I'm Kristie."

"So, you came down here with girlfriends?"

"Yes, and it looks like you came down here with friends also?"

"Yes, these are guys I went to high school with. What part of Birmingham do you live in?"

"Helena, just south of the Galleria."

"Oh, okay. I'm somewhat familiar with that area."

I guess going to the Flora-Bama by one's self is not such a good idea, thought Kristie. She knew she should get away from this creep. She could just say she needed to go, and then leave, but would he follow her out? There's enough security at the Flora-Bama, she could get someone at the entrance to make sure she reached her car and wasn't followed.

Kristie finished her beer quickly and said, "It was nice meeting you Eric, but I drove down here today, and I'm a little tired. So, I'm heading out."

"Nice meeting you too, Kristie, be careful and have a great time down here."

"Thanks, you too, Eric."

With that, Kristie stood up and walked through the maze that was the Flora-Bama. No one was following her, so she walked to her car by herself, got in, and drove back to the condo.

When Kristie let herself in the door, she found Donna sitting outside on the patio. Everyone else had gone to bed. Donna again indicated that she didn't like that place.

"Well, Donna, you've been dying to go there, and then it took you less than five minutes to decide you hated it."

"I thought it would be a little classier, something different."

"That's the Flora-Bama, and it will always the Flora-Bama. "

"Does Kenny Stabler have an interest in it?"

"I don't know, but he does frequent it a good bit. Interested in Kenny Stabler? Don't know what his marital status is at the moment, though."

"That's okay, he wouldn't have anything to do with me, anyway."

"You never know."

Eric, Eric Channing, thought Kristie as she was lying in bed waiting for sleep to come. That's who that was. He's changed some since high school. Now, Kristie wished she hadn't acted like such a bitch to him. She did look good that night, and she would have liked to have seen the look on Wiley Martin's face when he discovered that she was Kristie Tidwell.

Back at the Flora-Bama, the guys were giving Eric some lip about being turned down by the sexy dark haired girl he was trying to pick up.

"Guess she just wasn't interested in snuggling up with you this evening," said Wiley.

"Actually, she's a nice girl. I could tell the moment I started talking to her. She works for an insurance company, is a season ticket holder at Bama, and does volunteer service work."

"Not for you tonight," proclaimed Wiley.

"Did you find out where she was from?" asked Jimmy Harpo.

"She lives in Birmingham."

"But has she always lived in Birmingham?"

"I don't know, she didn't mention any other town except Tuscaloosa."

"According to Wiley, she looks a lot like he remembers Kristie Tidwell looking."

"Well, Kristie is her first name."

"That's her, I knew it," said Wiley.

"When I told her I was from Wentworth, she didn't bat an eyelash."

"I don't think she comes around Wentworth much, except to visit her mom and dad. I had some business with them several months ago. They asked me some things, and I told them I graduated from Wentworth High School, and when I graduated. Then they said their daughter graduated in my class and told me her name. I said I remembered her. That was about all I said because her mom and dad were so nice, and I treated Kristie like dirt when we were growing up."

"Anyway," said Eric, "She was totally unresponsive when I told her I was from Wentworth. Maybe if you hadn't been so cruel to her when we were in high school, she might have talked to me or talked to all of us."

"You think she recognized us?" asked Wiley.

"I wouldn't be a bit surprised if she did and just ignored us. Anyway, thanks a lot, Wiley."

"Hey, hey, hey, there are plenty of women around here, we'll find one for you. Kristie Tidwell, why would you want her?"

"Go to hell, Wiley, you haven't grown up a bit, have you?"

Eric had broadcasted the signal that he was newly divorced and needing a woman. However, the only women who showed any interest in him that evening were some of the regulars who looked like they had been ridden hard and hung up to dry. Pretty Kristie, where was she staying? When they were close to wasted, the guys went back to their condo, with Eric having failed in his quest for a woman.

Waking up the next day, he was in a bad mood, and still wanted a woman. Damn Wiley Martin, damn all the rest of the guys. He was convinced that the girl from last night was Kristie Tidwell from Wentworth. And even though Kristie gave off the vibes of being a nice girl, Eric thought he could at least have coerced her to cuddle up with him somewhere. Damn, damn, damn.

CHAPTER 25

As Kristie's career progressed, she continued to travel to major cities in the United States, usually by herself. In her field, she came to be well respected nationally and started seeing a guy, who was a business associate, from Philadelphia. While Kristie liked the guy, she didn't want to move to Pennsylvania. Also, the guy was an atheist, and she knew this would never work out because of her strong Christian faith.

When Kristie was at the peak of her career, her department was moved to the offices of the parent company in Indianapolis. While Kristie had a chance to transfer to Indianapolis, she elected not to. Her dad had passed away a few years ago, and her mom was now in assisted living. Being an only child, she felt obligated to stay close.

Because there were no other jobs in Birmingham like the one she had, Kristie decided to change fields and chose computer programming. For nine months, she lived off severance pay while studying twelve to fourteen hours a day. The studying paid off, and Kristie landed her first IT job right about the time her severance was nearing depletion. After getting that first job, Kristie changed jobs twice, and was subsequently promoted to IT management.

CHAPTER 26

While Eric loved Rhonda Jarvis and thought he wanted to marry her, something was holding him back from popping the question. Good looking girls were abundant in Nashville, and Eric found his eyes wandering on many occasions. Then one evening when he was having drinks with friends after work, he started talking to a girl who was also with friends, and was sitting at a table next to him and his friends. When happy hour was over, he asked the girl if she would like to go to the adjacent restaurant and get something to eat with him. She accepted.

When they finished dinner, Eric asked the young lady if she would like to go over to his apartment for a while, and she said yes. Eric had a roommate, but the roommate was engaged and mostly stayed over at his fiancé's place. So, the apartment was empty when the two of them arrived. The girl's clothes came off quickly, and Eric thoroughly enjoyed a meaningless romp in the hay. Afterward, the girl announced that it was time for her to leave because she had to work the next day. So, in less than ten minutes, she was dressed and out the door. Eric never bothered to find out her name, nor did he get any contact information from her.

Because Rhonda was your typical nice girl, she and Eric had never gone all the way. In fact, Eric never had any success in getting

Rhonda completely out of her clothes. Even Rita in high school was giving him more, after dating for about a year.

Eric soon found himself going out drinking almost every night, and discovered there was no shortage of women who were willing to either go home with him, or take him to their places. Occasionally, he would run upon the so-called nice girl who was nothing but a tease and wanted a relationship. But, most of the time, he lucked out. Besides rediscovering sex with no strings attached, he began, again, to smoke pot. He found it made the sex more satisfying, if that was humanly possible.

On the weekends, he continued to see Rhonda, and planned on marrying her one of these days, just not anytime soon. While Rhonda would occasionally drive to Nashville to be with Eric, most of the time, he drove to her apartment in Huntsville. Then, occasionally on those Sunday mornings, he would drive an hour south to Wentworth to visit his parents.

During his last visit to see Rhonda, Eric could sense some pressure being applied to him to get married and start a family. She was talking about applying for a Tennessee teacher's certificate and was researching the Nashville area school systems. While marrying Rhonda was somewhat appealing, and he would finally get to see her naked, starting a family scared him to death. The plan to marry Rita while he was in college was forgotten.

Eric did, though, start thinking about his lifestyle. So far, there had been no STDs or unplanned pregnancies. He never asked any of the girls if they were using birth control, nor had he ever considered using a condom. In this, the age of rampant STDs, he was taking too many chances. Maybe he would start using condoms. Yes, that's what he would do.

It was Mother's Day, and Eric had just arrived at his parents' house. He spent Friday and Saturday night at Rhonda's. Then they both departed out of Huntsville. Rhonda went to Birmingham to see her mom and dad, and Eric went to Wentworth to see his mom and dad.

Not much of a churchgoer, Jack Channing was sitting in the den of his house listening to the Methodist Church service broadcasting live on the radio. Dorothy, along with Sandy, now a junior at Jacksonville State and Roger, a senior at WHS, had gone to church. The house was comfortable, and the smell of the roast in the oven was making Eric's mouth water.

When Eric asked his dad what had been happening around Wentworth, his dad told him that Jake Stanley was caught dealing drugs in Blount County and would likely go to the penitentiary for a while. Johnny Morton, who had graduated from Auburn the year before, moved to the west coast in search of fame and fortune. And lastly, Wiley Martin, who had returned to Wentworth to take over the family appliance business, was doing just that. In fact, Wiley was considering expansion, perhaps opening a second store in the booming little town of Boaz. Then maybe he would open another store in the Falkville/Hartselle area. Bad boy Wiley was having a good life, and he was assured of a good life for many years to come.

Shortly after twelve, Dorothy, Sandy, and Roger arrived at the house looking solemn. Before putting her apron on and finishing Sunday dinner, Dorothy asked Jack to turn off the radio in the den and sat down on the sofa beside Eric.

"Got some bad news, Julie Yarborough was found dead in her Atlanta apartment early this morning. They don't know what caused her death, but it looks like she may have overdosed on heroin or some other dangerous drug."

Eric immediately went cold. If he had not taken her to Jake Stanley's apartment that fateful night, this surely wouldn't have happened. After the attack by Jake Stanley, Julie muddled through the remainder of her senior year at Wentworth. After graduation, her parents sent her to Emory University in Decatur, Georgia, a suburb of Atlanta. There were rumors that Julie was into drugs and the Atlanta party scene, but Emory was tough academically, and Julie was smart. Eric always thought she would get her degree, get a job somewhere, and never return to Wentworth. Eric moped through Sunday dinner as did the rest of the family. He would forever feel responsible for Julie Yarborough's difficulties and untimely death.

CHAPTER 27

It was May, and they had both been out of college for one year, but Eric had made no moves in the direction of taking Rhonda for his wife. He was making decent money selling pharmaceuticals, and Rhonda was getting by on her teacher's salary. School was going to be out for the summer in a couple of weeks, and by the first of July, Rhonda was required to advise the Huntsville school district if she would be returning for the next school year.

From Friday afternoon when he arrived at Rhonda's until Sunday morning when they both parted ways to celebrate Mother's Day, Rhonda talked nonstop about getting a Tennessee teacher's certificate. She clearly wanted to get married and make a perfect little home for her and Eric. She would continue to teach a few years while Eric sold pharmaceuticals. Their combined income would allow them to live comfortably while Eric worked his way up the corporate ladder. Then it would be time to buy a house and start their family.

But Eric had the best of both worlds. He had Rhonda, the respectable school teacher from a respectable middle-class Birmingham family, plus he had all the women and sex he could handle during the week in Nashville. In fact, there were a couple of girls whose names and phone numbers he had. If he couldn't find someone suitable for the evening, he would call one of these girls and ask to go over to her place for a fun time. He even had the occasional three-some. While that once disgusted him, he was now into it. What harm could it do now that he also had a respectable girl with whom he would eventually marry and start a family?

While Eric did most of his business in the Nashville area, he made occasional trips to the Chattanooga and Knoxville areas.

One afternoon in Knoxville, a few weeks after Mother's Day, he was having a few beers at a neighborhood bar when two young women asked him to join them. They told him they were lesbians, but liked having a man with them at times. They were into watching each other perform with a guy. It sounds like I have my evening planned, Eric thought to himself.

After settling the bar tabs, Eric followed the girls to their house in an upscale suburb of Knoxville. The pot they gave him was high grade, and the beer was Heineken, the perfect combination. At one point, one of the girls put a cotton ball under his nose and told him to sniff, which he did.

In less than a minute, the music was more intense. The girl who gave him the cotton ball to sniff looked so much better. He had two women, and was turned on to an experiencing-enhancing drug. Eric passed out.

Hours later he woke up on the floor beside the giant waterbed. The two girls were curled up naked in each other's arms asleep. Looking at the clock, he had a little over an hour before his appointment at one of the Knoxville area hospitals.

He didn't know how to get back to his hotel. Guess he would have to wake up the girls and find out. When he tried to move, everything ached, and once he stood up, he became dizzy and sat back down. He was naked and didn't know where his clothes might be. He decided to call in sick with a stomach virus and cancel his appointments.

Eric crawled over to the waterbed and started patting one of the girls on the back, telling them to wake up. He found his clothes and dressed. After making him breakfast of eggs, bacon, and toast, one of the girls wrote out the directions for getting back to his hotel. Driving back, Eric went over and over in his head what had happened last night. Uh oh! He didn't use anything. Then he remembered sniffing a cotton ball. What in the world could have been on that cotton ball?

While Jake Stanley might have been okay with this, Eric had a real uneasy feeling. Sex and hard drugs. Maybe this kind of life wasn't for him. When he arrived at the hotel, Eric called his boss and told him he had canceled his hospital appointment for that morning, but would re-schedule for later today or tomorrow. Then he fell into bed and took a long nap. After taking care of business the next day, Eric headed back to Nashville. It was Wednesday, and he had something paramount to do before he left for Huntsville to see Rhonda on Friday afternoon.

In one of Nashville's upscale jewelry stores, Eric looked at diamond rings and wedding sets. Now was the time to get married and settle down. He didn't want any more evenings like the one he had with those Knoxville girls. While he found some rings he liked, he didn't want to purchase just anything. He and Rhonda would be wearing these rings for the rest of their lives. He wanted her to have a say in this also.

When he returned home from the jewelry store, he called Rhonda and asked her if she could, instead, come to Nashville for the weekend, and she said, of course. Rhonda was insecure in her relationship with Eric, but she loved him very much. While she hadn't seen anyone else since they were students together at North Alabama, she surmised that Eric was seeing other girls.

After school ended for the day, Rhonda left Huntsville and headed north to Nashville with a smile on her face. She was so in love with Eric and looked forward to seeing him on the weekends. Rhonda was technically a virgin, and while she and Eric had done some serious fooling around, they never went all the way. Maybe it was about time. Maybe after this weekend, she would make an appointment with her ob-gyn and get a prescription for birth control pills.

When Rhonda visited Eric in Nashville, he would grill steaks for the two of them on Friday night. Then on Saturday night, he would take her out to eat and maybe out dancing afterward, even though Eric was not much of a dancer. When Eric returned to his apartment on Friday afternoon after a full day of sales calls, he sat down with a beer and the evening paper to await Rhonda's arrival. The steaks were marinating in the refrigerator, and the salad was made. Because Eric didn't like microwaved baked potatoes, he would put the potatoes in the oven to bake as soon as Rhonda got there. Eric had rum and lime concentrate to make daiquiris for Rhonda. He didn't care for them, but she did.

At 5:45, the doorbell rang, and it was Rhonda at the door. Even though she looked tired and her makeup was smeared, Eric thought she was beautiful and told her so. After getting her suitcase from the car, Eric put the potatoes in the oven, made the daiquiris, and fired up the grill. For appetizers, Eric took a bag of potato chips from the pantry and a carton of French onion dip from the fridge and put them on the coffee table. Eric was a guy, and that was one of the things Rhonda loved about him. If he had served the chips and dip in serving bowls, it wouldn't be right.

After dinner when they were sitting on the sofa listening to the stereo and talking about various things, Eric blurted out, "If you want to, we can get married. I'm ready. In fact, I've already been looking at rings. If you want to marry me, let's go to the jewelry store tomorrow."

Rhonda almost choked on her daquiri, but told Eric that she did want to marry him. That was another thing Rhonda loved about Eric. He didn't have a romantic bone in his body.

The next day, Rhonda and Eric went to the jewelry store and picked out an engagement ring and wedding ring for Rhonda. They also picked out a wedding band for Eric. After they purchased the rings, Eric got down on his hands and knees in the jewelry store and asked Rhonda to marry him. And she said yes. There were a few customers in the shop at the time, and they clapped and congratulated the happy couple.

That evening, Eric and Rhonda talked about plans, deciding to have a January wedding, but in the meantime, Rhonda would move to Nashville come summer and try to get a teaching job in a Nashville area school.

As she drove south to Huntsville on Sunday afternoon with a diamond on her left ring finger, she had never been as happy in her whole life. There would, for sure, be difficulties. Their marriage in the state of Alabama would be a mixed marriage, but they could deal with it. Maybe she and Eric would spend the day of the Alabama-Auburn football game apart each year. This coming week would be the last of the school year, so, Rhonda would let the school system know that she would not be returning for the following year. The wedding would take place in her home church in Birmingham. She wanted a large formal wedding with at least nine bridesmaids and groomsmen. Like all young women, she had dreamed of her wedding day all her life.

Back in Nashville, Eric was not sharing Rhonda's happiness. Only a few days ago, he had been with two women and took some kind of drug. Could one or both of these girls possibly get pregnant? Could he have caught an STD from one of them? They were apparently into everything.

This past weekend, he and Rhonda did some fooling around, but again, they didn't go all the way. Rhonda did tell Eric that she would make an appointment with her doctor to get a prescription for birth control pills. It was about time, thought Eric.

Eric was more worried about STDs than he was about pregnancies. He never got the names of these girls, and he didn't think they had his name. He would just have to watch for symptoms. If he escaped from this little escapade unscathed, he would give up all women except for Rhonda.

Because Rhonda's apartment lease didn't expire until August, she and Eric decided that she would stay in Huntsville for the summer and get a summer job to make some extra money. In the fall, she would rent a small apartment in Nashville in hopes of landing a teaching position.

CHAPTER 28

On Thursday morning after the weekend he and Rhonda got engaged, Eric received a call from his boss's boss in Oklahoma City. Corporate was pleased with his work and wanted him to take a promotion into senior level sales, a fast track to management. Because there were no senior sales positions open in Nashville or in the state of Tennessee, he would have to move to another regional office. The one they had in mind for him was Dallas. It was almost unheard of for a first-year sales rep to be placed on the management fast track. But Eric was an exceptional employee, demonstrated leadership qualities, and had learned the business in record time. They wanted him in Dallas in two weeks.

The company would pay any fees he might be required to pay to get out of his apartment lease, and, of course, they would pay for his moving expenses. There was no doubt that Eric had to take this position. To turn down a promotion would be career suicide with his company and he liked his company. Rhonda would have to move to Dallas.

When he broke the news to her that night, she was excited for Eric, but not sure she wanted to move to Dallas. They agreed to talk when Eric visited her for the weekend. So, instead of visiting her parents in Birmingham and showing off her new ring, she stayed in Huntsville.

Dallas was a great town, and by the time Eric arrived in Huntsville on Friday evening, Rhonda had warmed up to the idea of Dallas. Now, it was time to decide what they would do about the wedding and her teaching job. After hours of serious talking, they agreed that Eric would move to Dallas. Rhonda would stay in Huntsville and teach another year. Somehow, they would work out visits. They also postponed the wedding from January until June. They would still have a formal wedding in Birmingham. Both were young and had plenty of time to be married and have children.

Eric packed and moved to Dallas leaving Rhonda behind in Huntsville. Even though Dallas was flat, hot, and lacked the vegetation he was used to in Tennessee and Alabama, he fell in love with the city and enjoyed his work. He moved into an apartment in an upscale area, and soon began to enjoy the Dallas nightlife. And the Texas women? He had never seen as much big blonde hair in his life. Even though he and Rhonda talked at least three times a week, Eric was a man and couldn't resist taking what was being offered to him. This time around, he was careful and carried protection in his wallet, and always remembered to use it. While he kept telling himself he was in love with Rhonda and wanted to marry her, he was not looking forward to next June when he would have to settle down.

Come fall, Eric missed Alabama football and SEC football. While Dallas and Texas had the Cowboys, the Longhorns, the Mustangs, and the Aggies, it just wasn't the same.

One Sunday night when Eric called Rhonda, a guy answered the phone. Thinking he had a wrong number, Eric asked if this was Rhonda's number. The guy said yes, and that he would get Rhonda. "Who's the guy?"

"A neighbor who just moved in several doors down, he's a nice guy."

So, you're playing welcome wagon?"

"Eric."

"Well, I just miss you."

"And I miss you too."

"Thanksgiving's coming up, and we have to make some plans."

"Eric, we have plenty of time to talk about that."

"I guess we do. I'll let you get back to your guest."

"Okay, bye, love you."

"Love you, too."

Eric knew that something wasn't right about that conversation. Maybe the two of them needed to have a long talk over Thanksgiving. Eric was having a good time, and wasn't sure he wanted to get married. Also, Dallas was a great town if you were single, but he wasn't sure he wanted to raise a family there. Eric was enjoying his job and the money that went along with it. Maybe he should have a good time, save as much as he could, retire early, and go back to Alabama. Then he could spend time doing what he loved best, hunting and fishing. Did he even want to get married at all?

As Thanksgiving drew close, Eric and Rhonda decided that Eric would have Thanksgiving dinner at Rhonda's parents' house in Birmingham. He would drive to Birmingham from Dallas. On Thursday evening, they would drive to Huntsville in separate cars and spend Friday and Saturday together. On Sunday, they would drive again, in separate cars, again, to Eric's parents' house for Sunday dinner. Rhonda would drive back to Huntsville to begin school the next day. Eric would spend the night in Wentworth, and drive back to Dallas on Monday.

With the Alabama – Auburn game on Saturday, things might get a little tense. Eric always got upset when Alabama lost a football game. Rhonda cheered for Auburn, but got on with her life immediately after the game, whether Auburn won or lost. She thought Alabama fans were spoiled brats, who thought it was their birthright to dominate college football.

On Thanksgiving night, after arriving in Huntsville, Eric and Rhonda talked a little while about sports and current events before Rhonda told Eric that she had seen her doctor and was now on the pill. Eric was pleased, and for the first time, he and Rhonda would be having real sex.

From their fooling around, Eric knew Rhonda was a virgin, but tonight, something was different. When he entered her, there was no resistance, no pain, and no blood. Rhonda wasn't a virgin.

As soon as he came, Eric pulled out and sat upright on the bed. "You're not a virgin," he exclaimed.

"What do you mean, yes I am, or was?"

"Whenever we've been together, you've been tight, and you would tell me if I was hurting you."

"Some women have it easy their first time, and some don't. I guess my first time was easy."

"Nice try, honey, but you have lost your virginity somewhere along the way, and it wasn't to me."

"Well, you're not exactly pure as the driven snow."

"I lost my virginity when I was seventeen and told you about it. I've also told you about other women and admitted I was a womanizer before I met you."

"Do you want the ring back?"

"Yes, yes I do."

Rhonda took off the ring and handed it to Eric. It took him about ten minutes to dress, gather up his things, and walk out of the apartment, and out of Rhonda's life.

CHAPTER 29

Eric got into his car and drove to the nearest phone booth. He called his parents' house and told Dorothy that he was headed to Wentworth, and to leave the back door unlocked. He would explain everything in the morning.

As he drove down I-65 toward Wentworth, he felt like a ton of bricks had been lifted off his back. Being a man, he was convinced that his fooling around was okay. But for women, it was different. Wasn't it? Somewhere he had read that women associated sex with romantic love. However, a man could hop from bed to bed and not even think about the woman he was with, and still love his wife or girlfriend.

On Monday after Thanksgiving, Eric drove to Dallas, a happy young man. He was now free to enjoy the best Dallas had to offer. He loved his job, and he was free.

Eric continued to work as a senior sales representative in Dallas for the next three years. Shortly after his fourth anniversary with the company, he was promoted to sales manager, and was able to remain in Dallas. While he was still quite the ladies' man, he settled into real dating, the kind where you took a woman out to dinner and sent her flowers. While he enjoyed the company of several women, he didn't fall in love, and would let the relationships fizzle after three or four months.

One morning, just before his fifth anniversary with the company, Eric was summoned to Oklahoma City for a manager's meeting. Could this be something serious? The company had always been frugal, and it was a rare occurrence for anyone to be called up to headquarters.

It did turn out to be serious. The company had been bought out by a larger firm headquartered in Columbus, Ohio. Some employees would be getting offers from the new company; others would be laid off. Within the next month, sales department personnel would know their fate.

Driving back to Dallas that evening, Eric was mad and frustrated. He had a feeling that he would be one of the folks the company would let go. Heading south on I-35, he ran into some severe thunderstorms, and heard on the radio that the area he was driving through was under a tornado watch. The rainfall was torrential, and the thunder was some of the loudest he had ever heard, even though he grew up in Wentworth, Alabama, a tornado and severe storm magnet. Even though the weather was bad, Eric wasn't paying much attention to the road and allowed his speed to creep up.

The next thing Eric knew, he was lying flat on his back in a hospital room. While he could barely move his head, he was able to make a few noises which brought Dorothy and Jack Channing to their feet.

During the storm, Eric caught himself about to run into the back end of a tractor-trailer on I-35. He slammed on the brakes, causing his car to skid and turn over a couple of times. His badly injured body was transported to Dallas where he was hospitalized at the Baylor University Medical Center. His injuries included three fractured vertebrae, broken ribs, two broken legs, a fractured wrist, and numerous deep bruises. Luckily, there were no injuries to his head area, nor to his spinal cord. The wounds would eventually heal, but the restorative process would be a long one.

Dorothy and newly retired Jack decided that it would be best to keep Eric in Dallas during the major part of the healing process. When he could ride and walk, they would move him to Wentworth or Birmingham for the remainder of his care and therapy. Because the accident happened in the course and scope of Eric's employment, workers' compensation took care of the expenses. Through a combination of worker's comp benefits, sick leave, and short-term disability, Eric would collect about two-thirds of his salary.

He was in Baylor for about six weeks while the bones mended and the bruises healed. Then he was transferred to a rehab facility in Dallas to continue the recovery process. Jack and Dorothy stayed in Eric's apartment and were with him throughout the ordeal.

When Eric could walk with a cane, he flew from Dallas to Birmingham where Sandy, now an accountant, married to another accountant met him at the airport. Having driven to Dallas in the family car, Dorothy and Jack drove back to Wentworth, an eleven hour drive.

Sandy and her husband had just purchased a house in the Trussville area, and offered to take care of Eric and see that he got to his thrice-weekly therapy sessions at UAB. But seeing as they both worked, and Sandy was trying to get pregnant, the family decided that Eric would live with Jack and Dorothy in Wentworth, and they would drive Eric back and forth to his therapy sessions.

Eric had several therapists working with him while he was a patient at UAB. One of them was an attractive brunette named Gina Hanover, who began working with him about a month before he was scheduled to be dismissed. During his first session with her, Eric guessed that she was in her early twenties, and noticed that she wasn't wearing a wedding ring.

Reviewing his chart, Gina noted that Eric was living in Wentworth where she was born and raised. Of course, she let this handsome patient know that she was also from Wentworth. Being five years younger than Eric, and having attended WHS, she remembered Sandy and Roger.

Much to his dismay, Eric was one of the employees scheduled to be laid off by his company, due to the buyout. However, he was kept on the roles until his injuries from the accident had healed. With multiple severe injuries, Eric incurred some disability, and was given a generous settlement by the company.

Deciding to make a clean start in North Central Alabama, Eric flew to Dallas and arranged to have his belongings moved to

Wentworth and stored. Then he took up temporary residence at Jack and Dorothy's. They were overjoyed to have their son home.

CHAPTER 30

Eric was twenty-eight years old and had a large bank account. So, what was he going to do for the rest of his life? If he continued to work and let that bank account grow, his retirement would be secured. Wiley Martin's appliance business was doing well, and he recently opened a new store in Fultondale, just north of Birmingham. The store needed a manager. Hearing Eric was back in Wentworth, Wiley called his old buddy and offered him the manager position. However, Eric knew nothing about the appliance business, and didn't want to work for someone who was a friend of his. Instead, he took a job at one of the banks in Wentworth as a loan officer. While he didn't know anything about banking either, he could learn, and his friendship with Wiley wouldn't be affected.

A relationship between Gina and Eric snowballed, and by the time Eric was dismissed from therapy, they were falling in love. Because Gina lived in an apartment in Birmingham, and Eric was living with Jack and Dorothy, they only saw each other on the weekends. After three months, Eric proposed to Gina and she accepted. He unloaded the wedding ring set he had purchased for Rhonda and bought a beautiful new set for Gina.

This time things worked out, and Eric and Gina were married at the St. Paul's Lutheran Church in Wentworth. Gina resigned her position at UAB and went to work as a therapist at Wentworth

Medical Center. Of course, her parents were ecstatic to have her back in Wentworth. Following the wedding trip, the couple purchased a three-bedroom, two bath ranch style house in a fashionable Wentworth subdivision. Life was good.

While Eric was happy with his position at the bank, and was content to work there forever, Gina had become dissatisfied with her job at WMC. She wanted to do more with her life and felt her career would accelerate if she went back to Birmingham. Her goal was to open a private rehab facility, and Birmingham would be the optimal place to do it. Also, Gina liked nightlife and became bored living in a county where alcohol sales were against the law. Every weekend she would nag Eric about driving to Birmingham, having dinner at a nice restaurant, and then going out clubbing.

"Look, I'm just a country boy, a farm boy, and since I don't get around too well, I'm not about to dance."

"And why not?"

"I would look so stupid out there shaking my booty."

"No, you wouldn't."

"I don't dance, and I'm not going to dance. You knew that when you married me."

"Then let's just have dinner and listen to some music."

"I guess we could."

About once or twice a month, Eric and Gina would go to Huntsville or Birmingham on Saturday night.

One Saturday evening when the couple was having dinner at the acclaimed Highland Grill and Bar in Birmingham's trendy southside, they ran into Gina's old boss at UAB and her husband. Gina's former boss told her about a position at Brookwood Medical Center in the "over the mountain" suburb of Homewood. It was a management position for which Gina was qualified. Laney gave Gina the name and phone number of the person she should contact if she were interested.

On the drive home, Gina approached the possibility of her applying for the position with Eric, who was less than enthused.

"Look, Eric, you could get transferred to Birmingham with the bank, and we could sell the house and buy one in Birmingham. Things wouldn't be that complicated."

"Look, I'm just a small-town guy. I'm satisfied in Wentworth."

"Okay, I know you're happy and have your friends."

Later that night when they were in bed, Eric started having regrets for what he had said to Gina earlier.

"Look, sweetie, why don't you check into the Brookwood job. It might pay well into six figures, and then I can retire and be a house husband."

"You mean it?"

"Sure."

"Thanks, I'll call the person Laney gave me on Monday," said Gina as she was going to sleep.

Gina did make the necessary contacts, sent her resume to Brookwood, and interviewed with everyone, or so it seemed. Ten days later, the Brookwood rehab unit made her an offer she couldn't refuse. Brookwood would pay her almost twice what WMC was, she could commute, and the two of them would still be better off financially.

While Gina loved her new job, she found the everyday commute a challenge. Eric liked the extra money she was bringing in, but couldn't be persuaded to ask for a transfer with the bank. Eric had his friends in Wentworth, and Gina had her friends in Birmingham. While Eric encouraged her to reach out to the wives of his friends and to her high school classmates, Gina wouldn't do it, and clung to her friends, most of whom were single.

More and more, Gina started spending the entire week in Birmingham. She had a good friend, Tammy, who had just purchased a home in one of the upscale neighborhoods in north Shelby County. Gina was always invited to stay at Tammy's house during the week. The house was big enough, and Tammy like having Gina there. Gina would work during the day, and the girls often went out at night. This was decreasing her gasoline bill and the wear and tear on her car.

Gina got into the habit of staying two weeks out of the month with her friend, and the other two weeks in Wentworth with Eric. To compensate Tammy, Gina paid slightly less than one-fourth of Tammy's house payment. This went on for about a year, with Gina starting to dread the weeks she spent with Eric in Wentworth. And,

Eric started dreading the weeks he had to spend with Gina, and decided he liked being alone. He had developed a talent for cooking and would often have friends over during the week for spaghetti, or his famous beef stew and cornbread.

Gina kept trying to talk to Eric about moving to Birmingham, but Eric would hear nothing of it. Gina, on the other hand, was talking with two other therapists about starting their own business. Even though Eric and Gina had been married for almost six years, there was no talk between them about starting a family. Sadly, they were growing apart with each passing week.

One Friday afternoon in April, as Gina was driving to Wentworth to spend a week with Eric, she decided she wanted out of the marriage. She and Eric would have to talk about what each one wanted out of life. If Gina and the other girls started their own business, she would need to be in Birmingham full time. Eric would either agree to move to Birmingham with her, or the marriage was over. She really wanted her own business and couldn't understand why her husband was content to work at a Wentworth bank.

On Tuesday night, Gina approached Eric with her demand and things didn't go well. Eric refused to entertain the idea of moving to Birmingham and thought her plan of starting her own business was risky.

"All you think of is yourself," exclaimed Gina.

"Ditto," said Eric.

And they both knew it was true. The following weekend, Gina packed up most of her clothes and drove to Tammy's on Sunday afternoon. If she was going to live in Birmingham, she would have to find a place of her own. Maybe an apartment until the business started making some money. Then she would purchase a house.

Gina found an apartment, bought some furniture, and moved in. Eric was relieved. Even though she grew up in Wentworth, Gina was a big city girl. Eric would engage the services of their attorney in Wentworth and file for divorce. He would stay in the house and have her name removed from the deed. She would get her car, and he would maintain ownership of his truck.

Both agreed to a trial separation of two months before Eric would have the divorced papers filed. This way, they would be sure of their feelings. As the two-month trial separation was coming to an end, there were no changes of hearts, and Eric contacted their Wentworth attorney.

Gina was working fourteen-hour days which included her current position at Brookwood and the work she was putting in with her two partners in preparation for starting their own business. They hoped the business would be up and running in about six months.

As Gina was unpacking a box of miscellaneous bathroom items, she found her diaphragm and spermicidal jelly. She should have had a period about two weeks ago, but she hadn't. Oh no, could it be she thought, bursting into tears? She removed the diaphragm from its box and filled it with water. Sure enough, there was a tiny leak in the rubber shield. Then she took out the jelly tube and found that the jelly had expired.

Panic set in and she drove to the nearest drugstore and picked up a home pregnancy test. After returning home, she took it, and the results were positive. Gina felt that abortion was cold-blooded murder, but she did believe in a woman's right to choose. Eric was pro-life, no exceptions. Get a grip, she told herself. Go to the doctor as soon as possible just to be sure.

Her doctor did confirm that Gina was pregnant. That night she called Eric and told him.

"Well, whose is it?" he asked her.

"Whose is it?" she screamed back. "Of course, it's yours."

"You know what they say, mother's baby, father's maybe."

"Eric Channing, do you hate me that much, do you distrust me that much?"

"Well, it's been a while since we were together."

"The last time we were together was about four weeks ago, and I'm four weeks along."

By this time, Gina was crying uncontrollably. How could he say such things to her?

"I hate you, Eric Channing," she screamed and hung up the phone, slumping from the sofa to the floor. Lying in a heap for what seemed like forever, Gina cried and cried. Why was Eric acting this way and accusing her of things that he knew weren't true?

Then she remembered. Eric's first fiancée was supposedly a virgin the whole time they were seeing one another. But the first time they had real sex, she wasn't a virgin. Gina knew Eric was hurt, so maybe that's why he was so hard on her this evening.

Having no desire to get up off the floor, Gina curled up into a fetal position and continued to sob, not realizing the phone was off the hook. Finally, sleep came for her. The next thing she remembered, someone was knocking on her front door. It was the middle of the night. Who could that be? Should she answer it or call the police? Then she heard Eric yelling her name. Getting up off the floor, she walked to the door and opened it.

"I think your phone's off the hook," he said. And sure enough, it was.

"I'm so sorry I was such a butt on the phone, but a pregnancy was the last thing I was expecting."

"Yeah, me too."

"When I couldn't get you on the phone. I got in my car and drove down here. Are you okay?"

"Does it look like I'm okay?"

"No, but I think we should talk."

But they were both too tired and wrung out to talk. After Eric asked if he could stay for the night and Gina saying yes, they both went to bed in Gina's bed. After a few minutes, Eric started kissing her, and she kissed back. Then he removed her nightgown and soon they were making love.

The next morning both called in sick, deciding to spend the morning discussing what to do now. Gina pointed out the obvious, that Eric could get a transfer and move to Birmingham. It was much too late to give up on her business, and it wouldn't be fair to her partners. Moving down here would be so simple. But again, Eric refused.

After talking most of the morning and into the afternoon, they both decided a divorce would be the best solution. Even though both were still physically attracted to one another, they didn't love each other anymore. During the pregnancy, Gina would continue to live in Birmingham, and Eric would live in Wentworth, but he would be there for her until the baby was born. Afterward, they would make the necessary decisions. They also decided to put the divorce proceedings on hold until after the baby came.

Eight months later, Gina gave birth to a healthy, beautiful baby girl they named Tanya. Now that she had her own business, she could take the baby to work with her. Gina was the parent of custody, but Eric would have visitation rights and would pay monthly child support. Eric filed for divorce, and soon they were husband and wife no more.

CHAPTER 31

It was the first day of May, and Kristie was loading her SUV for a weekend trip to Nashville to see her favorite entertainer and his band in concert at Bridgestone Arena. As she was making sure everything needed for the two-night stay was in the car, she heard the phone ring from inside the house. It was 8:00 am. Who could be calling at this time of the morning? Thinking it was a telemarketer, Kristie didn't hurry in to answer the phone. As she walked into the house, a high school classmate was leaving a message for her indicating this was a reunion year. The reunion was going to be held during the third weekend in June with events on both Friday and Saturday nights. After briefly explaining the events and the cost, the classmate indicated there was a website for the class and left the URL. Kristie stopped in her tracks and replayed the message, writing down the website address. Why? Just curious she guessed. Forget the reunion, Kristie didn't like those people then, and didn't think she would like them now.

After arriving at work, booting up her computer, and getting settled in, Kristie navigated to the class website where she viewed photos of classmates during their senior year, along with some photos of them now. Some were good, and some weren't so good. She looked at pictures of families, including children and even some grandchildren. In reviewing the jobs held by some of her classmates, especially the women, most were impressive, but so was her job, IT Programming Manager.

Kristie wasn't going. Besides the Friday night event conflicted with a concert she was planning to attend with her friend Natalie. So, if she did decide to go, she would only attend the Saturday night event.

The week after she returned from Nashville, Kristie thought long and hard about the reunion. If she chose to attend the Saturday night event, she would only be out a few dollars and a few hours. She had a good job, her looks were still intact, and her car was not an embarrassment. Besides, if she was having a lousy time, she could walk out and head home. It was as simple as that. Also, Kristie had changed so much since her high school days, and she'd be a fool to think that everyone else in her class had stayed the same. Maybe it was time for her to do a little bit of growing up after all these years.

Okay, Kristie changed her mind and would attend the Saturday night celebration at the Renaissance in Wentworth, Alabama, about an hour and fifteen minutes from her home, located just south of Birmingham. Kristie printed out the reunion registration form, wrote out her check for the fee and the picture, and put it in the mail. What are those folks in charge of the reunion, folks who had lived in Wentworth all their lives, going to think when they receive Kristie Tidwell's registration form?

The next thing Kristie did was upload some information to the webmaster. While some folks told their life stories and uploaded numerous pictures of themselves and their families, Kristie only submitted information about her employer and job title. She didn't feel the need to provide any phone numbers, email addresses or website addresses. Just the basics, that's all any of those folks needed to know about her.

After receiving her information to upload, the webmaster, who was in a class several years ahead of Kristie's, emailed her, asking her to send a current photo. He had access to her senior picture, but wanted a current one. Oh, what the hell, thought Kristie, and sent him a recent picture. In this photo, her eyes were prominent, her dark curly hair cascaded over her shoulders, and her face was turned in such a way so there was no hint of a double chin. After receiving the photo, the webmaster emailed her and said it was a great photo, and shortly after that sent her a Facebook friend request, which she promptly confirmed. At the time, Kristie had very few Facebook friends from her high school days at Wentworth.

A week or so after Kristie submitted her reunion registration and uploaded the photo and her information, she received a friendship request from classmate Eric Channing. Kristie knew Eric, but never hung out with him or with the crowd he "ran with." Eric was an outstanding football player, and had an attractive girlfriend all through high school. While everyone assumed Eric and the girlfriend would get married and live happily ever after, Kristie found out, at some point, that they had not married, but parted ways after Eric graduated. While Eric was good looking, he was someone Kristie had never thought about, the Gulf Shores trip of the nineties was forgotten.

In Eric's write-up, he mentioned a daughter, but not a wife. He owned a house somewhere in Wentworth County and was recovering from surgeries related to injuries earlier in his life. He had suffered a severe knee injury while playing college football, and also suffered multiple injuries from an automobile accident during a stormy night near the Texas/Oklahoma state line.

Shortly after Kristie confirmed friendship, Eric would comment on many of Kristie's posts or would just "like" what she was posting. They loved Alabama football, were of the same political persuasion, and were Christians. Also, his Facebook profile stated that he was single and interested in women. Even though Eric was someone in which Kristie might be interested, she still had negative feelings toward Wentworth and the folks in her class.

CHAPTER 32

On the reunion Saturday, Kristie planned to sleep until she woke up, then she would leisurely get ready for what was going to be the scariest night of her life, her class reunion. It was June in Alabama, and the humidity was off the chart.

She decided to wear a black knit dress with an empire waist, silver platform sandals, and chunky silver and turquoise jewelry. Simple, but elegant. A few days before, she had her hair trimmed and colored. It was dark brown, almost black. Even though she wanted to be a little slimmer, well, a lot slimmer, she was still confident.

The big day was here and Kristie, after a good night's sleep was ready to prepare for the night's big event. Natalie told Kristie she and Tim would meet her for drinks if she wasn't having a good time and decided to leave.

Natalie had previously told Kristie that she would never go back to a high school reunion. She didn't like those people then, and she doubted she would like them now. For Natalie to attend a high school reunion, she would have to travel about fifteen hours by car. Kristie had to drive maybe an hour and fifteen minutes to get to her reunion.

Kristie was indeed scared, maybe as scared as she had ever been in her life. Wentworth was a dry county, and Kristie wanted to shock some of those people, so she packed a cooler of beer. Then, as an afterthought, she filled several Tupperware individual salad dressing containers with passion fruit tequila and put them in her glove compartment. Despite the humidity of Alabama in June, Kristie was having a good hair day.

Because she was unsure about the location of the Renaissance, Kristie left her house early for the drive to Wentworth. After locating the facility with no trouble, it was still about an hour before the reunion was to begin.

On this particular Saturday, downtown Wentworth was deserted. So, Kristie found an out of the way place to park, downed about 1-1/2 of the tequila shots, and waited until the warm liquid calmed her nerves. When it was time for her grand entrance, she said a prayer, got out of her SUV, and walked the half block to the Renaissance, through the double doors. To her right were name tags, but before Kristie could find hers, people were yelling, "KRISTIE! It's so great to see you, we're so glad you're here." A few even said they were worried about her when she didn't respond to previous reunion notices.

Kristie tried to speak to everyone, but it was impossible. However, some class members informally decided that the class would try to get together on a quarterly basis since most everyone had grown up and issues in the past were just that, in the past.

Kristie sat beside, and spent much of her time talking to Eric Channing. She was one of the last ones to leave, and thus would not be meeting Natalie and Tim for drinks.

On the brief walk to her vehicle, Kristie heard a man's voice, and footsteps behind her. "Kristie, Kristie, I'm not going to let you get away this time."

Kristie turned to see Eric Channing grinning down at her. "Did I ever get away before?" asked Kristie, a bit confused.

"Well, no, but I love your Facebook posts, and you're one of the people I wanted to see and talk to at this reunion."

While conversing with Eric during the reunion, Kristie found out that Eric was divorced and had a young teenage daughter. The woman he married was from Wentworth, but was several years younger than Eric and Kristie. Kristie never knew her. Eric told her she hadn't changed a bit. Even though Eric had aged some, Kristie still saw much of the younger Eric, and was attracted to him.

After standing beside her car and talking for a while longer, Eric asked her to come out to his house, which was in the country, west of Wentworth. "I have beer, and I have whiskey. I also have some better food than we were served here tonight. Come on, follow me."

Kristie followed Eric up and down hills, and over bridges. Where was he taking her? She would never be able to find her way out of this maze. Eric would have to lead her out when she left his place. They eventually arrived at his small, but charming brick home. Kristie liked the big front porch, complete with a swing, and the big front yard. Her garden home in Helena had neither.

The house had simple, but quality furnishings, including a sectional sofa, two wingback chairs, and a large recliner where Eric probably sat. Also, in the living room, was a large flat screen TV, and a dated looking stereo system. The kitchen appliances looked new. There were dirty dishes in the sink, and the floor needed sweeping. Eric apologized, saying he wasn't exactly the best housekeeper on earth. Kristie laughed and said neither was she.

"Are you still drinking beer?"

"Yes."

Eric reached into the fridge and retrieved two beers. Then he opened a drawer and retrieved two koozies, put the beer in the koozies, and handed one to her.

"Want to see the rest of the house?"

"Ugh, yes." Would the bedroom be their last stop? Kristie had been through this mating dance many times before. The guy shows you his apartment, house, condo, or whatever, and the tour concludes in his bedroom.

Feeling apprehensive, Kristie wondered what she had gotten herself into. She never spoke to this guy when they were in high school except for the occasional "hi," and here she was, at his house in rural Wentworth County. What if he was weird? She had no idea how to get to the interstate. Oh Lord, hear my prayer.

God does answer prayer, because after showing her his bedroom, Eric led the way back to the living room and flipped on the TV to Fox News. Through their Facebook communications, each knew the other was a conservative and an Alabama football fan.

They sat beside each other on the sofa and finished their beers about the same time.

"Want another."

"Sure."

Eric went back to the kitchen and brought out two more beers. They talked until just before midnight; mostly about football and politics. Eric was somewhat surprised at Kristie's football knowledge. One thing they didn't have in common, though, was Kristie's love for computers and technology. Kristie had a smartphone while Eric still had something several years old. Eric's desktop computer was ancient and slow, while Kristie's system was state of the art. Also, Kristie had been a software engineer before getting into management. Eric did remember her as being very smart, and beautiful as well.

When Kristie asked him about his daughter, he indicated that he and her Mom didn't always agree on her upbringing, with Eric feeling that his ex-wife was way too lenient. Kristie could tell he loved Tanya, and it pained him that he didn't get to see her more often.

After finishing her second beer, Kristie announced it was about time she started toward home, and asked Eric if he would take her back to the interstate. She would never find her way out alone.

"Oh, it's not that bad, it just looks worse at night."

"Well, it's night, and I'll never get out of here without your help."

"Okay, okay, I don't mind at all, pretty lady."

With that, Eric put his arm around her and began to kiss her. His kisses at first were light, then they became more intense. Suddenly

Eric stopped and said, "It's been a long time since I've been in a woman's arms."

"Do you still like it?" questioned Kristie.

"Of course." And they continued to kiss.

"I need to get going because I'm really getting sleepy."

"Stay here."

"Huh?"

"Oh, come on, we're both adults, and I'm not going to rape you or anything. I'm not going to force you to do something you don't want to do."

If Kristie spent the night with Eric Channing, even if they didn't do anything, would she be the talk of Wentworth or what? But being extremely sleepy, she didn't think she could drive to Birmingham. But once Eric led her back to the interstate, she could head toward Wentworth and stay at one of the hotels just off the interstate. Kristie owned the house and land where she grew up, but the water was turned off at the house, so it was an unsuitable place for her to spend the night. Anticipating she might want to spend the night at a hotel, Kristie did pack a bag with a nightgown, panties, and her cosmetics.

Noticing that she was getting droopy-eyed, Eric said, "Please stay here tonight, you're too sleepy to drive anywhere. Tomorrow you'll see that getting to this place is not as bad as you think."

"Well, I did pack a bag in case I decided to stay over."

"Uh, huh. You planned this," Eric said with a sly grin.

"Come on, let's go out and get your bag. If you want, you can sleep in the guest room."

As they walked to and from Kristie's SUV, they kind of leaned against one another. When they got inside, Eric asked, "Which room?"

"Take it to the guest room," Kristie answered.

CHAPTER 33

This is awkward thought Kristie, we haven't even had a real date, and I'm about to spend the night with this guy. Eric placed Kristie's bag on the floor, kissed her, and said he would see her in the morning.

Before slipping into her nightgown, Kristie went to the bathroom, brushed her teeth, and removed her makeup. Then she went back to the bedroom where she put on the nightgown, a silky pale yellow gown that fell to just above her knees and was slightly see-through. After getting in bed, Kristie was having mixed feelings about this. Thirty minutes ago, she and Eric were kissing passionately in his living room, and now they were sleeping separately. She wanted to be near him and to be held by him tonight.

As she was about to fall asleep, she heard a light tapping on the door. It was Eric, asking if he could come in. When Kristie opened the door, Eric reached for her and pulled her to him.

"Let's not sleep alone tonight. Don't you think it's absurd that we're in the same house, yet sleeping by ourselves?"

"Yeah, kind of."

And with that, Eric steered her into the master bedroom.

"I won't do, or force you to do anything you're not comfortable with, but I'm a man, and you don't have on a bra. I was wondering earlier if they were real, but now I know they are."

"And how do you know?"

"Oh, I can tell, believe me, I can tell."

Both Eric and Kristie were so tired that they were asleep within five minutes after getting in bed with each other. Being in an unfamiliar place, Kristie woke up multiple times during the night, only to find Eric asleep and snoring.

Suddenly, she woke up to the morning sun streaming through Eric's bedroom window, but there was no Eric beside her. She crawled out of bed and walked to the living room where she found him drinking a cup of coffee and watching Fox News.

Realizing that Kristie was standing behind him, he stood up and kissed her good morning.

"Was that okay?"

"Of course."

"Would you like some coffee?"

"No, I'm not much of a coffee drinker?"

"Now, that's just downright un-American, but what would you like?"

"You don't have any Diet Coke, do you?"

"It just so happens that I do. I'll get it for you."

Kristie sat on the sofa waiting for Eric to return. When he did, with a Diet Coke and a glass filled with ice, he sat beside Kristie, put his arm around her, and drew her close to him.

"How long have you been up?"

"A couple of hours, we country boys get up early while city girls like you sleep the day away."

"I have to admit I'm not a morning person."

"Are you hungry?"

"Starving."

"How do bacon, eggs, and biscuits sound to you?"

"Wonderful. You have all that here?"

"Sure. Out here you can't just run to the closest Hardee's and pick up something."

"Guess not."

Eric stood up and started toward the kitchen.

"Can I help?"

"You can come in here and keep me company."

Kristie stood and realized she had her nightgown on which was ever so slightly see-through. Eric, though, was wearing shorts and a t-shirt. Again, this was awkward. Should she ask Eric to borrow one of his t-shirts, or just be relaxed about the whole things? Deciding on the latter, Kristie sat in the kitchen with her Diet Coke, talking to Eric while he was cooking breakfast. Just before the food was ready, Kristie found where Eric kept the plates and silverware and set the table for them.

Eric was quite the cook, and Kristie told him so, with Eric admitting that he liked to cook, and often cooked for his friends' parties. Kristie was forced to admit she did little cooking.

"I can, but I would rather spend what little free time I have doing other things."

"Such as?"

Well, following current events, politics, and Alabama football. I also love to read and listen to music."

"What kind of music do you like?"

"Mostly modern country."

"Gee, I would have never thought Kristie Tidwell would be interested in country music."

"What kind of music do you like?"

"Even though I live in the country, I'm pretty much straight rock."

When they were finished eating, Kristie rinsed off the dishes, and put them in Eric's dishwasher. Looking out the window in front of the kitchen sink, she saw how well-kept Eric's backyard was. There was a vegetable garden, along with several flower beds. In the distance, she saw what looked to be a fish pond, and asked Eric if it was his.

"Yes, do you fish?"

"I used to with my daddy when I was a child, but I haven't been fishing since I was in college."

"It's mostly stocked with crappie and some bass. I like to have friends over to fish. After we clean the fish we catch, we'll have a fish fry."

Catching, cleaning, and frying up fresh fish was something from way back in Kristie's childhood, something else she hadn't thought about in many, many years.

After cleaning up the dishes, Kristie told Eric that she needed to shower, get presentable, and head back to Birmingham.

"I think you're presentable just like you are, but suit yourself."

So, Kristie showered, put on her makeup, and put on the dress and shoes she wore last night. When she stepped out of the bathroom, she heard a woman's voice. Kristie entered the living room and saw a woman sitting on the sofa talking to Eric, who was sitting in his recliner. The woman looked like she had been ridden hard and hung up to dry.

Eric immediately introduced the two women, and Kristie exchanged courtesies with her, saying it was nice to meet her, etc. Immediately following their exchange, the woman said that she had better be on her way.

"Where are you going to go?" asked Eric.

"I think I'll go up to my sister's for a while. She's probably at church, but I'll wait outside until she gets home."

"No, stay here."

Staring at Kristie, the woman said that she needed to go.

Eric walked her to the door, telling her to be careful and to come by if she needed anything. After the woman drove off in a rusted out, beat-up car, Eric told Kristie that the woman's husband was an alcoholic, and had physically abused her many times. In fact, a few times, she had to be hospitalized. Eric went on to tell Kristie that the husband stayed out all night and just returned to their house in a drunken rage. She was scared he might kill her this time, luckily, she was able to get away.

"She doesn't need to sit outside at her sister's until the sister gets home from church. Call her and tell her to come on back here."

"You mean call her on her cell?"

"Yes."

"She doesn't have a cell. They don't' even have a landline."

"Do you know where her sister lives?"

"No."

"I guess she left because I was here."

"Look, it's a sad situation, but the only answer would be to kill that son of a bitch, and don't think I haven't thought about it, along with everyone else in this neck of the woods."

"I guess I need to get going, and, by the way, will you please get me out of here, to the main highway at least?"

"Kristie, I'll lead you out, but I think you know where you are."

Getting a piece of paper, Eric drew a map which led to the main highway, which led to I-65.

"This isn't far from where my dad grew up. Okay, maybe I can get out of here on my own."

Chuckling, Eric said, "Sure you can, but call me when you get to the main highway, so I'll know that you're heading home."

Eric took Kristie's bag to her car, and after he had put it in the back, he put his arms around her and kissed her.

"I'll call you later this week."

"Okay. I had a great time with you and a great time at the reunion."

"Me too."

CHAPTER 34

Kristie found her way out of west Wentworth County, and smiled all the way back to Birmingham. Last night was exciting. Had she continued to turn her nose up at the people she went to school with, she would have missed out on so many friendships, and the opportunities to be with great people. In the next few days, Kristie doubled her number of Facebook friends.

Kristie liked Eric and was open to pursuing a relationship with him. He had decorated his house tastefully, and his yard, both front and back, looked great. But the other homes in the little community were low-income and rundown. She surmised that Eric was the main guy in the neighborhood with the best house. What did he do on weekends? Did he ever go out to eat? And if so, where? Could Kristie ever live there? No way. If the two of them did start a relationship, would she be driving up there for the weekends?

The following Wednesday, Eric texted Kristie and asked if he could call her that night.

"Sure. I'll be at home. I'm looking forward to it," she texted back.

When Eric called, they talked for over an hour with him asking her if she was doing anything special this weekend.

"No, just hanging around here."

"Would you like to meet me, say, in Gardendale Saturday night for dinner?"

"Sure, tell me where."

"Do you like Outback?"

"Yes."

"Then let's meet there. It gets crowded, so why don't we meet about 5:00?"

"Sounds like a plan to me."

"Are you sure?"

"Yes."

"Then we'll do it. 5:00."

Kristie could hardly wait. She had a date, with a guy. How long had it been? It seemed like Saturday would never arrive, and when it did, Kristie found herself not knowing what to wear. And Kristie always knew what to wear.

Outback was a casual restaurant, but she wanted to wear something other than shorts and a top. But what would Eric wear? She guessed khakis and a polo shirt. She needed to wear something that would match anything he might wear. After deliberating, she chose black knee-length walking shorts and a black and white trendy top. This ensemble should match up well with anything Eric might wear.

Not wanting to arrive too early at the restaurant, Kristie googled to see how long it would take to get there from her house. It was forty minutes, so she decided to leave at 4:25. That way she would be a fashionable five minutes late.

Just as she stepped out of the shower, about 3:30 on Saturday, her cell phone went off. It was Eric. Thinking he was having second thoughts about going out with her, Kristie expected him to say, "I'm sorry, but something's come up." Much to her surprise, though, Eric said that he had been at his sister and brother in law's house in Trussville, helping them rebuild a deck. Instead of meeting up in Gardendale, why don't they meet somewhere closer to where she lived?

That suited Kristie. So, they decided to go to a neighborhood Italian restaurant in Hoover, which was about ten minutes from her house. Perfect. Eric would drive to Kristie's and arrive around 5:00. Then they could go to the restaurant at whatever time they chose. Kristie didn't think this restaurant would be that crowded, even though it was Saturday night.

A little before five, Kristie uncorked a bottle of red wine and put it on the coffee table in the living room with a dish of cheese straws. In a few minutes, Eric drove up in his big silver pickup truck. After letting him in the house, Kristie looked up at him as if expecting a kiss, and he obliged. She then invited him to sit down and poured him a glass of wine. They sipped wine, nibbled on cheese straws, and chatted for over thirty minutes before they decided it was time to go to the restaurant. Eric was hungry from all the work he did at his sister and brother in law's house earlier.

The restaurant was owned by a Greek family and featured Greek dishes as well as Italian dishes. Both ordered small Greek salads. For her entrée, Kristie ordered veal marsala, and Eric ordered the baked lasagna after Kristie told him they had the best red sauce in town. Eric also ordered a bottle of Chianti. They split the entrees and had some left over to take home. Plus, they ordered two baklavas to eat later. Eric said he liked the place and made references to going there again.

When they finished dinner, it was only 7:30, but Eric was ready to go back to Kristie's and unwind. Bless his heart, he was tired from the day's work on his sister's deck. At Kristie's, they decided to go out on her deck and sit for a while. It was a mild summer night, and Kristie had a nice deck. When Eric saw Kristie's Big Green Egg, he immediately suggested that the next time he would bring steaks and grill them.

While sitting on the deck and listening to one of the "lite" rock stations in Birmingham, they talked for a couple of hours about anything and everything, often giggling.

"Ready for the baklava?" asked Eric.

"Sure, do you like Bailey's Irish Cream?"

"Absolutely."

So, they went in the house where Kristie put the baklava on dessert plates, took out two dessert forks, and poured two small glasses of Bailey's. Eric and Kristie took the food to the living room where Kristie turned on a cable radio channel, turned off the lights, and lit several candles.

As Kristie sad down, she leaned against Eric, who put his arm around her and began kissing her. Baklava and Bailey's forgotten, they smooched on the couch until Kristie announced they still had dessert.

"Can't let good baklava go to waste."

"I agree."

And they managed to eat the baklava, drink their Bailey's, and continue making out on the sofa.

Eric, having man thoughts, wanted to try out Kristie's bed because making out on the sofa was uncomfortable. But he wasn't going to suggest it on their first, well maybe second date, if you counted last weekend as a date.

Much to Eric's disappointment, Kristie didn't suggest the bedroom, but she did lean back on the sofa making it comfortable for both of them to sort of lie down. Even though Eric knew things might not go much further, he decided it was too early to give up. He would stay a little while longer.

After a while, Kristie went to the bathroom, and when she returned, Eric was sound to sleep on the sofa. She could only imagine how tired he must be, so she left him alone, blew out the candles, and went back to the master bedroom, put on a nightgown and crawled into bed.

It seemed as though Kristie had just fallen asleep when she felt someone getting into bed with her, and it wasn't the cat.

"Oh hey, you fell asleep on the sofa, so I didn't bother you."

"Is it okay if I get in bed with you?"

"Of course, come here."

This time more than sleep took place. To Kristie, making love with Eric seemed like it was her first time. She felt her body responding to him in ways she had never known before. While Eric was gentle, he had a forcefulness that let her know he was in charge.

Kristie's body was soft, and Eric liked soft. He couldn't imagine making love to any of the stick figured women, whose bodies were popular these days. Kristie had curves, and just enough flesh on her bones that he felt he could hold her without breaking her. Making love to Kristie was nice. Well, not just nice, it was fabulous. He could make love to her every day for the rest of his life.

After making love, Kristie and Eric fell asleep in each other's arms until both were abruptly awakened by the alarm.

"What the...?"

"It's time to get up and get ready for church, want to go?"

"Ugh, to church?"

"Yes, to church. Remember Jennie Browning? Her husband, Phil, pastors the church I attend. It's about twenty minutes from here. I've been attending their church since a year ago last Easter."

"I don't have suitable clothes for church."

"To Jennie and Phil's church, you can wear anything you want. During the summer, I wear shorts, and sometimes Phil even wears shorts. Think about it while I shower."

But Eric wanted to go back to his house which was over an hour's drive from Kristie's. He also didn't want to wear the same clothes he wore last night to church this morning.

When Kristie stepped out of the shower and into the bedroom wrapped in nothing but a towel, Eric said he would go to church with her soon, but not today. He was ready to get back to his house in west Wentworth County.

"Okay, that's fine."

"I'll let myself out since you shouldn't go to the door in that, the neighbors might be watching."

"Oh yes, they're going to be watching all right after they saw your truck parked outside my house last night.

"Tell you what, I'll call you tonight, how's that?"

"Perfect."

"Look, I really had a great time last night and this morning too. I'll go to church with you soon, I promise?"

He gave Kristie a brief kiss and left the house.

When she heard the front door close, Kristie lay back on her bed and sighed. For the umpteenth time in her life, she was falling in love. Uh oh, if she was going to get to church on time, she had better hurry.

CHAPTER 35

Eric did what he said he would do, and called Kristie just after 8:30 that evening. They talked for over an hour. A week from today was the fourth of July, and Eric asked Kristie if she had plans.

"Nothing special."

"Would you like to come up here? We could fish in the pond, then clean and fry what we catch for supper."

"What?"

"Just kidding. We'll swim in the pond."

"Huh?"

"Just kidding again. Sandy and I have a lot with a dock and boathouse and boat on Jones Lake, but we've never built a house on it. It's about ten minutes from my house. We could take the boat out for a while, then grill some chicken and ribs, maybe boil some shrimp."

"Sounds wonderful, I accept your invitation."

Because Kristie had a busy week ahead, they decided not to try to see each other until Saturday when she would drive to Eric's house and spend the weekend.

With one of her coolers filled with potato salad, coleslaw, a couple of packages of lettuce, and a key lime pie, she drove to Wentworth. She also brought a caramel cake from Edgar's. Eric was going to provide everything else.

Tonight, he was going to grill steaks. For tomorrow, they would take the boat out around mid-morning. When they had had enough of the water and sun, they would return to Eric's house where he would grill chicken and ribs and boil some shrimp. Depending on how they felt, they might drive into Wentworth for the fireworks show.

The long holiday weekend was one of the best Kirstie ever had. Eric was a marvelous cook, and unlike Kristie, he enjoyed cooking. After dining on ribs, chicken, and shrimp late Sunday afternoon, they opted to stay at Eric's house rather than go into Wentworth to see the fireworks.

Kristie knew Eric had a daughter who was in her early teens, but he never talked about her. On Sunday night after dinner, Kristie got up enough nerve to ask about Tanya.

According to Eric, she was conceived during the time he and his ex-wife were having problems and were about to file for divorce. But a couple of weeks later, Gina called him, telling him she had taken a home pregnancy test after missing a period. The pregnancy test was positive. After the phone conversation, which didn't go well, Eric tried to call her back, so they could talk reasonably. When Gina didn't answer, he drove to her apartment in Birmingham, and they talked way into the night before falling asleep. Both missed work the next day. With a baby coming, they made the difficult decision to get a divorce after the baby was born. It would be much better for the child to be cared for by parents who were not together than it would for the child to be raised in a house where the mama and daddy didn't love each other.

Eric was very much a part of the pregnancy and delivery, but the day Gina went home with baby Tanya, Eric went back to Wentworth, a new, single father. After that, he only saw Tanya when Gina needed a babysitter, and when she needed money, even though Eric regularly sent a check for child support. Now that Tanya was growing up, he saw her even less, but was paying most of the bills. Sensing he was bitter about things regarding Tanya, Kristie let the conversation drop.

Until a late-night thunderstorm forced them into the house, Kristie and Eric sat on his front porch in the swing talking and cuddling. The next morning, they fixed a light breakfast of fruit and whole wheat toast with Smart Balance and strawberry jam. As much as Kristie didn't want to, she knew she needed to leave. It was back to the real world and her job that was getting harder with each passing day.

After breakfast, Eric went out back to do some work in his garden while Kristie watched Fox News. When he returned, he found her lying on the sofa, her face pale. Thinking she may have gotten sick, he sat down and shook her softly.

"What's wrong sweetie?"

"Nothing, guess I'm just depressed about having to go back to the real world tomorrow.

"Something wrong at work?"

"Nothing more than usual. Upper-level management is continually evaluating resources and making threats of change. One of the guys who reports to me is not performing up to their standards."

"If he's not doing his job, then maybe you should fire him."

"It's not that he's not doing his work, it's just that he's older, pushing sixty. He tries so hard to do his best, but at some point, the brain gives out. I'm afraid he can no longer keep up, but that's not his fault. "

"Is there something else he can do within the company?"

"There are so many things he could do, and do well, but the organization doesn't like for its employees to take lesser positions with cuts in salary. He's a good guy, and doesn't deserve what's happening to him. He wanted to retire with the company, but it looks like that won't happen. I don't know that I could do his job and I'm younger than he is. If I were forced to go out and get a high-level software development position, I'm not sure I could keep up. I was doing some research the other day and learned that the maximum age for maximum performance for a software engineer or software architect is about forty-five. After that, engineers and architects need to get into a management or administrative role because their brains are no longer sharp enough to stay abreast with ever-changing technology."

"Are you scared about your job?"

"Sort of. If I can't bring this guy up to standards, we both could lose our jobs. I just want out of that hell hole."

"Then get out, do something lesser for lower pay. Do what's best for you."

"Eric, that's easier said than done."

"Come on, cheer up. We've had a wonderful weekend. God will take care of you, he always does. Why don't you think about starting your own business, computer training or something like that? Tell those corporate jerks to go to hell. Hang around here for a while, and I'll fix some lunch from yesterday's leftovers. Then you can go back to Birmingham and get ready for the week ahead knowing God loves you and will never let you down.

Eric was right. Kristie stayed until about 2:00 and thought she would faint from the July heat while loading her vehicle. About the time she arrived at I-65, the bottom fell out. As Kristie drove south on the interstate in the pouring rain, thunder, and lightning, she thought of the old song by the long defunct group, Atlanta Rhythm Section, "The dog days are scorchers, southern torture."

What would be so horrible about living in west Wentworth County? Did Eric have enough income to support her? He had recently left the bank after twenty years and now did free-lance writing. But Kristie knew that if her job was going great, there would be no thoughts of moving to Wentworth and becoming fully supported by Eric. She didn't even know how he managed his money. Was he cheap? How much would she be able to spend on clothes, hair, nails, etc.? Kristie was high maintenance, and how would that country boy/farm boy feel about that?

CHAPTER 36

Following the Fourth of July, Kristie and Eric saw each other every weekend when possible, and occasionally, Eric would drive to Birmingham to meet her for dinner during the week. This continued until the end of the summer, with late summer bringing on football season, and subsequently hunting season for deer and several types of fowl.

Eric was an avid hunter and spend many weekends from mid-October to late January at a hunting and fishing camp on Lake Guntersville, owned by Wentworth friend, Jimmy Harpo. As a bachelor and an early semi-retiree, he had nothing better to do than spend his weekends at the camp. In fact, Eric was the cook for the other guys staying there.

Kristie was an Alabama season ticket holder, and spent her Saturdays in Tuscaloosa when Alabama was playing there. Because she attended few away games, she would usually be at home on the weekends when Alabama was on the road.

Kristie had three seats and her old college roommate, Cindy, had one seat adjacent to Kristie's seats. Most of the time, Kristie sold her extra two tickets to another friend of hers, Shanna, who also lived in Tuscaloosa. Football weekends in Tuscaloosa were a big thing.

Because Kristie's friend didn't always need both extra tickets, she wanted Eric to attend some of the games with her. While Eric was just as enthusiastic about Alabama football as Kristie, he was hesitant about going to the games. His knees and hips were not in the greatest of shape, and Kristie told him that he would have to walk up one of the circular ramps. Then he would have to walk down thirteen steps with no handrail to get to her seats. Plus, their parking place was about a half mile away from the stadium. While Kristie's seats were undoubtedly good seats, he did have some reservations about attending games with her.

After talking it over, they decided that Eric would spend his weekends at the camp when Alabama was playing in Tuscaloosa. Then he would spend the weekends with Kristie when Alabama was playing out of state. Eric sensed Kristie was not happy with this arrangement and asked her why.

"My priorities are God, family, work, and Alabama football. Alabama football is something we both love, and I want so much to share it with you., but you would rather spend these weekends with Jimmy Harpo."

"Honey, please understand, I'm not sure I'm physically able to go to the games."

"Cindy, Shanna, and I will hang on to you as you walk down those thirteen steps. Also, if I start now, I can get us a handicapped parking place about a block and a half from the stadium."

"Sweetie, let's just play it by ear. If you have an extra ticket to any of the games, we'll talk."

"Okay."

While Kristie felt better, she was not entirely satisfied with their agreement. Kristie was in love, and wanted to share every minute with Eric that she possibly could.

Since they had started seeing one another, Eric would talk about various Wentworth people; most of whom Kristie didn't remember or could barely remember. One of Eric's good friends was none other than Wiley Martin. Eric admired Wiley, mostly for his business acumen, and also felt that Wiley was a good husband to his wife, a good boss to his employees, and a good friend to his friends.

When they were in their thirties, they took many trips together. When Eric was telling Kristie about one particular trip, she had a far-away look in her eyes.

"You're sad, why?"

"No, I'm not."

"Yes, you are. Look, it's not like my ex and I have a thing for one another. I've told you before that I was so ready to get out of that marriage. Come on, let me see that smile. I'll take you to Hawaii, to the Bahamas, to the Florida Keys. We'll dine and party until we fall over from exhaustion. At night, we'll make love like you've never made love before. Say okay."

"Okay."

"That's my girl."

Eric and Kristie couldn't get together without Eric talking about Wiley Martin and what a great guy he was. Maybe he and Wiley should start dating, she humorously thought to herself.

One evening, Kristie snapped, and informed Eric that she didn't
care for Wiley.

"Why don't you like Wiley?"

"Because he was mean to me when we were growing up, and
when we were in high school."

"Well, I find that a little strange coming from you, you who
preached that our classmates should put their petty issues aside, go
forward, and be there for each other. Talk about disingenuous."

"I'm sorry, but Wiley's an exception. I just can't get over my
dislike for him. I know he's one of your best friends, but that doesn't
make any difference. I hate him."

"How long has it been since you've seen him or talked to him?"

"Remember that night at dinner at Perdido Pass? Then later at
the Flora-Bama?"

"So, that was you?"

"Yes, it was me?"

"You blew me off that night."

"Yes, I blew you off that night because it was you and you were
with Wiley. And because I knew what you wanted."

"You hated us that bad?"

"At the time, I did."

"Wow, we thought it was you, but when I told you I was from
Wentworth, you didn't bat an eyelash. You said you were from
Birmingham and went to the University. You didn't mention
anything about Wentworth."

"That's right. Why should I have mentioned Wentworth?"

"Because it's your hometown. Wiley was the first one who recognized you and thought you were Kristie Tidwell."

"Big Woo!"

"Look, let's not fight over Wiley Martin."

"You're right, he's not worth it."

"Kristie!"

"Okay, okay, so Wiley's one of your best friends and you admire him a lot. I'll just have to accept that. Have you told him you're seeing me?"

"No."

"And why not?"

"Because it just hasn't come up in conversation. Keep in mind that guys don't sit around talking about women like you girls sit around and talk about men."

"Well, are you going to tell him about me?"

"When the time comes, yes."

"What about the next time you talk to him or see him?"

"We'll see."

"Are you ashamed of me?"

"Of course not."

"Then why don't you tell him?"

"Okay, okay, you win. The next time I talk to Wiley, I'll tell him we're seeing one another socially. Come on, let's forget Wiley Martin and concentrate on us."

CHAPTER 37

That was the first fight Eric and Kristie had as a couple, and they hoped it would be their last. Realistically, they knew there would be more hisses. But their hope was for more kisses than hisses.

Was Jimmy Harpo helpless or what? It seemed he could not spend time at his hunting and fishing camp unless Eric was there to do the cooking. Eric would leave for the camp on Thursday evenings and return home on Monday mornings. This routine started in September, even though deer season did not begin until October.

Supposedly, Eric was to spend the weekends with Kristie when Alabama was playing out of state, but something always kept him from seeing her. Kristie was in love, but Eric didn't seem to care about her anymore. So, what else was new in her life? She had been through this before, and could go through it again. However, this time it was going to be different. She was not going to drive this relationship. Eric would have to push it and make the moves.

Early during the second week of October, Eric called Kristie and said, "You'll be happy to hear this. Wiley Martin has lung cancer. It's the bad kind, small cell or small tumor, I think. He has about six months to live."

"First of all, I'm not happy to hear it. Wiley is too young to die. Even though I don't care for him, I do wish him the best, and hope that he knows the Lord. I'll pray for God to take care of him."

"He does, and right now he still has a good quality of life. Some of the guys are going to go down to Gulf Shores this weekend with him. We'll probably drive down on Thursday and come back on Sunday."

"Have a good time."

"Okay, I'll call you in the next few days."

This was a good weekend to go to any of the beaches on the northern Gulf of Mexico. The weather was going to be beautiful, and Alabama didn't have a game on Saturday.

When Kristie was talking to Natalie the next day, Natalie said that she was taking her mom and aunt, her mom's sister, to Panama City for a long weekend.

"You know," said Kristie, Eric and some of the guys are going to Gulf Shores, but I just might drive to Panama City."

Kristie didn't want to intrude on Natalie's trip, but the beach sounded great.

"Well, come on down. We have a two-bedroom condo reserved, and it's across the street from Pier Park. It'll be great."

Kristie, thinking they might be cramped in a two-bedroom condo, said she would book a room at a hotel about a mile east of where their condo was located. This hotel was nice and not too expensive. Unless Eric inquired as to what she was planning for the weekend, she was not going to let him know that she was also going to the beach. Besides, he could just wonder what she was doing.

Even though Eric said he would talk to her later in the week, he never called.

On Thursday, Kristie got into her convertible and drove to Panama City. Because she decided to work a half day, she didn't arrive and get settled until after 6:00. When she called Natalie to see what they were doing, she found out that Natalie's mom and aunt, for some reason, wanted to eat at the Red Lobster. They had just been seated and invited Kristie to join them. She didn't know where the Red Lobster was located, and thought to herself, if I'm at the beach, I'm sure not going to the Red Lobster. Instead, she chose to dine at one of Panama City's famous restaurants, Captain Anderson's. Being a lone diner, she knew she would have to sit at the bar, but that was okay.

The restaurant was packed and noisy with several large parties dining there. After getting a seat at the bar, she ordered a drink and requested a menu. Why did she need a menu? She always ordered the grilled shrimp appetizer and the broiled stuffed flounder for her entrée. This was too much food to eat in one sitting, but her hotel room had a microwave and a refrigerator. She could have the leftovers for breakfast or lunch tomorrow.

As she was finishing her salad, she heard a voice from behind.

"Hello Kristie."

Turning around, she was face to face with Eric.

"What are you doing down here?"

"Last time I checked, it was a free country. I can go anywhere within its borders. But I think the more important question is what are you doing here. I thought y'all were going to Gulf Shores?"

"Change in plans. We were able to get a couple of three-bedroom condos for a great price, so we decided to come here instead. What made you decide to come to the beach this weekend?"

"Nice weather, Natalie, her mom, and her aunt are down here. Plus, Alabama has this Saturday off."

"I guess I'll accept that."

"Excuse me, you'll accept that?"

I kind of thought you might show up in Gulf Shores knowing we were going to be there."

"Eric, what's this all about?"

"You're one of those women who tends to smother, and I don't like to be smothered. I guess you'll be going deep sea fishing tomorrow, and you'll be on our boat."

"For your information, I'm not going deep sea fishing tomorrow, not that it's any of your business. By the way, how did you know I was here?"

When the guys and I were leaving, I recognized your car in the parking lot, personalized license plate and all."

"Look Eric, I promise you I will not try to contact you this weekend, and if, for some reason, I cross paths with you and your buddies, I won't embarrass you by saying hi."

"Enjoy your dinner and your weekend," said Eric, as he turned and strolled out of the bar.

"Did you find your friend?" asked Wiley Martin when Eric returned to the truck.

"Yeah, he's down here with his wife for a few days. It's their twentieth wedding anniversary," Eric lied.

"Guess he doesn't want to hang around with the guys?"

"Not this trip."

After that exchange, Kristie felt like she had been kicked in the stomach. Why was Eric so nasty to her? She knew, though, it was because she told him she didn't like his good friend, Wiley Martin, and now Wiley was terminally ill.

Because Kristie was suddenly sick at her stomach, and couldn't eat a bite of her flounder, which just arrived, she asked for a go-box, paid her bill, and headed back to her hotel. Eric didn't ask her where she was staying, and didn't tell her where he, Wiley, and the rest of the guys were staying.

It would be impossible for Kristie to have a good weekend, following her confrontation with Eric. She might as well pack up and drive back to Birmingham tomorrow. The next day, after a restless night, she did.

CHAPTER 38

Kristie wasn't the only person to toss and turn that night. Eric couldn't get to sleep either. He had been an asshole, and he knew it. If he had played his cards right, he might be in Kristie's bed. Yes, Kristie tends to smother, and he was ticked off at her because she didn't like Wiley, but Wiley was mean to her when they were growing up. He'd call her tomorrow, apologize, and maybe tomorrow night, he could spend the night in her hotel room. After all, Eric was a real man with real man thoughts.

The boat, which the guys had reserved, was leaving at 5:30 am, so they needed to be at the dock around 5:00. After getting little sleep, Eric considered backing out of the day of fishing, but for Wiley's sake, he sucked it up and got on the boat. He wanted to call Kristie, but knew better than to call her at this time of the morning. He'd call her as soon as they left the boat this afternoon.

While not a great fishing day, the guys caught enough fish to fill up a cooler. With packing, the fish would keep until they arrived in Wentworth on Sunday. Sunday night, they would have a fish fry at Wiley's house to celebrate the weekend.

As the guys, all sweaty and fish smelling, were returning to their condos, who should Eric cross paths with but Natalie, her mom, and the aunt. They were staying at the same condos where the guys were staying.

"I thought y'all were going to be in Gulf Shores this weekend," said Natalie.

"Didn't Kristie tell you we had a change in plans? Got a great deal on two units here and decided to come to Panama City instead. Luckily, we didn't book a boat in Gulf Shores."

"Kristie's not here. She called this morning and said she was heading back to Birmingham. Something came up."

This time Eric felt like he had been kicked in the stomach. After leaving Natalie and the other women, he hurried up to the condo and called Kristie, getting no answer. But what did he expect after the way he had treated her last night.

After the women were seated at their table at Reggae J's, Natalie said that she was going to call Kristie to make sure she got back to Birmingham, and was okay.

Natalie's mom piped up, saying, "You stay out of it. Something's going on with those two. Let them work it out."

"Mom, I'm just going to make sure she got home. I'm not about to tell her I saw Eric."

"Just don't get knee deep in it."

Kristie, lying on her bed, staring at the ceiling, ignored Eric's call, but picked up when Natalie called.

"Did you get back okay?"

"Yeah."

"You okay?"

"Yeah, I guess. I'll talk to you when you get back up here. Have a great rest of the weekend."

"You too."

Eric didn't leave Kristie a message because he didn't know what to say or where to begin. Had he been a jerk or what?

Because the guys were tired and sun-drenched, they decided to go across the street to where else, but Reggae J's, for dinner. And they were seated next to Natalie's table. Fortunately, the women were almost finished eating. It was awkward. Eric felt as though Natalie, her mom, and her aunt were staring a hole through him.

The guys were much too tired to go out drinking after dinner, so they went back to the condo where Eric immediately went to his bedroom and fell into bed. But not before trying to call Kristie. Again, she didn't pick up, but this time he left a message saying he was sorry for everything, admitting everything was his fault. He ended the voicemail asking her to please, please call him, no matter what time it was, because he had to talk to her.

Playing back the message, Kristie smiled. He sure sounded upset. Should she call him back immediately or make him squirm for a while? Or, should she tell him she never wanted to see him again, and that he could go to hell?

When Kristie told Eric she didn't care for Wiley, she also said that she hated him. She knew Eric was disappointed and thought she should cut Wiley some slack since what had taken place was a long time ago. Eric also reminded Kristie that she had said many times, people should grow up and put their petty issues behind them.

Kristie ultimately decided to call Eric and suggest that they talk when he and the guys were back in Alabama. When Eric picked up, he didn't even say hello. Instead, he began by saying that he was so sorry. But yes, he was miffed that Kristie followed them to Panama City.

"Followed you to Panama City, I thought y'all were going to Gulf Shores."

"Didn't I call you Wednesday night and tell you we had a change of plans?"

"No, you didn't."

"I thought I did."

"Well, you thought wrong."

"I assumed you came down here to stalk us. I had no idea that Natalie, was here also, with her mom and aunt."

"To stalk you, what kind of person do you think I am?"

"I'm sorry. It's just that my ex used to stalk me after the divorce was final."

"I'm not your ex. Well, ex-wife that is. Look Eric, this conversation is going nowhere. Let's talk when you get home."

"Okay, we'll talk face to face as soon as I get back, which will probably be late Sunday afternoon. I'll call you."

"Okay."

"I really care a lot about you, you know that, don't you?"

"Right now, I'm not sure about anything."

"Will you think about me and pretend you're holding me tonight?"

"I guess I can do that," and Kristie smiled.

Although she had Eric begging for forgiveness, something didn't correlate between the conversation they had at Captain Anderson's and tonight's conversation. At Captain Anderson's, Eric didn't mention anything about calling her on Wednesday, telling her he would be in Panama City as opposed to Gulf Shores. She had some serious thinking to do before Sunday evening, and was glad she didn't have a football game to worry about tomorrow.

Eric had approached her and accused her of things that weren't true. But he did appear to be hurt that Kristie wasn't Wiley Martin's biggest fan. But then, he had never warmed up to Natalie and Tim either. She knew she should break it off with Eric. He had a temper and jumped to conclusions. Is this something she wanted to put up with for the rest of her life, should things between them reach that point?

CHAPTER 39

Eight guys went on the trip. One large SUV and two large pickup trucks took the guys to the beach. So, when Eric asked Wiley if he would mind riding back with someone else since he had a friend in Birmingham he wanted to drop by and see, Wiley said okay. There was plenty of room because guys going on a guys' weekend don't need a bunch of stuff like women do.

As Eric drew close to Birmingham late Sunday afternoon, he called Kristie, told her he was about twenty minutes from her house, and asked if he could drop by.

"Sure."

"Okay, I'll see you shortly."

Kristie let Eric in the house when he rang the doorbell, but there was no hello kiss. Instead, there was a definite awkwardness in the air. After picking up the kitty cat and scratching his ears, Eric sat down on the sofa and said, "I guess I should start this. I'm an asshole, a son of a bitch, a jerk, and every other term you women use to describe men like me."

"Continue," said Kristie.

"I was wrong to accuse you of following us to Panama City when I told you we were going to Gulf Shores, and then ended up in Panama City. When I saw you having dinner at the bar, I should have been glad to see you, and said to the guys, look who's here. Then I should have paid for your dinner and made sure you got back to your hotel. Then I would have stayed with you in your hotel room because I'm a man."

"But what did I do? I accused you of things that weren't true, or even reasonable. I didn't even ask where you were staying because I thought you probably made arrangements to stay at the same condos where the guys and I were staying. But how could you have known where we were staying? In fact, I don't even think I told you where we originally planned to stay in Gulf Shores. Nor did you ask."

"I ran into Natalie and company. They were staying at the same place where we were staying. Why weren't you staying with Natalie?"

"Their condo was only a two-bedroom, and it would have been cramped. Besides, Natalie's mom and aunt can be crabby."

"Yeah, I got that impression when were seated at a table next to them at Reggae J's."

"Y'all sat next to them at Reggae J's?"

"Yep, and they stared daggers through me. It wasn't pleasant."

"Back to where we were. I screwed everything up this weekend for you, for me, and for the guys. They could tell something was bothering me. And probably for Natalie, her mom, and her aunt. Did you have to pay any extra for checking out of the hotel early?"

"No."

"If you had, I was going to reimburse you."

"That won't be necessary."

"Look, I'm just so sorry about everything, and if I could turn back time to when I first spotted you in Captain Anderson's bar, I would, believe me, I would. There are too many things that I'm sorry about, and would appreciate not having to list them as my short-term memory is not what it used to be. So, can I just say I'm sorry for everything? I'll do whatever I can, whatever you want me to, in order to make amends for everything I've done to you and to everyone else. In fact, I'm going to apologize to the guys, and I'd like to apologize to Natalie, her mom, and her aunt."

After a few moments of silence, Kristie buried her head in her hands and started to cry. Eric had hurt her, and she wanted him out of her life. They had been seeing each other for less than six months. Would there be episodes like this again? Did she want to take that chance? But did she want to lose what might be her last chance for love and maybe marriage?

Eric wanted to put his arms around Kristie, hold her, and wipe away her tears, but he felt it was best not to approach her.

"I'm sure I hurt your feelings when I said I didn't like Wiley Martin, knowing he's one of your best friends."

"Yeah, I was kind of surprised after your soliloquy about our classmates putting their frivolous issues aside and going forward as a group."

"Guess I couldn't let go where Wiley was concerned."

"I think if you saw him and talked to him, you might be able to get past things. Like every one of us, he's changed too. Look, Kristie,

I want you, and I care about you. I'll do anything you want me to, just take me back, please."

"Well, I do have one condition."

"Anything."

"Within twenty-four hours, I want you to tell the guys you went to Panama City with, including Wiley, that you and I are seeing one another."

"Is that all?"

"Then report back to me what Wiley Martin said."

"I can, and I will."

Eric departed giving Kristie a chaste kiss on the forehead. He had to be at Wiley's for a fish fry soon, but concluded it would be best not to tell Kristie.

Eric and the guys ate fried fish, hushpuppies, coleslaw, and potato salad that evening. Eric did not keep his promise to Kristie that he would tell his friends the two of them were seeing each other socially. He was afraid to do it, afraid of what Wiley and the others might say.

Was he ashamed of Kristie? Kristie, a prominent member of two local clubs, one of which she was vice president. She knew several former Alabama football players, and had other friends in high places. Whenever they went out, she dressed impeccably, and her hair was perfect. For some reason, though, he just couldn't tell the Wentworth guys he was seeing Kristie Tidwell.

CHAPTER 40

The regular football season ended. Thanksgiving and Christmas came and went for Kristie and Eric. Eric, Tanya, Sandy, and Sandy's husband drove to Hilton Head, South Carolina to visit Roger and his significant other for Thanksgiving, while Kristie spent the holiday with Natalie, Tim, and their family. For Christmas, the Channings gathered in Wentworth to spend the holiday with their one remaining aunt. Kristie spent Christmas with her old college roommate, Cindy, and her family in Sylacauga.

With New Year's Eve looming, Jimmy Harpo's sister, Jan Franklin, who also lived in Wentworth, was hosting a New Year's Eve party. Hosting it with her was Jimmy's wife, Ruthie, and Jimmy's sister-in-law, Kathryn Harpo, wife of Jimmy's brother, Sam. Eric, of course, was invited.

While Kristie was less than enthusiastic about going to Jimmy Harpo's sister's house for New Year's Eve, she said she would go and make finger sandwiches of pimento cheese, chicken salad, and cream cheese and pineapple.

Eric booked a room for them at the Holiday Inn Express in Wentworth to minimize the amount of driving that they would have to do on New Year's Eve.

Eric and Kristie arrived at Jan and Jeremy's house about 8:00 pm. Many of the guests had already arrived. Some, already on their way to getting smashed, would probably not make it to midnight. As they walked in the door, Eric was greeted with loud, obnoxious hollering from some of the guys who were in school with them.

While Eric was talking to a few of the guys, Kristie put her coat and purse in one of the bedrooms, then went to the kitchen to set out the sandwiches she had brought.

Recognizing Kathryn Harpo, Kristie made her way to where Kathryn was standing with a rather homely looking woman who Kristie didn't recognize.

"Oh, there's Eric Channing, the guy I want you to meet," said Kathryn. "He was a hunk in high school."

The woman had salt and pepper hair, pulled back in a straight ponytail. She wore glasses, no makeup, and was dressed in black pants, sensible shoes, and a white turtleneck sweater. There was no hint of jewelry.

Kathryn and the homely woman walked over to greet Eric.

"Eric Channing, this is Carole Jameson."

"Hi Carol."

"Hi Eric."

Oh my, thought Kristie, if there's one name I hate, it's Carol. Kristie had once worked with an older snobbish lady whose name was Carol, plus Steve Conley's wife's name was Carol. Then, there was Robert Redford's girlfriend in the movie, *The Way We Were*, whose name was Carol.

Kristie wore a black and silver metallic sweater, black jeans, and black boots. She accessorized her outfit with a chunky silver bracelet and large silver earrings. Her hair was its usual thick and curly. Her eyes were accentuated with subtle pink, gray, and black eyeshadow. And on her lush lips was a perfect shade of dark red lipstick. The mousy little Carol couldn't hold a candle to Kristie's elegance.

Eric was smiling at Carol and appeared to be engaged in a conversation with her. Then he saw Kristie and started to make his way over to her, not looking happy. Apparently, Jan Harpo Franklin had planned to introduce Eric and Carol in hopes that something might develop between the two of them. But, they failed to tell Eric they wanted to introduce him to a friend of theirs. And when Eric accepted the invitation to the party, he didn't inform Jan that he was bringing someone. Eric was stumbling and bumbling in his explanation to Kristie.

"I think you, Kathryn, and Jan need to have a little meeting to discuss just who is going to be your girlfriend tonight. If the decision is Carol, take me back to the hotel so I can retrieve my stuff and my car and head back to Birmingham, drunks on the highway and all." Kristie hated New Year's Eves.

"Now Kristie, calm down, that woman is not attractive, and she's the last person in the world I want to kiss at midnight, much less do anything else with."

"She's not exactly attractive, is she?" laughed Kristie.

"Come on, let's go outside for a second," said Eric.

Eric led Kristie outside the house and over to the side of his truck. Then he put his arms around her and held her close.

"I guess I'm not as cultured as you. I should have told Jan I was bringing someone to the party, and that's my fault. I can't believe Jan and Kathryn think so little of me that they would try to fix me up with someone so unattractive."

Then Eric said to Kristie, "I'll give you two options for the evening. We can stay here until midnight and kiss passionately in front of these old married couples, or we can leave a little before midnight, and go back to the hotel room. We did leave some champagne in the ice chest in the room."

"I don't know, they both sound tempting. But I would like to lay a slurpy kiss on you at midnight just to spite Jan and Kathryn."

"You still have some issues with folks, don't you? I wish that wasn't the case, but I'll go along with it since I'm also ticked at Kathryn and Jan for thinking I'm the caliber of Carol."

As he promised, Eric grabbed Jan and Kathryn and directed them to one of the bedrooms just as soon as he and Kristie entered the house. "You didn't tell me you were planning to fix me up with someone," Eric yelled at Jan.

"Well, you didn't tell me you were bringing a female guest."

"You and Kristie Tidwell," exclaimed Kathryn. "Who would have thought of you two as a couple.?"

"What's wrong with Kristie?"

"Ugh, nothing's wrong with Kristie, it's just that she's so, and you're so."

"Didn't you and Kristie hang out when we were in school together?"

"A little."

"I think I'll get Kristie, and we'll go back to the hotel."

"Eric, please don't," whined Jan. "I've gone to a lot of trouble to make this party a success, please stay."

Eric shrugged his shoulders and went back to the party. He eyed the room and saw Kristie talking to some women who were in their class. She was laughing and appeared to be having a good time. So, Eric felt free to talk to some of the guys who were at the party. None of the men recognized Kristie. When they realized Kristie Tidwell was Eric's guest, they were shocked. Kristie was beautiful, and Eric knew it.

When Kristie went to the kitchen area to freshen her drink and get something to eat, Jan and Kathryn approached her, telling her they were shocked that she came to their party.

"Eric asked me to be his guest, and I said, yes."

"Well," said Jan, "we really wish we had known."

"Look, both of you. Eric asked me to come to this party with him. He should have told you he was bringing a guest. It was not my responsibility to make sure you that knew Eric was bringing a guest, and that guest was me. If either of you have a problem with me being here, Eric and I will gladly leave. In fact, Eric has already told me if I was uncomfortable that we'd leave. We'll celebrate New Year's Eve in our hotel room."

"Oh no," Jan said. "You don't have to leave. It's a free country and Eric can do what he wants. It's just that we thought he and Carol would be perfect for each other. One of us should check on her. I'm sure she's embarrassed because of what has happened this evening."

"If Carol is embarrassed by this evening's circumstances, it's not my fault," glared Kristie.

"Okay," said Jan to Kathryn. "Let's go find her and make sure she's having a good time."

Apparently, those two don't care if I have a good time, thought Kristie. How caddy can you get?

Kristie needed some fresh air after that encounter, and felt that she and Eric should leave. She departed Wentworth many years ago, vowing to never return except to see family. Then after having a wonderful time at the reunion, Kristie changed her mind about Wentworth and the folks with whom she went to school. But now, for Kristie Tidwell, there was no going back. Sure, she had some friends among those in her class, but this group tonight was just awful to her, or at least Jan and Kathryn were horrible to her. Where was Wiley Martin? She made a mental note to ask Eric about that.

CHAPTER 41

As Kristie left the house to go outside for some fresh air, tears rolled down her cheeks. She tried the door on the passenger side of Eric's truck and found it unlocked. She slipped into the passenger seat and saw tissues in the glove compartment. Thank goodness it was a mild evening temperature wise.

Where was Eric? She wanted to get out of this place if it was the last thing she would ever do. He was probably talking to his buds, and acting as stupid as they did in high school. And the last thing he wanted was to have to be attentive to a woman, even if she was his guest.

The next thing Kristie saw was the front door open. Jan, Kathryn, and Carol were coming outside. The three of them walked to a car that was probably Carol's. Guess she felt there no need to stay since Eric already had a date, Kristie thought to herself. Kathryn and Jan didn't bother to tell Eric that they were inviting a woman for him to meet. Eric didn't bother to tell Jan, the hostess, he was bringing a guest, a woman. But in the end, it was her fault for just being Kristie. Even though she had made many friends within her class after attending the reunion, people from Wentworth were still people from Wentworth with narrow minds. They were not open to meeting new people, and were nothing but a clique.

Did Kristie dare go back in the house? If she did, how would Jan and Kathryn treat her? Would Eric blame her for this evening, even though he was the one that asked her to go with him to the party?

Kristie spent time making finger sandwiches for this party, and she and Eric both brought beer and wine. She was anxious to see if the finger sandwiches had been eaten, and she also needed another drink. So, into the house she went, directly to the bar to pour herself a glass of wine, and to get a plate of food. The sandwiches were gone. Kristie washed and dried her serving plate and put it in the bedroom with her coat and purse. Then she fixed herself a dish of what was remaining: potato chips and dip, sausage balls, cheese and crackers, veggie dip, and miniature quiches. Then she looked around for an out of the way place to sit.

Finding a seat on one of the sofas, she sat down, putting her plate and wine glass on the glass top coffee table on top of some cocktail napkins. Then she leaned back, wine glass in hand, and closed her eyes. She was not having a good time. Kathryn and Jan were treating her like dirt while Eric was ignoring her, preferring to act like a juvenile with his friends.

What should she do to get back at Eric? Turnover and go to sleep as soon as they returned to their hotel room? Maybe he didn't want his buddies seeing him being attentive to Kristie Tidwell. If he didn't want these guys seeing him being kind to her, then why did he invite her? In fact, why was he having a relationship with her if he wasn't willing to show her off to his friends? Getting the milk for free, maybe?

Kristie awoke as the lights were turned low and the revelers were singing *Auld Lang Syne*. She saw some folks kissing, and she was alone with no one to kiss. Then she felt someone grab her and plant a kiss, with tongue, on her. It was Eric. When *Auld Lang Syne* was over, Eric said to her, "Why are you way over here? I didn't know what happened to you. I thought you might have called a cab and left. You're not having a good time, are you?"

"You're right, I'm not. Kathryn and Jan have been hateful to me because I'm here with you, and they wanted to fix you up with Carol."

"I guess we all screwed up this evening."

"I'll drink to that now that everyone is blaming me."

"I'm not blaming you, and I don't think Jan and Kathryn are either. Let's go talk to them."

"Wait, I don't have anything to say to those bitches. The thee of y'all screwed up and the three of y'all should be apologizing to me. But I wasn't born yesterday. This is Wentworth, and even though I was born and raised here, I don't belong here. I hate this town, and wish I had never gone to that stupid reunion."

"Are you ready to go"? asked Eric. "You have most of a drink and some food left."

"I'm not hungry or thirsty anymore."

"Okay, get your coat and your purse, and we'll go."

As soon as Kristie retrieved her coat, purse, and her serving plate, she and Eric headed for the door together.

After they got in the truck, Eric said, "We need to go back in and thank the Jan for hosting this party, and tell her we had a great time."

"You go tell her you had a good time. She and Kathryn were rude to me, and I had a lousy time. I made sandwiches, but ate very little. So, you go tell her you had a wonderful time acting like the jerk you were in high school.

Eric got out of the truck about the time that Jimmy Harpo and wife, Ruthie, were heading out. Kristie sat in the truck and watched the three of them talk for what seemed like an eternity. When they split up, Eric headed toward the house while Jimmy and Ruthie headed toward her side of Eric's truck, knocked on the passenger-side window, and motioned for Kristie to get out. Thinking Jimmy and his wife might want to apologize to her, she opened the door and stepped down.

Jimmy started by saying that his family had known Carol for a long time, and felt she would be perfect for Eric. They didn't know Eric was seeing someone, especially her, Kristie Tidwell. They were shocked when Eric showed up with her, and felt horrible for the poor Carol. Could Kristie possibly understand?

"Eric told me he was going to tell y'all after the fishing trip that he was seeing me."

"He didn't."

At that point, Kristie looked them in the eye and said, "All I did was accept an invitation to a New Year's Eve party from a guy I have been seeing for almost six months. And now it's my fault that your precious Carol has no one to kiss on New Year's Eve. I've had it with everyone, including Eric. As soon as we get back to the hotel, I'm gathering up my belongings, and heading home. I don't belong in Wentworth, and I was such a fool for thinking I could come back after all these years."

Jimmy and Ruthie turned and walked away.

CHAPTER 42

When Eric returned to the truck, he found a sullen Kristie.

"Baby, I'm so sorry that the party didn't turn out like we hoped, but the rest of the evening will be memorable. I promise."

"I wouldn't be so sure of that. You were supposed to tell Jimmy Harpo and the others you were seeing me soon after you returned from the fishing trip in October. By the way, where's Wiley tonight?"

"Wiley is in Cancun with Anabelle. I guess I forgot to tell the guys."

"You promised me you would tell them. In fact, if you had told them, Jimmy would have told Jan not to invite Carol."

"Come on Kristie, you're being just as childish as everyone else this evening. You don't like Wiley, but you haven't spoken to him since y'all were students at the University. Carol is a friend of the Harpos, and they wanted her to have a good New Year's Eve, though I'm still pissed that they thought she and I would make a good couple.

Neither Jimmy, Jan, nor Kathryn said a friendly word to me during the party. It was all about how disappointed they were that Carol didn't have a date. They had no idea you were seeing someone."

Just as she said she would do, Kristie started collecting her stuff to leave when she and Eric returned to the hotel.

"Now, Kristie, don't go. It's dangerous out there on a night like this."

"What's it to you?"

"I don't want anything to happen to you."

"Of course you don't, that would be the end of the free milk."

"What?"

When Eric finally understood, he glared at Kristie. "I think you've enjoyed it just as much as I have, don't give me that holier than thou attitude."

With that, Kristie jerked up both of her bags and headed for the door, but before she could open it, Eric heaved his lineman frame against the door, and blocked her from going anywhere.

"Eric, move away from that door."

"You're my woman, and you're not going anywhere."

"Let me go, or I'll scream. I'll call 911 and tell them you're attacking me."

"You're not going anywhere, and you're not calling anyone," said Eric as he continued to lean against the door, feet firmly planted.

As Kristie opened her mouth to scream, Eric grabbed her and threw her on the bed, but Kristie missed the bed and ended up sprawled on the floor in an awkward position. With a shocked look, Eric dropped to the floor beside Kristie and put his arms around her.

"Oh, sweetie, I'm so sorry, are you okay?"

After having suffered broken bones in two recent falls, Kristie wasn't sure, and she was also in shock. There was a knock on the door.

"I think you had better answer that," said Kristie.

"What's the trouble here?" questioned the rather nondescript looking gentleman at the door. Then seeing Kristie on the floor, the man, who was most likely the hotel manager, ran up to Kristie and asked, "Ma'am, are you all right?"

"I'm not sure," said Kristie, as she started to get up with the help of the manager whose nametag said Stan Monahan, Manager.

"I think I'm okay, nothing's broken."

"Ma'am, do you need assistance?" asked Stan.

"I'd like to leave; my vehicle is outside."

"Sure," said the gentleman.

"Do you have somewhere to go?"

"Yes, to my house in Birmingham."

While Eric sat on the bed with his head in his hands, Stan accompanied Kristie to her car.

"What do you want to do about him?" asked Stan, pointing back to the room.

"He can do whatever he wants."

"I can call the police, but you'll have to stay here and give a statement."

"That won't be necessary, but just make sure before he leaves the premises, he pays you."

As Kristie drove off, Stan made a mental note of her personalized Alabama license plate. With his connections, he could get the woman's identity in less than five minutes. But then, there was the matter of her friend or former friend.

Going back to Eric's hotel room, Stan found Eric still sitting on the bed with his head in his hands. Eric looked up.

"What can I say, what can I do? I'm so sorry. I guess I just lost my temper. I didn't hit her. I just grabbed her and tried to throw her on the bed."

"Dude, that doesn't sound good either. Do you live around these parts?"

"I live close to John's Landing."

"Have you been drinking?"

"A little, not much, though."

"I'll tell you what I'm going to do. I'm going to call the Sheriff's Department and have a deputy come and escort you to your house, because I don't want you to follow that lady."

"You don't have to do that. I'll go home. But I want you to know, I'm no thug, and I don't hit women. We just got into a fight of words, and she fell backward, she really did."

Yeah, and I'm the Easter Bunny. There's no way you're getting out of here and on the road unless you agree to an escort by a deputy. If I were that lady, I would have called the police and let your sorry ass rot in jail."

"Okay, okay, you can get a deputy out here to escort me home. I know most of the deputies anyway."

"The lady told me to make sure you paid for the room, but I'm not going to charge you because I want you out of here."

CHAPTER 43

Kristie was cruising down I-65 at seventy-five mph. She dared not speed. As she drew closer to the Birmingham area, traffic was getting congested, and she wondered how many people were behind the wheel tonight that shouldn't be behind the wheel. Kristie said a prayer asking God to get her home safely.

God answered Kristie's prayer because she got to her little garden home in Helena safe and sound. But as she turned into her driveway, she saw some flashing blue lights, and realized a policeman was parked in front of her house. Kristie opened the garage door and drove her car inside. Then she got out and went to see what the policeman wanted.

"Kristie Tidwell?" asked the officer.

"Yes"

"The Helena Police Department was notified by the Wentworth Police Department that there were some disagreements between you and your date this evening. The police officer in charge said you left Wentworth after the altercation."

"Well, it's a little more complicated than that, but I don't think any sort of crime was committed. I was uncomfortable and wanted to get out of Wentworth."

"The manager at the Holiday Inn Express in Wentworth has connections at the police department, and he wanted to make sure you arrived home, and that your friend didn't follow you. Are you comfortable staying at your house tonight?"

"Oh, yes. I doubt I'll see Eric Channing or any of his friends ever again."

"Okay, Ms. Tidwell, if you need anything, let us know."

"Thank you, officer, I will."

How did that manager know who Kristie was? He must have noted the license plate and checked things out. As the Helena police officer said, he has connections with the Wentworth Police Department. She'll have to track down the guy and thank him for his kindness and concern.

Wentworth Deputy Dwayne Salinas was making his way to the Holiday Inn Express where he was to escort some piece of shit to his house after he tried to beat up on his girlfriend. For a county with a reputation for its residents being devout churchgoers, domestic violence was commonplace.

Within fifteen minutes of his dispatch, Dwayne was driving up to the hotel where he saw an open door to one of the rooms with Stan standing in the doorway. Dwayne got out of the county vehicle and walked to the open door. Stan and Dwayne shook hands with Stan thanking for coming and taking this scumbag off his hands.

"Hey dirtbag," yelled Stan. "The deputy's here, and soon you're going to be somewhere other than here."

As Eric walked out of the room with his bag and the cooler, his eyes met those of Dwayne Salinas, the young deputy. While Eric was friendly with many of the Wentworth deputies, he didn't know that young Dwayne was now a member of the Sheriff's department.

"Dwayne?"

"Mr. Channing?"

"Dwayne, let's go."

"Okay, I'll follow you without a siren, but there had better not be any funny business."

When they arrived at Eric's house, Eric got out of his truck and walked up to Dwayne's county car.

"Look, Dwayne, what actually happened at the hotel was not the way it looked. My date and I had a misunderstanding, and I did grab her and push her, but not violently. I swear, not violently. I wanted to push her down on the bed, but she didn't get that far and stumbled onto the floor."

"Mr. Channing, I'm just doing my job. And just so you'll know, this will be kept confidential. No one will hear about it."

Sure, and I'm the Easter Bunny this time, thought Eric. In twenty-four hours, the whole town is going to know about this. But maybe Gina, who still lives in Birmingham, and Tanya, who is a teenager, would never find out.

As soon as the deputy and "boyfriend of the year" left the hotel, Stan wasted no time in calling the Wentworth police dispatcher, asking him to look up the woman's license plate. Kristie Tidwell? Kristie Tidwell, sure. She was Bobby and Mary Tidwell's daughter. Stan's aunt, his dad's sister was married to one of Kristie's uncles, one of her dad's brothers. He and Kristie were kissing cousins or cousin in laws or something like that. The dispatcher in Wentworth would get in touch with the Helena Police Department to make sure Kristie arrived at her home safely.

The next morning Stan planned to call his cousin by blood, Barry Tidwell, who was also Kristie's cousin by blood and tell him about Eric Channing. Would Barry try to harm Eric? No, but there were plenty of guys in the county that would put Eric in a world of hurt, and it wouldn't cost much.

CHAPTER 44

Eric unlocked the door to his house and walked straight to his bedroom where he would be sleeping alone. Kathryn and Kristie were friends when they were in high school, so why had Kathryn decided to treat Kristie like dirt? Jan ran around with the crowd that gave Kristie a hard time, but hadn't folks grown up? Maybe Kristie was too sensitive. But she told Eric on the way to Jan's house that she was looking forward to seeing Kathryn. She also seemed to be looking forward to the party.

When he talked to Jan, telling her he would attend the party, she should have said she was inviting a friend she wanted him to meet. Then he could have said he was bringing someone. But Jan said nothing. Yes, Kristie was obsessed with her long dark hair. She wouldn't go past her mailbox without makeup. What shade of lipstick should she apply? Does this top go with this skirt, shorts, jeans, etc.? Oh my, I wore this to the last meeting, I can't wear it again. Bad hair day, good hair day, manicures, and pedicures.

But Kristie was beautiful, and she liked, or used to like him. If there was one physical flaw with Kristie, it was her healthy appetite, making it difficult for her to control her weight. When she put her mind into it, she was good, but she could also be bad. But there was no denying that Kristie Tidwell was a beautiful woman, and this Carol person, oh pu-leaze.

Eric decided he was calling Kristie. He didn't care if he woke her up, he needed to talk to her. In fact, he was prepared to get in his truck and drive to Birmingham, if necessary, to make things right, and get Kristie back. Thinking about Kristie's white skin and dark hair falling over her shoulders, her big blue eyes, and her perfectly shaped lips drove him crazy. He was going to call her. She just had to answer the phone and talk to him, telling him the events of last night were forgotten. Then she would insist that he get in his truck, drive down, and celebrate New Year's Day with her.

But Eric had done the unforgivable. He grabbed Kristie and pushed her toward the bed. However, she didn't make it to the bed. Instead, she fell to the floor just shy of the bed. When that stupid manager knocked on the door, and he had no choice but to open it, the manager saw Kristie on the floor in tears. What was he supposed to think? What would he think if he were the manager? If he had been the manager, he would have punched the guy in the nose and asked questions later.

Yes, he was furious with Kristie, but no more furious than he had been at times with his ex-wife, Gina, or the first fiancée, Rhonda. Hitting or otherwise being aggressively physical with a woman was so far out of the scope of conduct. You just don't hit a woman, and he didn't hit Kristie, but he grabbed her and shoved her. But you just don't do that either.

Then he remembered an incident with his high school girlfriend, Rita McDonald. He was trying to get Rita's clothes off one night

when they were at a small farmhouse owned by a friend's father. A
drunken Eric yanked Rita's panties off, and was prepared to go all the
way with her. Rita screamed and fought him off. Then he passed out.
What would have happened had he not passed out? Guess alcohol
saved him that night. He was about to sexually assault Rita. What sort
of man was he? Not much of a man.

Sleep was not forthcoming. He had to explain things to Kristie
and ask her to take him back.

Eric walked into one of his spare bedrooms and opened a dresser
drawer. There was his loaded revolver. Eric wasn't a man, he was a
failure. Picking up his gun, he held it in his hand and stared at it.
Could he pull the trigger? Could he do this to Tanya, Roger, and
Sandy, his aunt, and his cousins? And what about Kristie? She was
the one who was driving him to this. If she had made even the
slightest effort to be friendly to the Harpo clan and be a part of his
group of friends, what happened at the hotel might not have taken
place. Killing himself would surely ruin the rest of Kristie's life.
Would she visit his grave and weep, begging him to forgive her? Eric
considered himself a Christian and felt it was a sin to commit suicide.
He was scared he would go to hell if he took his life. But wouldn't he
still go to hell for what he had just done to Kristie, and to Rita, so
long ago?

Putting the revolver back in the drawer, he wandered into his
bedroom and slipped into bed, hoping sleep would come, but he

knew it wouldn't. Eric lay awake until dawn when sleep finally consumed his fatigue worn body.

The next thing he knew, there was a loud knocking on his front door.

At 10:00 am sharp on New Year's Day, Stan Monahan called Barry Tidwell's home, with Barry's wife, Jackie answering the phone.

"Hey, Jackie, this is your cousin, Stan."

"Oh, hi Stan."

"Is Barry there?"

"Just a second."

"Hey Stan, what's going on?"

"Do you know Eric Channing?"

"Sure, he lives in John's Landing."

"Did you know he was with your cousin, Kristie, last night?"

"No, have Eric and Kristie been seeing one another? They both went to WHS."

"Up until last night, they apparently were. There was a nasty little scene in one of the rooms at my hotel. Kristie is okay, but frankly, I hope Eric's not okay or is ever okay again for the rest of his life."

Barry, beginning to feel anxious, asked what happened.

"After midnight I heard shouting. Then I heard loud noises and knocked on their door. Kristie was lying on the floor crying. It appears she and Eric got into a fight, and Eric either hit her, or shoved her to the floor.?

"You said Kristie was all right, didn't you?"

"Yes, she left and drove back to Birmingham, and I had a deputy escort Channing to his house, so he wouldn't follow Kristie."

"I'll check on things, Stan. Thank you for calling."

"What's wrong?" asked Jackie. Barry repeated what Stan had just told him.

"I think I'll pay a little call on Eric Channing," said Barry as he went to get his revolver.

"I know you think of Kristie as a sister, but please be careful. I've never known of Eric Channing to be violent in any way. I've never heard anything bad said about him."

"Well, a lot bad is going to be said about him, and something bad may happen to him."

Eric opened the door to a bug-eyed Barry Tidwell.

"What did you do to my cousin last night?"

"Nothing Barry, well, almost nothing, that is. What that manager saw was awful, but believe me, it wasn't what it looked like. In fact, if I were him, I would have punched my lights out."

Eric and Barry talked until Eric he had convinced Barry that things weren't as bad as they seemed.

"I love Kristie, and I want to marry her, but I've done the unforgivable, or at least some folks think I have. I'm scared I'll never be able to get her back. I don't suppose you could talk to her?"

"Look, Eric, we're both men and I have a temper just like you do, but blood is thicker than water, and you're on your own. I hope Kristie dumps you like a hot potato. She deserves better."

CHAPTER 45

It was almost time for the ballgame to start. Kristie and Eric were supposed to watch it together after a New Year's brunch of shrimp and grits. Last night scared Kristie to the point of not wanting to have anything to do with Eric Channing. She never wanted to see him again, or even talk to him. A few of his things were at her house, but she planned to box them up and send them to him. Also, she wanted nothing to do with Wentworth, Alabama. Maybe she would sell the acreage she now owned and never go back there again.

Kristie's top four priorities in life were God, family, work, and Alabama football. The bowl game was to begin in a few minutes, and it would make Kristie forget her troubles.

Alabama won easily, and at the end, things got emotional when Greg McElroy, senior quarterback, left the game, his last in an Alabama uniform. It was also moving when Mark Ingram and Julio Jones, juniors, who would likely declare for the NFL draft, left the game for their last times in Alabama uniforms. Sitting on her sofa, alone, Kristie teared up because it was the last time she would see Greg, Mark, Julio, and others in crimson. Eric Channing was forgotten.

When the game was over, the phone rang a couple of times. It was Eric. What could he possibly want, and why would she want to talk to him after last night? If the manager had not knocked on their door when he did, there was no telling what might have happened to her. Eric was in a mood that she had never seen before.

When Kristie didn't answer, Eric, sounding like he was crying, left her a message begging her to call him immediately. If she would just call him and talk to him, and hear him out, he would never ask for anything from her again.

After replaying last night's events over and over in her head, Kristie admitted to herself that things were blurry. Was Eric trying to hurt her, or was he just trying to get her to stay with him? He did have that wide-eyed Rhett Butler look when she fell backward onto the floor. He did rush up to her with tears in his eyes. Then the manager knocked on the door.

Did she owe it to him to listen to what he had to say? No. Would she listen to him and see what he had to say? That was the sixty-four-thousand-dollar question.

The phone rang again. It was a 256 area code, but a number that Kristie didn't recognize.

"Kristie, this is Barry, your cousin, are you okay? Did Eric Channing hurt you last night? And Roll Tide."

"And Roll Tide to you, wasn't that game fabulous? If we had played like that all during the season, we'd be back in the BCS. Think Mark and Julio are gone?"

"Probably, did Eric Channing hurt you?"

"No, we attended a party at Jan Franklin's house. Do you know her?"

"I know who she is."

"Well, the party was a disaster, and we had kind of a fight on the way back to the hotel. When I tried to leave, Eric didn't want me to. He said it was too dangerous to drive with all the drunks on the road. I was going to leave anyway, and he attempted to stop me by grabbing me, and pushing me onto the bed. But I missed the bed and landed on the floor. That's when the manager knocked on the door."

"You know who that manager, Stan Monahan, is, don't you?"

"No, who?"

He's Wilson Monahan's son."

"Oh my, he's a cousin on your Mom's side. I just didn't make the connection."

"He looked you up from your license plate, realized who you were, and then called me."

"I will make it a point to call Stan and thank him."

"I paid our Mr. Channing a little visit this morning, and he was beside himself. I told him the only thing keeping me from killing him was that I didn't want to go to jail. He then said he had thought about killing himself. He said that physically attacking a woman was one of the worst things a man could do. He admitted he no longer thought of himself as a man. I know people who know people who will make sure something bad happens to Eric Channing, and they work cheap. There are plenty of old, deep wells in rural Wentworth County where a body could be disposed of and never recovered. Just let me know what you want to do."

"Oh, Barry, I don't want to get involved with the Wentworth mafia. I just need some time to think."

After talking some more about the ballgame and the upcoming BCS. Barry told Kristie if she changed her mind about the Wentworth mafia, to let him know. Eric Channing could be disposed of without a trace, and the Sherriff's Department would only do a token investigation.

After talking to Barry, Kristie's phone started ringing about every fifteen minutes with Eric leaving a blubbering voicemail after each call. With so many voicemail messages on her phone, Kristie decided she had better talk to Eric and tell him where to go, so she could get on with her life. It was a new year.

The next time Eric called, Kristie picked up. Eric, startled that she was willing to talk to him, didn't know what to say. He was disturbed and kept telling her he was so sorry about last night, and everything was his fault. He even went on to say that they should have spent New Year's Eve alone and not at Jan Franklin's house.

Because Eric sounded so desperate, Kristie was afraid to tell him to go to the devil. What if he did something stupid? He wanted to drive down to Helena that evening to see her, but she told him she was not ready to see him, she needed time to think. Eric seemed to accept this and started sounding like his old self on the phone. He was ecstatic that Alabama won the game earlier. He also agreed with her that if Alabama had played that way all season, they would be in the BCS. He just wished he and Kristie could have watched the game together. After a few more minutes, their conversation ended with Eric saying he would call her in a few days.

CHAPTER 46

New Year's Day was on Saturday, and Kristie had to be back at work on Monday. When she didn't hear from Eric by Tuesday evening, she reconciled to herself that he was out of her life forever. They could live their lives, avoiding each other. Besides, Kristie was seriously entertaining selling the acreage, and leaving Wentworth, Alabama behind. She had a few friends, who were in her graduating class, but with the Harpo clan and Wiley Martin being the core of the Wentworth clique, she would never belong up there, nor would she ever be accepted.

Kristie was aware that this would be the first weekend in a while where she didn't have Eric. As nightfall approached, she sat in her living room with an unbearable weight on her shoulders. Work was not going well, and her boss was turning up the heat on Louis, the nice guy approaching sixty, who they felt was not pulling his weight. Kristie would be forced to do something before long.

After a few glasses of wine and a couple of sleep-aids, Kristie dozed off. She said nothing of this to Jennie Stewart. Tomorrow was church, and Kristie didn't know if she would be able to fake anything. The next morning, she called Jennie, telling her she wouldn't be at church because she had a migraine. As a migraine sufferer, Kristie was able to use having them as an excuse to get out of commitments, but it had been a while since she had done so.

Putting on a happy face was impossible, but Kristie kept telling herself that time heals all wounds. She would have to endure the dark clouds which were sure to hang over her for a while.

Shortly after Kristie dozed off on Sunday evening, her phone rang. She promptly answered it without checking the screen. It was Eric. He was at the bottom of the hill outside her subdivision and wanted to see her. She was in her nightgown and groggy from taking sleep-aids.

"I'm sorry you drove all the way down here, but I'm asleep, and I'll probably have a bad day tomorrow. I can't see you tonight."

"Please, Kristie! I have to talk to you. I promise I won't touch you. I just need to talk to you tonight. Please!"

He sounded so desperate that Kristie, against her better judgment, said okay. In less than a minute, Eric was pulling into her driveway. Kristie hardly had time to change into sweatpants and a sweatshirt before Eric was knocking on her door.

After sitting down in one of Kristie's wing chairs, Eric said that his limited vocabulary couldn't begin to describe how terrible he felt about New Year's Eve. He did something unforgivable and knew that Kristie had every right to tell him to stay away from her for the rest of their lives. But if she had any feelings at all for him, could she possibly give him another chance? He told her that all he wanted was one more chance. If he ever did something like he did to her on New Year's Eve, he would be out of her life forever. Feeling as though she had no other choice, Kristie said okay.

After a long moment, Kristie admitted to Eric that the crowd at the New Year's Eve party was not one with which she was comfortable, even though it had been decades since she had seen most of those people. This was the wild crowd, not the group with which she used to hang out.

"Look, Kristie, I know how you feel. You may not think I do, but I do. If you lived in Wentworth, I couldn't see you hanging around with those folks. You would be a better fit for the upper crust group. My group is made up of the wild gang who didn't care about grades, college, education, etc. They just wanted to have fun, smoke, drink, and have sex. They wanted high school to last forever, and wanted no part of life outside of Wentworth. In a way, I'm a part of them, and will always be a part of them. And I know now that you will never be a part of them. But that doesn't matter to me anymore. I know you don't like those folks, and I accept that. I want to be with you, and I'm trying to like your Birmingham and Tuscaloosa friends, I really am."

Eric and Kristie talked until after midnight. Then Kristie told Eric he needed to get on the road because she had to have a few hours of sleep before she faced what was sure to be a bad day.

"I don't suppose I could stay here tonight?"

"I'm not ready for that, you really need to leave."

Eric stood up and walked to the door, with Kristie getting up also. When Eric reached out and touched her shoulder, she backed away. "Don't do that Eric, I'm not ready."

"Okay. May I call you in a few days?"

"Sure."

In the weeks that followed, Eric called Kristie every day, with Kristie agreeing to have dinner with him after a couple of weeks. After dinner, they went back to Kristie's place where they held hands and watched a movie. After the movie, Kristie told him she wasn't ready to spend the night with him.

By the end of January, Kristie and Eric made love, and Eric told her he loved her and wanted to be with her. By the end of February, everything seemed to be back where it was before that fateful New Year's Eve. Spring would soon arrive in Alabama, and Eric and Kristie were looking forward to the months ahead.

CHAPTER 47

One warm April Saturday, Eric suggested to Kristie that they drive to Tuscaloosa. He hadn't been to the University of Alabama campus in a long time, and wanted to see the azaleas in bloom, something for which the university was known.

The azaleas were indeed beautiful. Walking hand in hand, Eric and Kristie talked very little. When they got to Denny Chimes, on the south side of the famous quadrangle, Eric suggested that they sit down on the steps for a moment. He put his arm around Kristie and told her he thought this was one of the most beautiful places on earth, and he was having the privilege of sharing it with the most beautiful woman in the world.

At that point, Eric pulled a little black velvet pouch from his shirt pocket. From the pouch, he pulled out a ring with a large center cut diamond, encircled by small rubies. It was a ring both had admired in a Birmingham jewelry store a couple of weeks ago.

"If you think I'm getting down on my knees, you've got another thing coming," grinned Eric. "But will you marry me anyway?"

"YES, YES, YES," screamed an excited Kristie. He put the ring, which was already sized, on her finger and kissed her.

"Looks like we've attracted a crowd," said Eric, as a few passersby gathered and clapped for them.

Kristie asked a young woman who had been out running if she would take their picture in front of one of Alabama's famous landmarks.

After thanking the woman, Eric said he was hungry and asked Kristie if she was up for an early dinner. Kristie was hungry too, so they decided to go to Cypress Inn. Maybe, by going this early, they could get a table with a view of the Black Warrior River.

Kristie and Eric were seated at a good table by one of the big picture windows overlooking the river, and had a great dinner. By telling the Maître d they had just gotten engaged, they received a free carafe of wine and free desserts. Kristie and Eric had a wonderful time eating their first meal together as a couple to be married.

On the way back to Birmingham, the happy couple discussed wedding plans. The wedding would start out as small as possible, knowing it would grow in time. Not wanting to wait forever, they decided on a Saturday in late June since they were reunited during their class reunion last June. They also decided the ceremony would be held in the morning, maybe 10:30 am. Because June is the month for many nuptials, folks could attend their wedding, then have time to get to an afternoon wedding, and then to an evening wedding.

"Can you imagine a day any more horrible than one where you had to attend three weddings?" commented Eric. "Makes me itch."

By the time they went to sleep that night, they further decided to invite everyone in their graduating class, plus immediate family members and guests. For invitations, they would ask Debbie Krebbs to send out a couple of emails about the wedding and keep up with who responded that they would be attending. For her efforts, they would get Debbie something nice. They also agreed that Phil Stewart, Kristie's minister, would perform the ceremony, and his wife, a childhood friend of Kristie's, would stand up with her. Eric hoped that his daughter would agree to stand up with him.

The couple decided to live in Kristie's house in Helena after the wedding. Depending on how things went with Kristie's job, they might sell her house and move to the Alabama Gulf Coast. Eric always felt if he had been more flexible, and had agreed to move to Birmingham when he and Gina were married, things might have turned out differently.

At church the next day, Eric and Kristie's engagement was announced. Phil would be happy to perform the ceremony, and Jennie was honored to be asked to stand up with Kristie.

They still needed a place to have the wedding, someone to cater the wedding, a photographer to take pictures, and a florist to arrange the flowers. Kristie knew she had better get started on Monday. She had a wedding to plan.

Sunday night, after Eric left for Wentworth County, Kristie lay in bed thinking, I'm engaged, and I'm going to get married. She often stared at her ring as it sparkled.

CHAPTER 48

Kristie started planning her moves for the next day at work. She and her boss were having some trouble. He seemed to have lost his sense of humor, and every time Kristie went to his office to consult with him about an issue, he made her feel stupid. Her boss was a knowledgeable person, and she wanted to draw off that knowledge. He worked with the other folks under him, but didn't seem to want to work with Kristie. He was also friendly to everyone except her.

Kristie liked her company and wanted to stay there, but she could not successfully work with her boss. Sometimes she would lay awake at night tossing and turning about things at work. She even had her resignation letter stored on her hard drive, ready to pull out if and when the time came.

She wasn't going to say anything to anyone at work about her engagement. Would her boss and her colleagues notice the ring? Probably not. Maybe she wouldn't say anything until June. But she would ask for a week or two of vacation after the wedding for a honeymoon. Then she would go in, throw her resignation letter on her boss's desk, work out her notice, and leave. She would need to discuss this with Eric because her actions would also affect him.

Sure enough, neither her boss, her colleagues, or the folks she supervised noticed her new ring. But after their weekly staff meeting on Thursday morning, her boss asked her to stay for a few more minutes. He wanted to know what Kristie was doing to bring Louis up to standards. Kristie indicated that Louis was stressed out, but was trying his best to take his performance to the next level, but things weren't working out for him. She then asked her boss if he had any suggestions.

"Just keep holding his feet to the fire, stress him out to a point where things either kick in or he fails. Oh, is that a new ring?"

"Yes."

"It's beautiful, is it an engagement ring?"

"Yes, I got engaged this past weekend."

"Congratulations, have you set a date?"

"No," Kristie lied.

"Well, we'll have to go out and celebrate."

"I'm for that."

Raj, a second generation Indian, wasn't sure about American traditions. While weddings were always a big thing in his culture, and called for days of celebrations, for Americans, they could be simple, or as elaborate as the bride and groom chose to make them. Sensing Kristie's hostility this morning, he decided not to ask any additional questions. In fact, he didn't know that Kristie was seeing anyone. Even though management personnel were encouraged to show interest in the personal lives of their subordinates, Raj hadn't shown much interest in Kristie. The only things he knew about her were that she was an Alabama football season ticket holder, she liked modern country music, and that she was politically conservative. Maybe not taking an interest in Kristie was a mistake. He made a mental note to talk more to her and find out what made her tick.

That afternoon, Kristie met with Louis and told him that upper management wanted him to make significant improvements in his work in the next three months. He wasn't on probation yet, but it could be on the horizon if there were not documented improvements. Kristie also told him if he found another job opportunity to take it. She couldn't guarantee he would be able to keep his job even if he did improve to the point that the higher up "mukkidy mucks" were satisfied. Kristie further indicated that she would do as much as she could to help him, but she understood that the brain at sixty just doesn't function like the brain at thirty-two. Louis was visibly upset, and so was Kristie. She suggested that he go home and chill out. But to his benefit, Louis responded that going home wasn't the answer. He'd stay a while and continue to work on his projects.

Kristie hated the IT department and her superiors. After she and Eric got married, she was quitting, even if she had to live in west Wentworth County and grow vegetables and catch fish out of Eric's pond to eat. Anything had to be better than this place.

Within a week, Kristie had made most of the wedding plans. Having a morning wedding helped because she booked a caterer, who would serve the food and bake the cakes, a DJ to do the music, a florist, and a photographer. Now it was time to work on her dress. With someone her age, a traditional wedding gown was out of the question. Instead, she opted to do the mother of the bride route, choosing something in a style and color good for her.

Eric contacted someone who had previously shown an interest in buying his small place in Wentworth County. This person was ready to complete the purchase, and Eric would take up residence at his sister and brother in law's house in Trussville until after the wedding. They talked about putting Kristie's house on the market and moving to a bigger house. They also talked about moving nearer to the Alabama gulf coast, an area they both loved.

Since men often don't talk about such things, Raj didn't mention anything to anyone at the office about Kristie's engagement, nor had Kristie discussed it with anyone, including him. Raj didn't even know when the wedding was to take place, but did approve a two-week vacation request in June for Kristie. He surmised the wedding would be taking place at that time. Guess he wasn't invited. Going out and celebrating Kristie's engagement never happened.

The Friday before the wedding, Kristie told Raj that she was leaving at 3:30 and would see him in two weeks. No one at work had bothered to give her a shower or take her out to lunch. And that was fine with her. After Raj received Kristie's email, he raced to her office because he was sure this was the weekend she was getting married. Much to his disappointment, Kristie had already left.

Raj felt terrible. He had been hard on Kristie, the nicest "American" he had ever known. There were several things that folks in the department did when someone was about to get married, but no one did any of those things for Kristie. He didn't know what kind of wedding she was having, and he didn't get an invitation. Furthermore, he had not heard of anyone else in the department receiving an invitation either. Maybe he would call Kristie on her cell phone, but as soon as he returned to his office, one of the AVPs called and summoned him to his office. The call was never made.

That evening when Kristie and Eric were eating take-out Chinese, Kristie told Eric that no one said anything to her about the wedding. She had emailed Raj that she would be leaving at 3:30, and all he said was okay, nothing else.

"Well, when you get back to work, you just greet Raj with your resignation." Eric had never met Raj, but hated him just the same.

CHAPTER 49

While not exactly joined at the hip, Eric and Kristie spent a lot of time "hip to hip" on their wedding trip to Key West. Being an avid fisherman, Eric wanted to go deep sea fishing one day, and Kristie said fine. She could do some shopping and cruise around in the convertible. What in the world was Eric going to do with any fish he might catch? Closer to home, on the northern gulf coast, the fishing companies would pack the fish you caught. If you were staying at a place with a kitchen, you could cook, and eat the fish there, or keep the fish on ice until you got home, about a half day's drive.

Kristie occasionally threw fish on the grill, but she had never fried a fish and wasn't about to start now. Eric, though, had done everything possible there was to do with fish. They were staying in an upscale hotel suite with a small kitchen, but still, she didn't want the smell of fish in their hotel room.

Much to Kristie's surprise, the maritime company would pack your fish in dry ice and ship them anywhere in the southeast for a price, of course. Eric had the company send his catch, a substantial one according to him, to his sister's house in Trussville to keep until they returned to Birmingham. Sandy was sure to love that.

After a day of fishing, Eric was sunburned and exhausted, wanting nothing more than to crawl into the bed and watch TV for the remainder of the evening. Not wanting Kristie to feel like she had to stay with him while he slept, Eric suggested that she go out, perhaps to Jimmy Buffett's Margaritaville because Kristie was a parrot head and they hadn't yet been to Mr. Buffett's famous restaurant.

Because there was a wait to get a table at Margaritaville, Kristie decided to stroll down Duvall Street until her table was ready. When the hostess led her to her table, she was surprised to be seated, a lone female diner, right in front of the stage. Margaritaville had nightly entertainment, and Kristie was ready to listen to some good music. Being familiar with many Key West musicians, Kristie asked the hostess who was playing this evening.

Bo Dickenson would be entertaining, along with a special guest. The hostess winked, and Kristie thought, could it possibly be Jimmy? The band was on break from touring, and Jimmy did own a recording studio here, considering Key West one of his hometowns. Or could it be Kenny? Kristie heard that he was in town. In fact, Eric told her that while out on the water, they saw his yacht. Either way, this promised to be an exciting night.

When Bo took the stage at 10:30, he played a few songs and then introduced his special guest, Jake McPherson. Jake was well-known in Nashville music circles, but flew under the radar most of the time. He had won many awards for his singing and songwriting, and was a member of numerous halls of fame, including Georgia, Alabama, and others. Jake had a great life. His was not a household name, and his face was unrecognizable, but as Natalie would say, he laughs all the way to the bank.

Kristie loved Jake's music and owned all his CDs. She attended every concert of his she could, the ones which were within driving distance of Birmingham. The farthest she had ever traveled to see Jake was Savannah, Georgia. His concerts were usually in small venues, and ticket prices were almost always under $50.00. Jake recognized her and knew her name. Even though he was a busy man, he seemed to be informed about everything. She and Jake had talked about football, politics, the weather, you name it.

Jake's relationship status was one of the planet's best kept secrets. There was an ex-wife, and there were rumors that while they were no longer married, they were still together. She had also heard stories of girlfriends. Jake was born in northeast Alabama and maintained a home there. Being close in age to Jake, and being from the same part of the country, Kristie had developed a major crush on him, and at one time was seriously interested in him. Why shouldn't he ask her out? She was attractive and raised similarly to the way he was raised. But most importantly, Jake was a good person. Fame hadn't changed him.

When Jake took the stage, he looked down, saw Kristie, and subtlety jerked his head back. After performing a few songs, he announced that he would be at the Margaritaville store signing autographs. Kristie quickly paid her check and went next door to see Jake. After purchasing several items for him to sign, Kristie got in line to await her turn, and realized she had her engagement and wedding rings on, signaling she was off the market. Feeling somewhat guilty and somewhat not, Kristie slipped her wedding set off and made sure the rings were snug in a small zipper compartment in her purse.

What in the world did she think she was doing? Jake McPherson, with his blonde hair and blue eyes, could have any girl he wanted. Also, Jake met and talked to people all the time. He was not going to pay any attention to what might or might not be on her left hand. Kristie, you're horrible she said to herself, put those rings back on and tell Jake you're here on your honeymoon. When it was her turn to talk to Jake, he hugged her, saying it was great to see her. He also asked what had brought her to Key West.

"I'm here on my honeymoon."

"Where's the lucky guy?"

"He's back in the room getting over his sunburn." Kristie smiled, and Jake smiled back.

"Well, Kristie, I'm almost finished, would you like to go somewhere other than here and get a cup of coffee?"

"Sure."

Jake and Kristie walked to a little out of the way place that served sandwiches and desserts.

"I'm going to have a piece of their key lime cake, it's good. Would you like a piece, or maybe something else?"

"The key lime cake sounds good, and a large glass of water with extra ice to drink."

"Jake smiled a knowing smile at her and went to get their orders.

When he returned, Jake wanted to know about Kristie's husband and the wedding. He was somewhat surprised that her husband was someone she knew in high school, but had only now begun a relationship. In turn, Kristie asked him how his children were doing. He said they were busy with their careers, but still, lazy as ever. Jake then asked Kristie about some other people from Birmingham they both knew.

When they were ready to leave the little café, Jake said, "I guess you're off the market, and that's my misfortune. "

Kristie then blurted out, "You've known me for a while, why didn't you ask me out?"

"I don't know, just busy, just apprehensive about some things. But you are one of my most beautiful fans. You've seen what most of my fans look like, haven't you?"

"Yes." And they both laughed.

"If you weren't married, now is the time I would ask you to come back to my hotel for a nightcap. Instead, I would like to escort you to your hotel, if that's okay."

"It is okay. I would be honored and grateful."

The walk back to Kristie and Eric's hotel was a pleasant one. Due to a storm off the coast, a cool breeze was blowing. When she and Jake reached intersections, Jake would take her elbow as they stepped off the curbs and crossed the streets. When they were about a half block from the hotel, Jake stopped, turned to Kristie, and said, "Is it okay if I leave you here?"

"Of course."

"You always struck me as the independent type. Many times, you would show up at my shows alone. You would get into your vehicle and drive anywhere."

"That's me. And it's not going to change just because I'm a married woman."

Jake kissed Kristie on the forehead and told her he looked forward to seeing her soon.

Entering the room, Kristie found Eric in bed asleep with the television tuned to the Sean Hannity replay. As Kristie was puttering around, Eric woke up and asked her how Margaritaville was.

"Great, and you will never guess who was performing there."

"Kenny Chesney? He is in town."

"Not exactly."

"Jimmy?"

"No, but that would have been great."

After several more guesses, Eric gave up.

"Okay, who?"

"Jake McPherson."

"Jake McPherson, really now. Did you tell him you were on your honeymoon?"

"Yep."

"And what did he say?"

"Congratulations. Look."

Kristie pulled a CD out of her bag and handed it to Eric. It was one of Jake's early ones.

"Well, open it."

Inside the CD, Jake had written, "To Kristie and Eric, all the best as you journey through life together."

"Isn't that sweet. Jake obviously didn't ask you out because you once said if he ever beckoned you, that I was history."

"And you once said if Sandra Bullock ever winked at you, I was history."

While Kristie was out, Eric slept for a few hours and felt like a new man. When Kristie climbed into bed, she was immediately grabbed by him. He was ready for his sixth night of marriage.

A couple of hours later, Kristie turned on her side, facing away from Eric. Yes, Jake McPherson, with his blonde hair and sexy blue eyes had kind of beckoned her, but Kristie was in love with Eric and felt nothing for Jake other than a slight physical attraction.

When you're used to the beaches of the Florida panhandle and the Alabama gulf coast, the beaches of Key West are disappointing. Lying on the beach for hours in Key West is not what most tourists do. It was a great wedding trip, though, but both Kristie and Eric were anxious to get back to the real world. They planned to drive up Highway 1, spend the night in Miami, head up to Orlando, spend the night there, and then head home.

By the time Kristie and Eric reached Marathon Key, it was time for lunch with Kristie suggesting a place called Hog Fish, located at a marina. She had eaten there before and liked it. The hostess seated Kristie and Eric at a great table overlooking the water.

While waiting for their food to arrive, Kristie was looking around. Four tables away, she saw none other than Jake McPherson.

"Jake," yelled Kristie.

Seeing Kristie, and smiling, he made his way over to their table. After Kristie introduced Eric and Jake, they talked for a few minutes before Jake went back to his table where he was dining with three other gentlemen.

"So, that's the great Jake McPherson?"

"In the flesh."

"I can see why you like him."

"I do like him. He's a great person, and has a great voice. Plus, he's an Alabamian, and was raised like we were raised. Through his many successes, those values remained intact."

Eric had yet to attend a Jake McPherson concert, but Kristie was hoping to get him to one soon. Could Eric be jealous of Jake? Jake was semi-famous, wealthy, and a mover and shaker in the music business. Even though Kristie had a major crush on him at one time, and had fantasized about being with him, what would someone like Jake McPherson want with someone like Kristie Tidwell? Oops, Kristie Channing.

CHAPTER 50

Wiley Martin passed away from cancer in the early morning hours two days after Kristie and Eric returned from Key West. Widow Anabelle Martin wanted Eric to be a pallbearer, and Eric was honored to have been asked. He would have to be at the viewing on Sunday afternoon and of course, at the funeral on Monday morning.

Because Kristie had not spoken a word to Wiley since they said "hi" to one another in Bidgood Hall when they were students at the University of Alabama, she didn't feel an obligation to do the funeral thing. However, Wiley had been a close friend of Eric's, and Eric wanted to be there when the viewing began. He suggested, though, that Kristie drive up later in the afternoon. Kristie agreed to this, thinking nothing of it, not questioning why Eric would want them to drive separately.

Kristie arrived at the Knoll funeral home about 2:15 to find numerous people present to pay their respects to Anabelle. Eric, looking all noble, was talking to a group of folks, mostly the Wentworth clique, people who were born and raised in Wentworth, and never left Wentworth. Kristie, dressed in a black pencil skirt, black and white top, and black low-heeled strappy sandals, walked up to Eric, who took her by the elbow, and introduced her to the group he was talking to as his wife.

Then came a shriek from Anabelle. Eric, with some of the other guys, rushed to her side. Homely Anabelle was having a "moment," and white knight Eric was the first one to get to her. Taking charge, Eric ordered people who were standing around them to get cold, damp, cloths to put on her head. As soon as Anabelle was stable, Eric and a couple of other guys escorted her out of the room to the back of the funeral parlor where she could relax and have something to drink.

After fifteen minutes or so, Anabelle's friends decided that it would be best to take Anabelle home, so she could get some rest. The viewing would continue with Jimmy Harpo, his wife, Ruthie, his sister, Jan, and Jan's husband, Jeremy, receiving guests. Anabelle and Wiley had no children, and Anabelle was an only child, both parents now deceased. Eric and Ron Griffin, another gang member, would take Anabelle to her house.

Kristie still had some hate inside of her for Wiley Martin that wouldn't go away. A few weeks before they were married, Eric told Kristie that Wiley, Johnny Morton, and Jake Stanley were pissed that she was first runner-up in the Miss Wentworth pageant when they were seniors in high school. For revenge, they were going to tie Kristie up, force her to drink straight whiskey until she passed out, gang rape her, and throw her into some snaky woods along one of the creeks that meandered through Wentworth. Were these guys going to do that to her just because she had placed higher in a stupid high school beauty pageant than their dumb girlfriends?

With Anabelle getting whisked home by Eric and Ron, there was no need for Kristie to hang around the funeral home. After getting into the convertible, she put the top down. Perhaps it was a little crass to drive to a dead person's viewing with the top down, but what the hell.

As soon as Kristie was about to start the car, she received a call from Eric, telling her that Anabelle would not be able to go back to the viewing and that Jimmy Harpo and family would handle things until it was over. Eric and Ron were going to stay with Anabelle for the next hour or two until Jimmy's wife and sister could get to the Martin house to spend the night. Eric suggested that she go on back to Birmingham. He would get there within the next two or three hours. Oh, how she hated Jimmy Harpo and his stupid sister.

"Wiley Martin, burn in hell," screamed Kristie as she sped down I-65 with the top down heading toward Birmingham. The next thing Kristie remembered was pulling into the driveway of her home, and it was still her home. There were no immediate plans to put Eric's name on it.

After shimmying out of her blacks and whites, Kristie put on an over-sized t-shirt, removed her bra, and left her panties on. Oversized t-shirt, panties, and no bra was the standard outfit for a woman living alone. The viewing ended at 4:00 pm. By the time the Harpo gang departed and made their way over to Anabelle's, it would be about 4:30. Kristie guessed that Eric would leave Anabelle's house about 4:45, putting him at her house about 6:00. Then they could have dinner together.

6:00 came and went, then 7:00, then 8:00. Kristie called Eric several times, but his phone went directly to voicemail. She didn't have the numbers of any of the Harpo gang, and Anabelle's landline was private. Just after 8:30, Eric drove up.

When Eric walked into the house, it was evident that Kristie was unhappy. When Eric asked her what was wrong, she screamed, "Where have you been? The viewing ended at 4:00."

"After Jimmy, Jan, Ruthie, and Jeremy got to Anabelle's, we sat around reminiscing with Anabelle about Wiley and about the good times we had when we were in high school, and up until the time we found out Wiley was dying."

"Well," replied Kristie, "I would have been out of place since I didn't hang out with that group. I was poor little chubby Kristie Tidwell until I placed high in the Miss Wentworth beauty pageant. Then I was shunned even more because I placed higher than any of their bitchy girlfriends, yours included."

"Kristie, is this what it's going to be like? Are you going to always be throwing something up to me about the Wentworth folks? I'm sorry you had a difficult time in high school, and you dislike so many of my friends. But if we're going to be husband and wife, you have to let some things go. Take a deep breath and move on. We don't have to hang out with those folks all the time, but most of them are my friends, and I'm not going to give them up just to hang around Tim and Natalie, and the other folks you consider your friends."

Eric grabbed a beer from the refrigerator and sat down at the kitchen table while Kristie went back to their bedroom and lay across the bed on her stomach. A few minutes later, Kristie felt Eric's weight on the bed. Putting his arms around her and laying his head on her back, Eric said, "Honey, what is it? I've never seen you act like this before. You're like one of those bridezillas on TV."

Eric went on. "You've never like Wiley. I know that, and I've accepted it. I also know you sometimes get irritated with me for spending so much time with the Wentworth people instead of with you and your friends like Natalie and Tim. It's just that I feel more at ease with the Wentworth folks. They're like home folks to me. Natalie and Tim seem so worldly."

"Natalie and Time, worldly? Natalie and Tim who went to South Beach and had dinner at Burger King?"

"Natalie and Tim ate at Burger King in South Beach, laughed Eric.

"Yes. After checking into their hotel, they were walking through the area and couldn't find a restaurant where the wait was less than two hours. So, they went to Burger King."

"Wow, there's no way I'd eat at Burger King if I were in South Beach. I don't care how long the wait was or what kind of table they gave me, when they were forced to seat a rube like me."

Kristie and Eric found themselves laughing as Kristie turned over and put her arms around Eric. Wiley Martin was forgotten, along with the chicken casserole.

CHAPTER 51

Wiley's funeral was to take place at 10:00 am at the Knoll Funeral Chapel in Wentworth, and Eric was supposed to be there at 9:00 am. Interment would immediately follow at a local cemetery.

"Didn't we miss something last night, like supper?" was the first thing out of Eric's mouth when they both woke up almost simultaneously.

"Want some breakfast?" asked Kristie.

"What time is it?"

"About a quarter till seven."

"I don't have time."

Eric jumped out of bed and padded down the hall to his bathroom while Kristie went across the room to the master bathroom.

"I need to leave here in an hour flat."

Kristie showered, put on her makeup, and once again shimmied into the black pencil skirt. But today, she dressed in a purple and gray top, wearing the same strappy sandals as yesterday, carrying the same bag. Kristie was scrunching and spraying her hair when Eric appeared at the door of the master bathroom.

"Oh, you're planning to go?"

"Do you not want me to?"

"I wasn't sure you'd want to go."

"Does anyone ever want to go to a funeral.?"

After a pause, Kristie said, "If you don't want me to go, just say so, and I'll go to work."

"I'd like for you to go, we can stop on the way and get some breakfast."

After Kristie put on her jewelry and dabbed her wrists and neck with cologne, they were off in Eric's big silver pickup truck.

When Kristie and Eric arrived at the funeral home, no one was there. Since they didn't stop anywhere to eat, Eric suggested that they drive over to the I-65/U.S. 157 exit and pick up some sausage and biscuits.

As soon as they started eating, Eric's cell phone rang. It was Jan Franklin, Jimmy Harpo's sister. Anabelle had a restless night, and would need some folks to help her get through the service. Jan thought she would require two men, one at each side to hold her up in case she fainted. Would Eric volunteer, along with Jimmy? What choice did he have?

Anabelle arrived at the funeral home, accompanied by the Harpos, about twenty minutes before the service was to begin. Because Eric had once again left her alone to be one of Anabelle's white knights, Kristie spoke to a few people she knew, including the minister of the First United Methodist Church, and the president of the Wentworth Chamber of Commerce. She also spoke to a few of her classmates who were eager to know how married life was treating her so far.

When the time for the service to start drew near, Kristie made her way into the chapel and took a seat near the back. Tomorrow, at this time, Wiley Martin would be six feet under, and maybe poor, poor Anabelle would be resting at her home, eating the food people had brought in, and making plans for the rest of her life.

Eric mentioned to Kristie on the drive up that Anabelle had no family in Wentworth, and would likely sell the house and move back to Huntsville. Kristie didn't care what Anabelle did, she just wanted Wiley and Anabelle out of their lives. Make that the same for the Harpos. Kristie had no use for them as they barely acknowledge that she existed.

Cindy Smith asked if she could join Kristie for the service. Kristie liked Cindy, though they had been competitors when they were growing up. Cindy was not a big Wiley Martin fan, but felt the need to attend the funeral because she and Anabelle did charity work together. Kristie admitted she was only there because Wiley and Eric were good friends, and she was now Eric's wife.

The service was nice. A soloist form the Methodist church sang *How Great Thou Art* and *How lovely is Thy Dwelling Place*. The minister read scripture and spoke of how Wiley had created numerous jobs in the Wentworth area and had helped many people. The minister also mentioned that Wiley worked hard and played hard. Kristie knew this was true, but she also heard things to the effect that Wiley was a crooked businessman and loved to throw his money around. This could have been true, but that revelation didn't belong at his funeral.

At the graveside, Kristie, along with everyone else was about to wilt under the late June sun. Jimmy and Eric got Anabelle seated on the front row under the tent, and then went to join the rest of the pallbearers. Standing by the casket, Eric looked somber and stoic, dressed in a dark suit. Sweat was popping up on his forehead and brow.

Friends would gather at the Martin house after the service, and, of course, Eric would not want to miss that. Unfortunately, Kristie also had to go since she and Eric drove to Wentworth together. Maybe she should have driven alone, then she would be free to go home, and not have to endure hearing more Wiley Martin accolades.

As Kristie expected, the attendees at the reception after the funeral were members of the old gang, and she did not feel close to anyone who was there.

After fixing a plate of food, and pouring herself a glass of wine, Kristie found a place to sit in silence, away from everyone else.

Eric, on the other hand, was in his element, shaking hands, hugging, and making sure everyone was comfortable, including Anabelle. At one point, Kristie saw Eric, the Harpo clan, and Wiley's high school girlfriend, with her husband, huddled together, most likely reminiscing about Wiley. Should she get up and join them? She was Eric's wife, and a member of Wiley's graduating class. No. She was going to stay out of sight. Kristie Tidwell, the fat girl, was going to hide as much as possible so the gang wouldn't see her and say mean things to her.

It was time for another glass of wine, so Kristie ventured to the wet bar, located the bottle of chardonnay that was on ice, and helped herself. Ruthie Harpo, Kathryn Harpo, wife of Jimmy's brother, Sam, and Jan Franklin, also known as the Harpo women, were in charge of the food and drink, but no one was around when Kristie poured her second glass of wine.

Before she knew it, it was time for a third glass of wine, which she once again poured for herself without getting noticed by anyone. Feeling herself getting tipsy, Kristie continued to nibble on the snacks that were available.

Because she was sitting close to the kitchen, she heard Jan say, "There's another honey baked ham and turkey breast in the refrigerator. There's also plenty of boiled shrimp, potato salad, coleslaw, and broccoli salad. Let's lay everything out for supper."

"Good idea," said Kathryn. "I'll count how many folks are here. I think it's mostly the gang."

"We have eleven still here, so there's plenty," said Kathryn, returning from the living room.

I wonder if Kathryn included me, thought Kristie. I'll sit here and see if anyone comes looking for me. When Kathryn mentioned the gang, Kristie knew about whom she meant, and Kristie was not a part of that group back then, nor was she now.

After a few minutes, Kristie heard Jan yell out to everyone that supper was laid out in the kitchen. Then she heard voices as the eleven were in line filling their plates. She heard Eric talking, but did not attempt to find her and ask her if she wanted to eat with him and the others. Had he not noticed that she had gone missing?

When everyone had helped themselves, and went to the dining room or the living room to eat, Kristie stood up and went to the kitchen, looking into the dining room. The gang she wasn't a part of, who had tormented her in high school, was sitting around the large dining room table eating and telling stories about Wiley. Eric was seated by Anabelle. No one from the dining room saw her. Should she fix a plate of the real food and take it back to her perch? If not, what should she do?

By sitting off to herself for so long, Kristie was showing a reluctance to be part of the gang and to be with her new husband. She had been married less than three weeks to the man she loved, plus she would soon be free from a job that was bringing her down. She should be happy, but was showing her dark side. Even though she loved Eric, did she also resent him? Was she in a love/hate relationship? It was too late to join Eric and his group of friends, many of whom didn't like her anyway, so she decided to sit back on the sofa in the den and feign sleep. She was, in fact, tired.

After eating, folks were saying that they needed to go. Tomorrow was a work day. Kathryn, Jan, and Ruthie told the guests not to worry about the cleanup. They could handle it. Besides, with paper plates and plastic flatware, there wouldn't be much to do.

"Kristie, wake up," yelled Eric.

"I guess I dozed off."

"Did you get something to eat?"

"I had some cheese and crackers, and some chips and dip."

"Jan, Ruthie, and Kathryn put out some ham, turkey, potato salad, and other stuff for supper. Did you sleep through that?"

"I suppose I did."

By this time several of the gang had surrounded her and Eric. Thankfully, she had set her wine glass in the kitchen. That's all she needed was for the gang members to say she got drunk, lying for the sole purpose of ruining her reputation and further making fun of her.

"Are you ready to go?" asked Kristie

"Yes."

"Then let's go."

With that, Kristie grabbed her purse, stood up, and walked out the door with Eric. As Eric shook hands with the men and hugged the women, Kristie didn't acknowledge anyone. When they got in the truck, Kristie asked Eric to stop somewhere so she could get something to eat. What she had consumed earlier was gone.

"Let's get you something from the house."

"Those bitches didn't exactly offer me anything after they discovered that I had fallen asleep in the den."

"Look, I'm sure they'll be okay with it."

"I'd rather stop at Jack's or McDonald's than eat their food."

"Okay, suit yourself, but I think you're misjudging a lot of those people."

With that, Eric started the truck and pulled out into the street. Because Kristie seemed depressed, Eric decided to stop at one of the town's barbecue places and get her something. She'd like that better.

While Eric thought Kristie was unreasonable, he could see her side of things. Wiley Martin was unkind to Kristie, and she wasn't a part of the group at the reception. Eric wanted to maintain his friendship with Anabelle, but knew it might be difficult. After getting Kristie a barbecue sandwich, fries, and a Diet Coke, they headed toward Birmingham. Kristie would be going to work tomorrow and turning in her resignation.

CHAPTER 52

Before she went to bed, Kristie forwarded a copy of her resignation letter to her work email address. She planned to print out a copy when she arrived at her office tomorrow and submit it to Raj.

Even though Kristie was on vacation, she checked her work email, finding nothing much was taking place, except that HR and Raj's boss were pressuring her to do something about Louis. Louis wasn't going to be her problem for long, neither was Raj, and neither was the IT department.

When Kristie arrived at her office for work the next morning, her message light was flashing. She had a message from Raj to come to his office just as soon as she could. But before heading to his area, Kristie printed her resignation letter, signed it, and put it in an envelope. No matter how many sinister things Raj may hit her with, she was getting the hell out of this place to begin a new phase in her life.

"I want you to let Louis go this week. Wednesday might be suitable. It will give him a chance to get used to the idea before the weekend."

"Before I went on vacation, Louis told me he would rather quit voluntarily and preserve his professional integrity rather than be fired. Do you mind if I approach him and give him an either-or?"

"I don't guess so, but upper management wants him out of here shortly."

"Okay."

"Oh, and here's something else."

Raj opened the envelope, unfolded the letter, and read it. His mouth dropped open.

"I never expected this. I thought you wanted to stay here until you retired."

"I did, but this place has changed so much, and I'm just not up to dealing with all the stress and pressure coming down on everyone. It's killing me emotionally and physically.

Then something snapped inside of Kristie.

"I've done nothing but work my fanny off for this company, and in the last few years, nothing was appreciated. The day I was hospitalized for heart problems, I came in and had to leave immediately because even you knew I was in distress. Throughout the day I kept you informed about what was taking place, but when I called you to tell you I was being admitted to the hospital, you were incredulous, saying I don't guess you'll be at work tomorrow. But I was back at work on Monday after being dismissed from the hospital on Saturday night. So, I was out a total of about two days. Then I asked if it would be possible during the first week after my hospital stay, to come in late so I could sleep until I woke up. You said okay, but I could tell you didn't much like it."

"A year later, I had the misfortune of injuring my shoulder which resulted in surgery. Following the surgery, I needed to go to therapy two times a week, and you didn't like that. I'll have you know I made up every minute that I took off to go to therapy. But still, you were a smart-ass about the whole thing. In fact, I didn't finish the therapy because I felt uncomfortable. You treated me as though I was goofing off. Also, I was one of the lucky ones because I had very little pain. Some folks are so wrung out after their therapy they have to go home and rest. I always came back to work and worked until at least 6:30 or 7:00. I had the surgery on Thursday and was back at work the following Tuesday, taking off three days, when most people are out between ten days to two weeks with that kind of surgery."

Raj lowered his head and said, "I didn't know you felt that way, keeping those feelings pinned up inside."

"Maybe if you had talked to me occasionally, you might have found out something."

"I guess it's too late now, but I never doubted your dedication. I wanted you to take off the week after your heart failure, but you said you didn't need to, that you were okay. I worried about you because these jobs are stressful. I didn't want anything to happen to you. After you had your shoulder surgery, you looked so tired, but you said you weren't in pain. One of the senior VPs kept seeing you leave in the middle of the afternoon to go to therapy and wondered what was up. When I told him about the surgery, he seemed okay with it, and even said he'd had several broken bones in his life and knew what that was about."

"Kristie, I think you imagine things. I've noticed that since I've been your boss. You can be moody at times, making me hesitant to approach you. I'm going to miss you, I really am. I have so much respect for you. A lot of times, Americans aren't friendly to us, but you've always been great to me, and to the other Indians who work here. In fact, you're everyone's favorite American."

Kristie teared up. "Do you want me to fire Louis?" Raj asked.

"Let me talk to him first and see if he wishes to resign. If he lets us fire him, he can collect unemployment. But if he resigns voluntarily, he can't collect his pennies, but he'll leave with his dignity. Either way, he could sue us for age discrimination, but it will be hard to prove. Louis is a professional and to do something like that would kill what he has left of his career, and I know he wouldn't want to do that. I'll let you know what comes out of our conversation."

After Kristie left, Raj took her resignation letter to HR.

When she returned to her area, she messaged Louis to come to her office and motioned for him to close the door. Kristie then told him he would have to turn in his resignation letter immediately or be fired. Louis must have already prepared his letter because he excused himself and was back within five minutes with his notice and handed it to Kristie. With that, she further assured him that she would check the "eligible for rehire" box when HR sent her the paperwork.

Raj was still in HR when Kristie arrived with Louis' resignation. Was it necessary to have her name changed at this juncture? Guess she should ask.

"I think this is a first," said Pat Jones, one of the VPs in HR. "We just received notice of your resignation from Raj, and now you're turning in a resignation from Louis."

"Yep."

Pat took the letter from Kristie and said she would be forwarding paperwork for Louis.

"By the way, Pat, I got married two weeks ago, Saturday, should I go through the process of changing my name since I'll soon be out of here?"

"Congratulations. I wouldn't bother to do it at this late date."

"Thanks."

Kristie realized as she was riding the elevator that Raj didn't ask her what she was going to do when she left. Did he know that she had gotten married? Probably not. Did he care? Of course not.

What should have been a happy day for Kristie was turning out to be just another horrible day at work. After calling in the three folks, including Louis, who worked under her, and telling them she was resigning, Kristie closed her office door and put her head down on her desk.

By now, it was after 11:00. Should she treat herself to a long lunch? Maybe she would call Eric and see if he wanted to meet her somewhere. Picking up her cell phone, she saw that Eric had called and left her a voicemail. In the message, he said he loved her and wanted to know how her day was going. *How nice, but my day is going to hell in a handbasket.* She phoned him, but it was his turn not to answer. She left him a message saying that she had turned in her resignation and her last day would be a week from Friday. Also, she told him she loved him and would see him at home that evening.

CHAPTER 53

After working out her notice, Kristie started making plans to start her own business. She was doing something she loved and was able to be with her new husband. During the remainder of the summer, while Kristie worked, Eric turned the backyard into quite a showplace. At night, they made love like a couple of twenty-somethings.

While Eric was undoubtedly happy and loved Kristie, he missed seeing his Wentworth friends and wanted to know how Anabelle was. After that disastrous New Year's Eve party at Jan Harpo Franklin's house, and Wiley Martin's funeral, Kristie made it clear she wanted nothing to do with the Harpos or with Anabelle Martin.

As much as he hated to admit it, Kristie was partially right about some of the Wentworth folks. They could be cliquey. The same crowd in high school was the same crowd now, except for spouses who were not from Wentworth. If someone in the clique married someone they met in college or met by some other means, the spouse was accepted. This was the case for Anabelle Martin and Ruthie Harpo. But if someone moved to Wentworth because of their job, he or she would never be accepted by the locals. Those folks would have to form their own cliques with other non-native Wentworthians. Or so it seemed.

Kristie's friends were much more accepting of new people. Being active in several organizations, Kristie had an extensive circle of friends who were always looking to meet other people. Kristie still had friends from her college days and friends from her earlier days in Birmingham. He also thought she kept in contact with a couple of folks from Atlanta. Eric could honestly say that he had never felt uncomfortable with or unaccepted by Kristie's friends, even Natalie and Tim. While they were all friendly to him, he couldn't say the same about how his friends treated Kristie.

Kristie's house was a bit small for the two of them who were used to having their space, but each knew it was temporary and were willing to deal with it. Kristie stayed in the room that served as her office, most days, while Eric worked in the yard. The backyard was natural, and Kristie had done nothing with it.

They also took some money out of savings and had the basement re-done to make a man-cave for Eric. He would spend hours down there watching TV, reading, and listening to music. In fact, this was working so well that the two of them thought about continuing to live in Kristie's house while they were in Birmingham. Then maybe spend some extra money and purchase a bigger home near the Alabama gulf coast. While Eric had sold his place in west Wentworth County, Kristie still had the house and acreage where she was born and raised.

At the end of the summer, Kristie and Eric attended their first Jimmy Buffett concert together in Nashville. Both Eric and Kristie loved Nashville and Jimmy. Kristie purchased excellent seats at the Bridgestone Arena for them. Hanging out with Eric and Kristie were

Natalie and Tim. Initially, Eric was not crazy about Kristie's best friends, but he soon warmed up to them and spent time hanging out with Tim while the girls did other things. The guys would drink beer together almost every Saturday afternoon at Hooters, and they also spent time at the Bass Pro Shop.

The weekend before the Buffett concert in Nashville, the four of them drove down to Panama City. Tim insisted that Eric go with him to a German restaurant about a mile from the hotel and spend Saturday afternoon drinking German beer. Kristie, not being a fan of the German Restaurant and their oom-pah music, didn't care, and neither did Natalie. The girls preferred spending the afternoon on the beach. When a late afternoon thunderstorm drove them inside, they showered and dressed in anticipation of dinner with their husbands.

It was getting a little late in the evening, and the girls were anxious for the guys to get back. Before calling them, Kristie and Natalie stood on the hotel balcony overlooking the parking lot and the street to see if they might be on their way. It was Kristie who spotted them first, stumbling their way back to the hotel.

"Natalie, I believe they're drunk," exclaimed Kristie as the guys were unable to walk in a straight line.

"Nah, what makes you think that?" said Natalie with obvious sarcasm.

When the boys reached their adjoining rooms, it was apparent that they were drunk, and Kristie was thankful they didn't get picked up on their way back to the hotel for public intoxication. The women put their respective spouses to bed and went out to dinner. When they returned, both guys were awake, but not feeling well. Those German lagers can pack a punch.

In Nashville the night before the concert, the four of them had dinner at a famous barbecue place in downtown Nashville, and then went to listen to music at one of the many clubs on Broadway. This time, Tim had a good bit to drink, but the others were all right.

On the way back to the hotel, Tim had to be held up by Natalie and Eric while Kristie walked behind them. As they entered the lobby of their hotel, who should they see, but Jake McPherson. Even though people were mingling in the hotel lobby, no one seemed to recognize Jake except the three of them.

"Jake," Kristie yelled, running up to him and giving him a hug. Natalie and Eric said hi to Jake, and Tim was too drunk to recognize him. Natalie told Kristie and Eric she thought she could get Tim up to their room, and for them to stay down here and talk.

Kristie, Eric, and Jake sat down on a sofa in the lobby lounge for about ten minutes and had a nice chat. Jake was at the Hilton visiting family who were in town for the concert. He was on his way to his Nashville condo for what he hoped would be a good night's sleep before flying to Chicago in the morning. The three of them were having trouble keeping their eyes open. When they parted ways, Jake indicated he would like to invite the two of them to some of the gatherings at his Alabama house, and would contact Kristie via

Facebook. As Jake left to retrieve his car, he gave Kristie a big "lean into" hug and shook Eric's hand.

"Well," said Kristie in the elevator, "It looks like we might be a part of Jake's inner circle."

CHAPTER 54

It was January 10. Kristie, after having her nails done, was in the mood for a nice lunch. A phone call to friend, Natalie, asking if she would like to meet for lunch resulted in a negative since Natalie was on her way to her nail appointment. Kristie was hungry and decided to drive from Homewood to Vestavia and have lunch at Mug Shots.

Even though the early week cold snap had ended, the weather was cloudy and dreary with a dense fog enveloping Shades Mountain. Mug Shots was located atop Shades Mountain in the trendy Birmingham suburb known as Vestavia Hills. Recognized for the best burgers in town, Mug Shots was also a favorite lunch place for the area's professionals.

Since her marriage to Eric Channing, Kristie Tidwell-Channing had been working on starting her own internet marketing affiliated business. Minimal upfront investment was required, but realizing any significant income would be slow. Money was not an issue for her and Eric because he had a nest egg, and generated income through his free-lance writing for several hunting and fishing magazines. Kristie also had a nest egg, plus she owned the property in Wentworth that she had inherited from her Mom and Dad.

All her life she had wanted to be married and felt that if she ever married, her problems would forever disappear. That wasn't the case.

As she climbed out of her SUV outside the restaurant, Kristie had never been so unhappy in her life.

A couple of days before Christmas, Eric got into a heated argument with his brother Roger, who was the head waiter at a trendy Hilton Head, South Carolina restaurant. Roger and his significant other, Henry, had arrived at Eric's sister's house in the northeastern Birmingham suburb of Trussville on December 22. On Christmas Day, the family, including Eric and Kristie, planned to drive to Wentworth to spend Christmas with Eric's only living aunt.

On December 23, Eric and Kristie had Roger and Henry over for an informal dinner, featuring Kristie's famous white chicken chili. In addition to the chili, Kristie was serving sandwiches made from her own unique recipe for pimento cheese. For dessert, there would be eggnog gelato and shortbread cookies.

Before the soup and sandwiches were served, Eric and Roger began to argue, and Henry took Roger's side. Both left the house, scratching off in the driveway. Even though she was uncomfortable with their gay lifestyle, Kristie followed Henry and Roger, and begged them to come back in the house, reconcile with Eric, and have supper. The two of them refused, citing both her's and Eric's adherence to scripture regarding gays, and their right-wing ideology which they felt was anti-gay.

After Roger and Henry drove off, Kristie went back inside the house, feeling that she was a failure as a hostess. As she was opening the door leading from the garage to the kitchen, she met Eric, suitcase in hand. Kristie screamed at him.

"Where are you going?"

Eric replied, "I've had enough, and I have to get out of town for a few days."

"But it's Christmas, and we're expected in Wentworth day after tomorrow."

"Tough!"

"But Eric, this is our first Christmas together."

"We're not joined at the hip and have been apart before. So, what?"

Kristie couldn't believe what she was hearing. Eric, because of a fight with his gay brother, was leaving town, and her, at Christmas. What was supposed to be one of their best times together was turning into a nightmare. No matter how much she begged and cried, Eric put his suitcase in his truck and took off, not telling Kristie where he was going or when he was coming back.

While Kristie had been shocked many, many times in her life, this had to be the worst. After Watching Eric's tail lights disappear, she went back into the house, put the food in the refrigerator, went to the bedroom, took two over the counter sleep aids with a shot of tequila and fell into bed.

Waking up the next morning with a dry mouth and throbbing head, by a bright sun streaming in the windows, a groggy Kristie recalled last night's events. This was no dream like she had the night before their wedding. This was real. Eric had left her. She didn't know where he was going or when he would return.

If there was ever a time for her to lie on the bed and cry, feeling sorry for herself, this was it. Today's plans were for her and Eric to spend a quiet evening alone with romance being a part of the evening. She was going to make shrimp and grits for dinner for the main course with caramel cake from Edgar's for dessert. They would start drinking margaritas about 4:00, then transition to Pinot Grigio with dinner, then later, Bailey's Irish Cream. All the while pacing themselves to ensure they were not hung over for Christmas Day at the aunt's house. Where did Eric go, and why did he leave her?

Even though Kristie was not sure how the fight started, she knew the Channings had short fuses, and didn't get along with each other. Eric had disagreements with siblings, cousins, and his aunt since he and Kristie had been together.

While Eric was prone to arguing with his family, she and Eric had very few disagreements, and when they did, they reconciled quickly. There were times she was scared Eric might hit someone, but with her he was always gentle, not wanting a repeat of last New Year's Eve.

After becoming engaged, she and Eric, like other couples to be married, discussed their expectations for their life together. Both had friends who were not necessarily friends of both, and each did things with close friends that didn't involve the other. Eric knew everyone in Wentworth, and his base was still in Wentworth. Kristie, however, had friends in lots of places, but her core group of friends was in Birmingham. Even though Kristie had renewed acquaintances and made friends with members of her graduating class after attending their last class reunion, she didn't feel as though many of Eric's friends, especially those who were not members of their class, accepted her.

Kristie pulled herself out of bed and gazed at her reflection in the mirror. Her face was swollen from crying, and her hair was a mess. She picked up her cell phone and checked to see if Eric had left her a text during the night. There was nothing. Eric was Kristie's husband, and he packed a bag last night and left their home, not indicating where he was going or when he was coming back. It was Christmas Eve, and they had plans for the day and plans for tomorrow. He hadn't contacted her, but she had every right to contact him, so she called him on his cell phone. She was not surprised when he didn't answer.

What a day, what a first Christmas with her husband, or instead, without her husband. So, what was Kristie to do? Going to Mrs. Channing's tomorrow without Eric was out of the question. Should she call his sister, Sandy? Henry and Roger were staying at Sandy's house. While Sandy wasn't crazy about their lifestyle, she accepted it better than Eric.

Deciding to call Sandy, Kristie reiterated last night's events to her. Sandy already knew there had been some drama. Finding out that Eric took off wasn't a total surprise to Sandy because he had done things like this before. Sandy told Kristie she had hoped those outbursts from Eric would stop when he married. Sandy, who didn't care for Kristie because she saw Kristie as having taken her big brother away from her, suggested they meet for lunch soon. Kristie had no idea that Eric was prone to outbursts such as packing a bag and leaving when things didn't go exactly right. She had known this guy since they were in junior high. Sheesh!

After hanging up, Kristie remembered something that might be a key to where Eric was and what he was doing. Early Christmas morning, Eric had planned to drive to Jimmy's place in Guntersville where he and some of the guys were going hunting. Then the guys would return to their families in the afternoon for Christmas dinner.

Kristie and Eric were going to exchange presents on Christmas Eve, then on Christmas morning, Eric would head to Marshall County to go hunting with the guys. Kristie would drive to Mrs. Channing's late Christmas morning. Kristie wasn't thrilled about this, but it had been a tradition with this group of guys for many years. Another reason Eric was so into going hunting was that this trip would be their first trip without Wiley.

How Kristie muddled through this day, she would never know. Eric stayed out all night and Kristie was hoping against hope that he would show up for their evening together. She called his cell phone again, and he didn't answer. Should she leave him a message? No, instead she texted him, reminding him of their plans for tonight, and that this was their first Christmas together as husband and wife.

God gives you strength when you need it, and this evening Kristie needed all the strength God was giving her. She spent the evening reading the Bible and praying for Eric. It wasn't about her, it was about Eric and the problems he was having. Once again, Kristie took two sleep-aids and fell asleep.

She woke up Christmas day alone. Their presents were wrapped and under the tree. She had nowhere to go for Christmas. She knew she could go to Natalie's and Tim's or to Jennie's and Phil's. But she, in her present state of mind, didn't need to be around anyone, and spoil their Christmas.

They say when things go wrong, your body has a way of kicking into survival mode, and you trudge on. This might have been happening to Kristie because she was out of bed, straightening the house, and thinking about what she was going to do for the rest of her life if Eric was gone for good.

Even though Kristie enjoyed working on her own little business, she thought about going back to work to bring in a steady paycheck. Or should she take Eric to the cleaners? Eric had only been gone a couple of days, and Kristie was already thinking divorce. Her insecurities about men were coming out again. Would there ever be anyone who would truly love her and cling to her?

Somehow, someway, Kristie managed to get through Christmas Day alone. No phone call from Eric, and no contact with Sandy. Kristie was dying to know if Eric had shown up at his aunt's house, but she was not up to calling Sandy to find out. Eric's aunt didn't bother to call Kristie to see what was taking place either. None of the Channings seemed to care for Kristie, and she didn't know why. The Tidwells and the Channings were two established Wentworth families, although Eric's mom grew up in Morgan County, just north of Wentworth County.

Eric was Kristie's husband. He disappears two days before Christmas and has been gone ever since. Kristie should know his whereabouts, but he wouldn't have any contact with her, making her decide to hire a private investigator to find him. Then what? She would cross that bridge when she came to it.

CHAPTER 55

After lunch at Mug Shots, Kristie talked to a PI, who was recommended to her by an attorney friend. All she wanted to know was where Eric was. The PI indicated that he shouldn't be too hard to find. He had the license plate of his truck and his cell phone number.

Sure enough, in two days, the PI called Kristie and told her they had located Eric. He was staying at a low-end roadside motel in Key Largo, Florida. After hearing this, Kristie asked the PI to keep an eye on him for two days and then report back to her on his activities.

What now? Did Kristie want to fly down there and confront him? What would he do if she did? Did she really know this man who had been her husband for slightly more than six months? Would he try to harm her? Would he refuse to talk to her? One thing was for sure, he had deserted her, and that was grounds for divorce. Did she love him, and would she take him back with open arms if he came to his senses? These were questions she couldn't possibly answer. And all of this because of a disagreement with his gay brother on December 23, two days before Christmas.

What were Eric's siblings doing? What was his aunt doing? Lunch with Sandy never happened. Also, no one else in his family had contacted her, and she was afraid to call any of them. She was alone in this.

After they married, she had Eric set up a joint checking account, a joint savings account, and a couple of mutual funds. But Kristie still had her own money, and Eric had his own money.

Checking the joint accounts, she found that no holds had been placed on them, nor had any withdrawals been made. He must be using his own money, she thought. But just because she could, Kristie put holds on their joint accounts.

While Eric had a temper, and could fly off the handle, he was gentle with her. Not once in their relationship had she been scared he would harm her except after that horrible New Year's Eve party at Jan Franklin's house. When they were alone together and intimate, he was the most wonderful person in the world.

What had happened? Unlike most guys, Eric loved affection and admitted to being a "touchy-feely" person. Most nights, she could count on a sensual back rub from him after their lovemaking and before they fell asleep in each other's arms. The first time she had one of her leg cramps when she was with him, Eric, being a former athlete, grabbed the leg, and massaged it in just the right places to relax the muscle. Afterward, he held her until she fell asleep. Some nights they would sit by each other on the sofa, his arm around her while they watched hours of TV. He was such a gentle, loving man, and at the same time, a virile man. He hated chick flicks and refused to dance to anything. Kristie loved him and thought he loved her. Oh, how life could change on a dime.

CHAPTER 56

After running out on Kristie, Roger, and Henry on December 23, Eric had replayed the scene hundreds of times in his head. Did he run away because of a disagreement with his gay brother, or did he run away from other people who were pulling him in different directions, or was he running away from married life?

Kristie was beautiful, and for some reason, she loved him, a big ugly galoot. Of course, she remembered the hunk he was in high school, and told him he hadn't changed as much as she thought.

But he was a small-town boy, as he liked to put it. Kristie was big city. While they both shared a love for Alabama football and politics, Kristie liked going to white tablecloth restaurants. He would never forget the dinner they had at Commander's Palace in New Orleans this past fall. She ordered some kind of oyster dish for an appetizer, which they split, then ordered the turtle soup. Followed by the rack of lamb and some weird side. The dinner culminated with pecan pie a la mode, the only ordinary thing she ordered. Eric ordered a Caesar salad, the filet mignon, and split the pecan pie with Kristie. She loved every second of their dining experience, while he was miserable.

Kristie wore a little black dress, her signature patent leather slingbacks, and her pearl choker, while Eric was miserable in his suit and tie. Why couldn't they have gone to Acme Oyster House or The Gumbo Shoppe where he could have worn khaki pants and a t-shirt?

On the night of the drama, Kristie was serving her famous white chicken chili with finger sandwiches of pimento cheese on wheat bread, crust trimmed, of course. Appetizers included boiled shrimp and meatballs in a sauce made from plain yellow mustard and plain grape jelly. For the wine, Kristie served a Merlot and a Pinot Grigio.

While Kristie was working hard to make everything perfect, Eric kept saying to her, "Why don't you just make some real chili and cornbread and serve beer with it?"

"It's Christmas, and I would like to do something nice."

"Well, okay, I'm sure the fairies will love it."

"Come on, Eric, this isn't that fancy."

"Whatever."

Did he pick a fight with Roger just to have an excuse to get away from Kristie? Did he really love Kristie?" After the reunion, she had set her sights on him, country boy and all. Then after she snagged him, was she trying to change him, to make him out to be something she wanted, someone who liked to eat out at fancy restaurants and go to the theater? There was no doubt Kristie was an intellectual and he was nothing but a red-neck.

It wasn't that Kristie was trying to change everything about Eric. In fact, it was the opposite. She was okay with him going to Jimmy Harpo's place three out of every four weekends. She loved his homemade beef stew and always made cornbread to go with it. Her cornbread, made in a cast iron skillet, was delectable. They both loved homemade peach ice cream and made it most weekends when Eric was home.

When it came to music, surprisingly, Eric was a little more rock while Kristie was a little more country. He wasn't into going to concerts. While Kristie loved them, she didn't gripe when he refused to go with her. Besides the Buffett concert in Nashville, he did go to that Jake McPherson concert with her in November. He liked Jake McPherson, but Jake's music was what Eric thought of as chick music. And he could swear that Jake had a crush on Kristie by the way he looked at her when he greeted them after his performance.

Kristie's plane had just come to a stop at the Miami International Airport. From here, she would pick up her rental car and drive to Key Largo, to her hotel. Once she got settled in, she would travel, followed by her private investigator and one of his operatives, three miles to Eric's hotel, hopefully, to meet with him. If trouble arose, the PIs would be there for her, at a price. Why, oh why, was she this scared of her husband of slightly over six months?

This was south Florida, known for its wealth, its decadence, its swamps, its big snakes, and its alligators. While Kristie had traveled through here numerous times, she felt as though she didn't belong here.

After getting settled in her hotel and phoning the PI, Kristie got in her rented Toyota SUV and headed toward Eric's motel. She could see the PI in a rusted out pickup truck several vehicles back. As she approached the hotel, her heart skipped a beat. There he was, crossing the road to the parking lot of a little fish place and bar.

Seeing this, Kristie made a turn into the restaurant parking lot where she saw Eric go into the establishment. Kristie parked, shut off the motor, and called the PI to update him. The PI told her to go into the restaurant, and he would be outside. In fact, meeting him in a public place would be preferable to going to his hotel room.

Kristie entered the place as Eric was taking a seat at the bar. A customer was to his left, but the stool to his right was vacant. Taking a deep breath, Kristie walked up to the empty barstool and climbed onto it.

Eric's head instantly turned to the right as he sensed his wife's presence. "What took you so long? I figured you would be down here well before now."

"I wanted to give you some time and space, hoping you would come to your senses."

Eric signaled to the bartender to bring Kristie a beer. She took a sip of it before going any further. "I'm your wife, and you're my husband, we took vows in the presence of God to have and to hold, and all the other. Now you've undoubtedly decided that being married was inconvenient, so you took off."

Eric stood up and said, "Let's get a table."

So, Kristie followed him to the back of the restaurant where they found an isolated booth. One of the waitresses, dressed in short cut-offs and a black tank top, approached the booth and brought them menus.

Eric asked Kristie if she wanted anything to eat. She shook her head. "I'm not very hungry right now."

Eric told the waitress to bring them an order of the steamed shrimp and another beer. "The conch chowder is excellent and so are the conch fritters.

"Sorry, but I'm just not hungry."

After the waitress left, the two of them talked until the shrimp came.

"Have some. How long has it been since you've eaten?"

I haven't eaten anything today."

"That's not good."

"I said, I'm not hungry."

"When and how did you get here?"

"I flew to Miami this morning and rented a car."

"Let me order you some conch chowder. If all you have is beer, you'll get buzzed way before you should be getting buzzed."

"Okay."

Eric signaled for the waitress to return to their table, and ordered a cup of conch chowder for Kristie and a grilled grouper sandwich with onion rings for himself.

"What do you want from me?"

"I want to know what your intentions are. I want to know where I stand as your wife. I want to know when you're coming home."

"I'm not sure I like being married, or maybe being married to you. I'll probably come home at some point, but I don't know when. Any other questions? Make me a proposal."

"Oh Eric, I can't believe we were making love on December 22 and talking about how wonderful our first Christmas together would be. Now we're sitting across from each other in a Key Largo fish joint having this protracted conversation.

"Things just changed, I guess."

"Things just changed, things just changed," screamed Kristie, not caring if anyone in the place heard her.

"I said make me an offer," replied Eric in a ho-hum drawl.

"Let's talk tomorrow. I'm tired from the plane ride, the drive, and everything else."

"At least have some supper. Here she comes."

The conch chowder was quite good, and so were the conch fritters served with it. Kristie and Eric ate in silence. When Kristie finished and was getting up to leave, Eric said, "the key lime pie is great also, want a piece to go?"

"No thanks," said Kristie, as she put a ten dollar bill on the table.

"That's not necessary. I may be an asshole. Correction, I am an asshole, but dinner, such that it was, is on me tonight."

"Can we meet tomorrow, maybe in your motel room?"

"Sure, is 10:00 okay?"

"Yes."

Reading her mind, Eric said, "I'll be there. If I ran out, you'd just find me again, right? Do you know my room number? Of course, you do."

"Good night, and thanks for supper."

"Bye Kristie," whispered Eric when she was out of earshot.

About two minutes after Kristie departed, Eric caught a glimpse of a large guy, who reminded him of Alabama offensive lineman, D.J. Fluker, exiting the restaurant. Wonder how much she's paying her goons, thought Eric.

As Kristie was making her way to her hotel, she called the PI and told him she would be visiting Eric at his motel the next day at 10:00 am. After affirming that Kristie felt safe in her room, the PI suggested that they monitor Eric's room throughout the night. Even though he indicated he would not run, you couldn't take him at his word. If he tried to sneak out, they would be on his tail. Kristie agreed.

CHAPTER 57

Back at her hotel, Kristie took two sleep-aids and washed them down with a shot of tequila. She needed a good night's rest to get up early tomorrow, and determine what she wanted from Eric to let him out of their marriage.

As the sleep-aids and tequila did their job, Kristie contemplated how a once happy and loving marriage had come to this. Her husband was hiding out in the Florida Keys, not wanting to have anything to do with her. Those times when people were mean and unfair to her, were paying off. Kristie was independent, and she was strong. She would get through this. Yes, she would get through this, not on her own strength, but through her faith in God. God had brought her to it, and he would see her through it.

At 6:30 am, Kristie was wide awake and felt refreshed. After showering and getting dressed, she sat down at the desk in the room and contemplated what she wanted from Eric, what her proposal to him was going to be. Sooner or later, she would have to engage the services of an attorney to get the inevitable divorce. She felt as though her expenses in traveling to Key Largo should be reimbursed, plus the costs of hiring a private investigator to find Eric and to protect her while she was in the Keys should be paid. After that, she was okay with splitting the joint accounts according to what each had contributed. Thankfully, she didn't put his name on her property in Wentworth or any of the other assets she had acquired on her own.

Kristie called her PI, who assured her that Eric was still in his room at the roadside motel. So, Kristie decided to make her proposal to Eric, pending any other recommendations her attorney might make.

Pulling onto Highway 1 and heading toward Eric's motel, Kristie prayed for God to help her get through this, one of the hardest things she ever had to do in her life.

At slightly after 10:00, Kristie was knocking on the door of Room 121. It was answered by Eric, looking freshly showered and dressed. He smelled so good, and Kristie wanted to grab him and melt into his strong arms like she had done so many times before. But this was different. At the door, Eric gave her a brief smile and motioned for her to some in.

During the months of their courtship, and in the months following the wedding, they could hardly keep their hands off one another when they entered a hotel room. Before going out anywhere, they always "tested the bed." Now things between them were antiseptic. What in the world had changed between December 23 and now? And that's how Kristie confronted him. What had changed to make him hate her?

"I'm a small town guy. You, on the other hand, are a city girl."

"We dated for a year before getting married. Did you just discover that about me and decide you weren't cool with it on December 23?"

"Well, you order escargot in restaurants, and I order fried shrimp."

"So," screamed Kristie.

"You're into fashion and have a closet stuffed full of clothes and shoes. You also have way too much jewelry, perfume, purses, and everything else. I have my khakis and t-shirts, plus three pairs of shoes. I couldn't believe you came back from Key West with six new pairs of flip-flops this past November."

"And I paid for them myself. Those shoes didn't cost you a dime. But don't tell me you haven't enjoyed seeing me dressed up."

"I guess I've enjoyed seeing some of those clothes on the floor."

At this point, Kristie slumped down on one of the beds and buried her head in her hands.

"All this time I tried so hard to make myself attractive to you, and you never liked any of it, not any of it?"

"Why do you need so many clothes, so many shoes, so much jewelry, and so many purses? Why do you have to cook things like white chicken chili? Why can't you fry chicken and make mashed potatoes from scratch?"

At this point, Kristie became emboldened, stood up, and faced her estranged husband.

"Eric, we dated almost a year before we married, and we've been married a little over six months. While we were dating, you were okay with what I ordered in restaurants, with what I cooked for us, and everything else I did. You told me you loved me and wanted to marry me. You said we would grow old together and cling to each other every night. What made you change your mind? And don't say it's because you wanted me to serve Roger and Henry regular chili and Bud Light instead of white chicken chili, finger sandwiches, and two kinds of wine."

"Kristie, I want a real woman, a natural woman, and you, my dear, are a fake. I'm so sick of coconut body wash, what's wrong with Ivory Soap? How much makeup, lipsticks, and cologne can a woman have? What's wrong with being natural? Why, you admit you won't go past the mailbox without makeup. Weekly nail appointments. What's wrong with plain ole nails, unpainted? You're a fake, nothing but a fake, and I want and deserve something better."

"Once again, Eric, listen to what I'm saying. You dated me for a year, and then we got married. You knew this about me. So, why didn't you stop dating me? Why did you ask me to marry you? Why did you marry me, why?"

"I don't know. I guess it was because I wasn't sure how much longer I would be getting the mild for free."

After that remark, Kristie wanted to slap him. No guy had ever said things like this to her.

With this, Kristie told Eric that she would file for a divorce. Furthermore, she would agree to sit down with him and their respective attorneys to split the money they held jointly according to the percentage each had contributed. She also let him know that she wanted reimbursement for any expenses incurred in connection with locating him, and pursuing closure to their joke of a marriage. Eric agreed to this and told her he would be awaiting service of the divorce papers.

Kristie grabbed her purse and portfolio to leave, and told Eric that he would be hearing from her attorney soon, real damned soon. Eric followed her to the door and then out to her rented SUV.

"Please don't take any of this personally."

With that, he kissed her forehead. She got in her vehicle and Eric closed the door, stepped back, and waved to her as she drove off.

CHAPTER 58

Eric noticed that Kristie drove off in the direction of Miami. Was she flying back to Birmingham this afternoon? She loved Key West. Why should she not head down there for a few days? He could see her now, alone in one of the island's upscale eateries, perfect makeup, perfect hair, and perfect nails, dressed to perfection from head to toe. Eric sang to himself the Alabama song, *She's a Lady, Down on Love.*

Although he was sure Kristie would have her goons watching him for a while, he wanted a natural woman, a woman like you would find in the Florida Keys. Faded short cut-offs, showing every crease, a see-through tank top, leaving nothing to the imagination, plus beat-up sandals. Reddish brown hair, no makeup, no perfume, and no jewelry, except maybe a belly button ring, would be great. He might even go foe a woman with a tattoo. That particular woman was Anita, the server who waited on him and Kristie last night. He wanted an "in the flesh" natural woman, and he was already getting excited at the thought of being with Anita.

When he first approached Anita about getting together after she got off work, she inquired about "little miss perfect," who he was with the evening before.

"I sent her packing."

"Are you sure?"

"Yes, she won't be anywhere around here tonight."

"Then it's a plan."

As he and Anita crossed the road heading toward his room, he noticed she smelled of fried fish. But she has been working in a seafood restaurant. Then in the room after her clothes were off, he thought to himself, is there any woman out there who still has her natural hair color. Then he noticed her hands. Not only did they smell strong of fish, but she had blunt, rounded fingers, nothing like the feminine tapered fingers Kristie had, fingers Kristie used many, many times to make him feel good. Plus, her nails weren't painted. But isn't that what he wanted. Well, that's what he thought he wanted.

When they were about to get down to business, Eric's efforts weren't working. He had lost his desire, and try as he did, he couldn't get it back. He told Anita he was stressed out from the day's events, and asked if she would agree to try this in several days.

None too happy, Anita accused him of still having a thing for Kristie and suggest that he not come on to her until she was out of his system. Well, so much for his search for a natural woman. There had to be one out there who would meet his requirements.

After sunrise, Eric decided it would be best for him to move in, if only a few miles down the road, perhaps to Islamorada. There were plenty of places where he could get a room. Even though Kristie's goons would be following him, he would text her and let her know his new address and where to serve the divorce papers.

Within two hours, Eric was checking into a motel in Islamorada. Should he have gone all the way to Key West? That was Kristie's place, besides it was too expensive to stay there for any length of time. His room in Islamorada was reasonable and half-way decent. He would remain there until the divorce papers were served, planning to agree to just about anything to get out of the marriage as long as it didn't make too big a dent in his nest egg. When he was settled, he texted Kristie, telling her where he was staying and where to direct the divorce papers.

In the text, he also assured her that he would not move anywhere else until he received the papers. Guess he had better not try to bed down any women until the divorce was final. Pretty Kristie, nice Kristie, Kristie, who somehow managed to fall in love with him. And that was her misfortune.

Kristie's plane from Miami landed on schedule at the Atlanta Airport. She would have about an hour layover before boarding another plane for the short flight to Birmingham. Walking down the concourse which led to the gate from which her flight to Birmingham was departing, Kristie ran into none other than Jake McPherson, the singer-songwriter. Traveling with Jake was a young man she guessed was one of his assistants.

"Well, if it isn't Kristie."

"Hi Jake, fancy meeting you here."

They hugged each other, and Jake asked how she was.

"Fine," Kristie lied.

Jake wasn't fooled, though. Kristie's eyes were bloodshot, her hair was a mess, and she looked sleep-deprived. Jake introduced her to his assistant. After exchanging pleasantries, they parted ways. While Kristie was one of his best-looking fans/followers, he never considered asking her out because his handlers had advised him to never get involved with fans. Something was wrong, and Jake sincerely hoped she would be able to work things out.

Oh great, thought Kristie, I see Jake McPherson, and I look and feel like a zombie. My husband wants a divorce and let me know he thinks I'm the most undesirable thing on the planet. Jake could have any woman he wanted, but after seeing me like this, he would never want me. A depressed Kristie did think she was the most loathsome thing on earth.

Kristie arrived in Birmingham after dark. Getting off the plane, collecting her bag, and walking through the parking deck, she was about as blue as a girl could be. It was cold, and she was alone. The one man she truly loved had rejected her. Could his rejection of her have been because she made white chicken chili and kept her nails manicured? What kinds of reasons were those? Had the argument with his brother caused him to snap? This made no sense.

When Kristie arrived at the house, she found that the kitty cat was glad to see her, but it was apparent he missed Eric. After taking two over the counter sleep-aids, along with a shot of tequila, Kristie was ready to go to sleep. She decided to contact her attorney tomorrow and start the divorce proceedings.

CHAPTER 59

Since Eric was in Islamorada, maybe he would drive down to Key West and see what was happening there. Even though it was where he and Kristie had spent their honeymoon, he wouldn't hold that against the town. Key West was Harry Truman's place, Ernest Hemmingway's place, and even Jimmy Buffett's place. Besides, there was lots of fishing and diving to do down there. But on the downside, there was a large gay community which made Eric uncomfortable. Wonder if Henry and Roger ever took part in the delights of Key West?

After a grouper sandwich and a couple of beers, Eric was ready to go to bed. Maybe he would drive to Key West tomorrow. It would be several days before the divorce papers could be drawn up and served. Besides, Kristie's goons would find him when the time came.

Then a light bulb went off in Eric's head. Didn't Anabelle Martin move somewhere down here shortly after Wiley passed away? He had lost contact with Anabelle soon after the funeral, mostly because Kristie had hated Wiley since she and Wiley were children. Of course, Kristie wanted nothing to do with Anabelle. Where was Anabelle? Jimmy Harpo might know, but more than likely, Jimmy's sister, Jan, would know. She and Anabelle were good friends. Kristie hated the Harpo family, but other than that New Year's Eve party, and maybe

Wiley's funeral, she had no reason to hate them, or hate any of his other Wentworth friends for that matter.

She had her own Wentworth friends, but they were the smart, talented people. They were the folks who never took up smoking, and only started drinking when they were in college or after they became adults. Most of them either saved themselves for marriage or were responsible adults before doing any fooling around. Eric was sure none of them had or would ever do drugs.

That wasn't his crowd, though. He was a country boy. He started smoking cigarettes and drinking alcohol when he was just sixteen, and lost his virginity with his sixteen-year-old girlfriend at age seventeen. Even though he was a college graduate and graduated close to the top of his class, he took the "regular" classes in high school. Kristie and her friends took the college prep courses.

Eric found Jan's number on his phone and placed a call to her. When she didn't answer, he left her a message to call him and let him know if she knew where Anabelle was now living. As he was falling asleep, he wondered if Jan would bother to call him back. Jan wasn't Kristie's biggest fan, so she would surely be glad to hear he had left her.

The next morning, Jan returned his call. Sure enough, she knew where Anabelle Martin was now living. It was in Knight's Key, not far from the Seven Mile Bridge, and not far from where he was staying in Islamorada. Jan assured Eric that Anabelle would love to see him because Eric had meant so much to Wiley. She didn't hesitate to give him Anabelle's address and her new cell phone number. During their conversation, Jan didn't ask Eric what he was doing in the Keys, nor did she ask about Kristie. This bothered him, because he was looking for someone to validate his feelings that Kristie wasn't the woman for him.

This gave a whole different meaning to his stay in the Keys. He'd call Anabelle, go see her, have long conversations with her, take her to dinner, and who knows what else. He was almost sure she would have a pool where they could lounge for hours, sipping wine and nibbling on the pink shrimp and stone crab that were famous in the Florida Keys. They could fish off the coast in the shallow waters. If he could catch enough fish for their dinner, he would clean them and grill them while Anabelle made a huge salad and whipped up some potato dish or something else to go with the fish and salad.

But wait, this is what Kristie would enjoy doing. This was the reason he left Kristie. She was just too hoity-toity at times. Shit! Was he two-faced? Yes. But Kristie didn't try to be a part of his crowd, and he didn't identify with her crowd, including banker Tim and his wife, Natalie, Jennie Stewart and her minister husband, Phil. Also, there was the Tuscaloosa gang that went to football games together. He couldn't stand any of them.

CHAPTER 60

Having been hurt because Eric had not contacted her since the day of Wiley's funeral, Anabelle was overjoyed to hear his voice. She had thought about Eric and wanted to see him and to talk to him, but he was married to Kristie, and Kristie hated Wiley, even in death. As a result, Kristie hated her. Kristie was more than likely the reason Eric and Anabelle had not talked to each other since the funeral.

When Anabelle asked if Kristie was with him, he told her that Kristie would soon be filing divorce papers on him on the grounds of desertion. He didn't want to be with her anymore. Then Anabelle asked if Kristie still hated Wiley and her.

"Yes," Eric replied. "She takes delight in the fact that Wiley is dead, Jake is in jail, and Johnny, living in Vancouver, is gay. She seems okay with some of the people from Wentworth, but hates others."

"Eric, would you like to come over for dinner tonight? I'll fix a chicken casserole and a salad or something else green. It's not Keys cuisine, but still, comfort food."

"Sure. I'm getting tired of fish sandwiches and conch chowder."

Eric arrived at Anabelle's house in Knight's Key about 5:30 pm. Much to his surprise, the house wasn't huge. In fact, it was about the same size as Kristie's garden home in Helena. There was a pool and patio area in the back where Anabelle was putting the finishing touches on a pitcher of margaritas when he rang the doorbell.

After hugs and a few "you look greats," Eric followed Anabelle to the pool area where she poured Margaritas for them. You're not a salt person, right?"

"You remembered."

To go with the margaritas, Anabelle served boiled shrimp with two kinds of cocktail sauce. She also served red pepper jelly over cream cheese with crackers. This was something Kristie also liked to serve.

While Eric told Anabelle she looked good, he lied. She had lost weight, and it brought out the wrinkles she had due to sunbathing and hours spent in tanning beds. Also, her hair was dry and brittle. She needed to have her roots touched up. Her once dark hair now looked brassy, almost the color or rust. Guess she hadn't found a good hair stylist in the Keys. Anabelle's legs were laced with ugly varicose veins, and Eric thought this was the first time he had ever seen Anabelle with her fingernails and toenails unpolished. Come to think of he, he had never seen Kristie with "naked fingernails and toenails."

If he and Kristie had moved to the Alabama Gulf Coast, Kristie would have insisted on going to Birmingham to get her hair done. Jennifer had been doing Kristie's hair forever, and she always said that only Jennifer, and maybe the girls who worked for here, were ever allowed to touch her hair. If something ever happened to Jennifer, Kristie didn't know what she would do.

Why was he comparing Anabelle to Kristie? Anabelle was a few years younger than him and Kristie, but if you linked these two women up side by side, you would think Kristie was ten or fifteen years younger than Anabelle. While Anabelle was beautiful when she and Wiley married, her beauty was no longer there. On the other hand, Kristie was beautiful when they were in high school, and she still was. Again, why was he comparing Anabelle to Kristie?

Because it was beginning to get a little cool as dusk was approaching, Anabelle suggested they go inside while the casserole finished cooking. Eric helped Anabelle with taking everything indoors and commented that whatever was in the oven smelled delicious.

The table was decorated with a colorful floral centerpiece and was set even fancier than something Kristie might do, even for a simple meal. Let's see, thought Eric. There are the bread and butter plates with the butter knife placed appropriately. Then, there's the water goblet, followed by what looked like a glass for the white wine and one for the red wine. Then lying above the dinner plate was a dessert spoon, even though there was the standard teaspoon to the right of the dinner plate. He had seen Kristie use a bread and butter plate once or twice before the night of the fight.

Anabelle filled their water goblets and asked Eric which he preferred, chardonnay or merlot. He said chardonnay, which was

Anabelle's preference also. She asked Eric to open one of the bottles of chardonnay and pour it into the white wine glasses, picking up the red wine glasses and taking them to the counter.

Oh shit. Kristie went that far one time, one evening a few days before they officially got engaged. Two different wine glasses, one for white and one for red. He couldn't remember which was which.

"For chardonnay, we'll drink out of the slightly smaller glasses," said Anabelle.

"Thank you. Remember, I'm just a small-town guy."

"Quite all right, most men think red wine is supposed to be served as chilled as white wine."

"Red wine is supposed to be served at cellar temperature, not room temperature. Kristie used to put the red wine in the refrigerator for about thirty minutes before serving it. I remember that much about wine."

Kristie sounds like a classy lady. We could have used more like her in my club in Wentworth."

"Yes, Kristie has a lot of class," Eric said in a far-off voice. "She'll be much better off without me."

"Is that what you're telling yourself?" asked Anabelle as she heaped white rice, casserole, and her famous garlic Brussel sprouts onto the dinner plates and set them on the table.

"I guess I am. But dinner's almost served, so let's not ruin our appetites. Everything looks and smells wonderful."

Anabelle placed a basket of rolls on the table, and Eric held out her chair while she sat down. They were dining in the large eat-in kitchen. Anabelle turned out the lights except for the decorative lamp hanging above the table.

Eric picked up his wine glass and toasted to a delicious dinner, and the renewal of a friendship he hoped would last forever. The chicken casserole was the same one Kristie made, and so were the Brussel sprouts. What was happening? Had Kristie decided to possess Anabelle? Of course not, Kristie hated Anabelle. What would Kristie think of him being here with Anabelle? Were her goons following him?

When they finished dinner, Eric helped Anabelle clean up and put the dirty dishes in the dishwasher. Then she suggested they have their brandy in the living room. This was beyond Kristie. To the best of his knowledge, Kristie had never served brandy. She had a sangria recipe containing brandy, so there was some at the house, but they never drank it correctly out of snifters. Anabelle poured brandy into two snifters, handed Eric one, and motioned for him to follow her into the living room.

Anabelle turned on some music from the sound system, took a candle lighter out of the piano bench, and lit some candles. Was she coming on to Eric? When he first met Anabelle, before she and Wiley married, she was beautiful, and Eric had normal man thoughts about her, as well as every good-looking woman he saw. But Anabelle no longer gave him those thoughts, but Kristie did.

Because he hadn't had any contact with Anabelle since Wiley's funeral, he asked her to bring him up to date on what she had been doing.

Anabelle moped around the house in Wentworth for about two months, then took the advice of a friend and got out of town for a while. She decided to purchase this home in the Keys because she had always liked this part of the country and preferred the warmer climate to that of the Alabama Gulf Coast and the Florida panhandle. With the millions she inherited, she was able to purchase this house on Knight's Key, not far from the seven-mile bridge. You'd love fishing off the old bridge, Anabelle told him.

Then the conversation turned to Kristie and Eric's pending divorce.

"What went wrong, y'all seemed so much in love?"

He told Anabelle about the fight with his brother and his brother's friend, which led him to packing a bag and leaving. Then after he got away from everything, he decided he didn't want to be with Kristie anymore.

Why didn't he want to go back to Kristie? That was a question he hadn't fully answered himself. Eric went on to air his gripes about Kristie to Anabelle. She was obsessed with her appearance, but the insider of her house looked like a tornado had been through there. She had too many clothes, too many shoes, too many purses, too many of everything. Her life was centered around nail appointments and hair appointments. If she never bought another lipstick or any more eyeshadow, she would have enough to last until she died. How can a woman be so high maintenance? What's somebody like me going to do with a woman like that? The truth was, Eric knew exactly what to do with a woman like that.

Then he got to the big one. She didn't like any of his friends, but expected him to embrace her friends, most of whom he couldn't stand. She resented Jimmy Harpo because Eric spent a lot of time at his house near Guntersville, just hanging out. Then he told Anabelle what took place on that New Year's Eve at Jan Harpo Franklin's house.

It was almost 11:00 and Eric had no desire to make any moves on Anabelle, so he left, telling her he would likely settle somewhere in the Keys when the divorce was final. While he was not physically attracted to Anabelle, he wanted to remain friends with her.

CHAPTER 61

Eric was not the only one who could take off on a winter vacation. After returning from the Keys, Kristie decided she would go to New Orleans to escape from the real world. She tried to call Eric, but he wouldn't pick up the phone, so she texted him that she would be there for a few days. Once again, she heard nothing from him.

Kristie had informed most of her friends about Eric's disappearance, and everyone seemed appalled that he would do something like that to her. Kristie planned to join Natalie and Tim in the Crescent City to listen to some music, eat some great food, and forget about life for a while. For Kristie, the real world had sucked the past few weeks, so she was anxious to get away.

Kristie arrived in the Big Easy on Wednesday night, in time to have dinner and make an appearance at Pat O'Brien's. Being a lone female in the French Quarter might not be wise, but Kristie didn't care. Besides, there were probably more undercover cops per square mile in the French Quarter than any other place on the planet.

After dining at one of her favorite Cajun restaurants, she went to Pat O'Brien's for a hurricane, then to Café DuMonde for café au lait and beignets. It was time to return to her hotel, and for the first time in a while, Kristie felt human. You can lose yourself in the French Quarter.

Did Kristie wish Eric was with her? Yes. But she craved shrimp, oysters, baby drum fish, red beans and rice, hurricanes, pralines, and the crusty New Orleans bread with lots of real butter. It didn't matter that she was alone.

The next morning, Kristie showered and dressed for a day in the quarter. She planned to have lunch at one of the quarter's original red beans and rice joints, now famous for its oyster po-boys. Then she was going to walk around, listen to the street musicians, and maybe do some shopping. As usual, there was a line to get into the restaurant. Kristie went to the back of the line and waited until it was her turn. Because she was by herself, she didn't mind sitting at the bar.

Making her way to the bar, she took a seat on one of the stools. When the waitress came to take her order, she ordered the oyster po-boy and a Diet Coke. It was a little too early for alcohol and Kristie was craving a Diet Coke.

After finishing her lunch and paying the check, she left the restaurant where there was still a line out the door. Suddenly, she heard her name called. Thinking it might be someone who was there for the music event, Kristie turned around to see who was calling her name.

It was none other than Jimmy Harpo, with his wife, Ruthie. They were lowering themselves to speak to her? She guessed there was no one from Wentworth around to see them talking to her.

Not in the mood to speak to the couple, Kristie kept on walking. She was sure Eric had been in contact with them, and they knew a divorce was pending.

Then she felt a hand on her shoulder as Jimmy turned her around and asked if she was okay.

"Well, I was."

Jimmy then asked Kristie, "What brings you to New Orleans.?"

"It's a free country, for the time being, at least, and I can go anywhere I please."

"Look, Kristie, I know you don't like me, my siblings, and my in-laws, but none of us dislike you. In fact, we were overjoyed when we found out that you and Eric were going to get married."

"I'd hate to see the way you treat people you really dislike. What about the New Year's Eve party and Wiley Martin's funeral?"

Those were unfortunate, and you never gave any of us a chance to explain."

"Now that Eric and I are getting a divorce, you definitely won't get that chance. Now if you'll excuse me, I really have to go."

CHAPTER 62

Having finished his dinner of meatloaf, mashed potatoes, green beans, and cornbread, Eric was contemplating what to watch on TV. He and Kristie usually watched the prime-time lineup on the Fox News Channel. Kristie was a part of the political blogosphere, and had created a couple of political blogs which were growing slowly, but growing just the same. She was so politically savvy that Eric thought she should run for Congress when the current representative from their district retired. But Kristie had never held public office and felt she wasn't qualified. He hadn't visited any of Kristie's websites in a while. Maybe he would do that soon.

Not only did she have political websites, she also had a couple of Alabama sports sites, emphasizing football. Kristie knew football, especially Alabama football. What didn't Kristie know about? Gardening. That woman didn't like getting her hands dirty and how could that be? She was Mary and Bobby's daughter. She wasn't adopted because she looks just like Mary used to look. She also favors Bobby.

Eric felt his eyes water. Maybe he'd call her or text her to see how she was doing. Kristie wasn't perfect by any means, but she loved him. The last time they saw one another was in Gulf Shores, Alabama just before the divorce was final. They were sitting on the beach as the sun was setting. Kristie was staying at a hotel, and Eric was staying with a friend. They stood up, collected their things, and walked toward Kristie's hotel, through the hotel lobby, and out to the parking lot where Eric's truck was parked.

Standing by the truck, Kristie started to cry.

"What did I ever do to make you hate me?"

"Nothing, Kristie, nothing at all."

Eric got in the truck and drove off.

He could always watch the news, but the CMA Awards were being televised on one of the country music channels. A few weeks ago, he read that singer/songwriter Jake McPherson had been nominated for a couple of awards. Ever since meeting Jake and attending one of his concerts with Kristie, Eric had sort of kept up with him and even considered him an acquaintance.

Settled. He would watch the CMAs and flipped to the channel. Just like in Hollywood, there was a red carpet leading up to the arena where the ceremonies were to be held. Various artists were being interviewed by the press as they made their way on the red carpet.

Every guy was wearing a tuxedo, some with western hats and boots, while the ladies were dressed in flowing evening gowns, sporting perfect hair-dos.

Speaking of perfect hair, Eric glared at the TV. There was a woman in a black evening dress with elbow length puffed sleeves. Her plunging neckline showed just the right amount of cleavage. When the camera zoomed in on her face and neck, he could see that she wore pearl drop earrings and a double strand pearl choker, completing her simple, but elegant look. After standing by her man as he was interviewed on the red carpet, the lady turned around, and guided by her man, walked into the arena. Her dark curly hair draped her shoulders while her gown swayed to the movement of her hips as she walked.

RECIPES

Kristie and Anabelle's Chicken Casserole
(In the book, Kristie and Eric never got to enjoy it together)

- 5 to 6 large boneless, skinless chicken breasts
- 1-1/2 cups mayonnaise
- 1/2 cup of cream of mushroom soup (can also use cream of chicken soup)
- 1/2 cup of sour cream
- 1 package of frozen broccoli, thawed
- Sea salt (optional)
- Fresh ground pepper (optional)
- Cajun seasoning (optional)
- Garlic powder (optional)
- 1 package finely shredded Monterey jack and cheddar cheese (you can actually use any type of cheese as long as it melts well in the oven)
- 3 to 4 green onions, chopped

Preheat oven to 350 degrees

Cook chicken breasts according to package directions and let cool until you are able to touch them. Cut chicken into bite-sized cubes. Sprinkle the chicken with sea salt, pepper, Cajun seasoning, and garlic powder to taste. Any or all of these spices may be omitted. Chop broccoli into small pieces if necessary and mix together with the chicken and place in the bottom of a medium to large casserole dish.

In a separate mixing bowl, combine mayo, soup, and sour cream. If desired, add some extra garlic powder and/or Cajun seasoning. Combine this mixture with the chicken and broccoli and cook in the casserole dish for 15 minutes. Remove from oven and place half of the cheese on top, then layer the green onion on top of the cheese, then sprinkle the rest of the cheese on top of the green onions. Turn the oven to broil and place the casserole dish in the oven and let it stay there until the cheese is bubbly. Serve over white or brown rice.

Note: This recipe was served to the author at a dinner at a friend's house several years ago. The friend gave the author the recipe, but she lost it. So, she made one up and it is similar to her friend's recipe. There are many chicken and broccoli casserole recipes out there, but this one is original and any similarity to other recipes is a coincidence.

Kristie's Shrimp and Grits

- One package of peeled and de-veined shrimp
- 1 stick of butter
- One medium sized onion chopped
- 1 can cream of mushroom soup (may use cream of chicken soup if desired)
- Fresh ground pepper
- Cajun seasoning
- Garlic powder
- 1/2 cup of sour cream
- 1/2 of one link of smoked sausage (can use more if you like smoked sausage)
- 6 to 8 servings of grits
- Shredded cheese of your choice (I use a mixture of cheddar and Monterey jack)
- 3-4 green onions chopped (optional)
- Paprika (optional)

Sauté the shrimp in the butter and onions and drain off the excess butter. Season the shrimp with pepper, Cajun seasoning, and garlic powder to taste. Combine the shrimp with the soup and sour cream. Cook the smoked sausage according to package instructions and chop into bite-sized pieces. Add to the shrimp mixture

Cook the grits according to package directions and combine the cheese and grits while the grits are still hot. You may use any amount of cheese that you wish.

Spoon the grits onto a plate or into a pasta bowl and scoop out a hole in the center. Fill up this hole with the shrimp mixture. Garnish with green onions and paprika.

Note: This recipe is totally and completely made up by the author.

Kristie and Anabelle's Garlic Brussel Sprouts

- Two packages frozen Brussel sprouts
- Olive oil
- Parmesan cheese
- Garlic powder

Prepare Brussel sprouts according to package directions and let cool. Cut each sprout in half and place in mixing bowl. Drizzle with olive oil and mix. Sprinkle with parmesan cheese and garlic powder and mix again.

Distribute sprouts onto baking sheet and broil until sprouts are just beginning to turn brown on the edges.

Note: This recipe is totally and completely made up by the author and can be made with other vegetables such as broccoli and asparagus.

A Sequel:

SUNSETS OF FIRE AND ICE

PROLOGUE

A crowd of twenty-five to thirty gathered close to the funeral tent on a cold January day. Gun metal colored clouds were forming in the western sky around a fiery sun. In a couple of hours, the folks of Wentworth, Alabama would be able to witness what some called a sunset of fire and ice.

Most of the graveside attendees were huddled close to the tent to catch a glimpse of the family and listen to the minister read scripture and weave into his sermon, accolades of the deceased. But about twenty yards from the crowd stood two lone figures. One was a tall gentleman who had wavy blond hair and a beard, and standing about ten feet to his side was an attractive woman.

As the minister was talking about the deceased's dedication to the Lord Jesus Christ, to family, and to work, the man, handsome in his own way, appeared to be very nervous, shifting his weight from one leg to another. With cell phone in hand, he was checking the screen almost every two or three seconds.

The lady had chestnut colored hair mixed with strands of gray. It would be obvious to anyone that she had once been a beautiful woman. In fact, she still was. Also straining to get a glimpse of the folks seated in the tent, she appeared as nervous as the gentleman standing a short distance from her.

While the woman was not able to see the folks seated on the front row, she spied someone in the second row who looked familiar. This woman had gray hair woven in with her very dark hair. But not being able to see her face, she couldn't be sure if this woman was Anabelle Martin.

The chestnut-haired woman and the blonde gentleman nodded to one another as the sermon continued. Neither had any idea who the other one was.

When the graveside service concluded, both of the lone figures slowly made their way to the tent. The woman saw Barry Tidwell staring at the casket and then she saw him look toward one of the people still sitting in a chair in front. Barry didn't look happy, but was anyone supposed to look happy at a funeral. The chestnut haired woman and the blond stranger arrived at the front row at the same time, both with tears in their eyes.

****

Be sure to check my website, for news and updates.
http://www.marienicoleharper.com

LOVE Y'ALL,
MARIE

Southland Bookworks